An

Everyday Hero

★

Also by Laura Trentham

An
Everyday Hero

Laura Trentham

St. Martin's Griffin
New York

First published in the United States by St. Martin's Griffin,
an imprint of St. Martin's Publishing Group

AN EVERYDAY HERO. Copyright © 2020 by Brandon Webb. All rights reserved.
Printed in the United States of America. For information, address St. Martin's
Publishing Group, 120 Broadway, New York, NY 10271.

www.stmartins.com

The Library of Congress Cataloging-in-Publication Data is available upon request.

ISBN 978-1-250-14555-0 (trade paperback)
ISBN 978-1-250-14556-7 (ebook)

Our books may be purchased in bulk for promotional, educational,
or business use. Please contact your local bookseller or the Macmillan Corporate
and Premium Sales Department at 1-800-221-7945, extension 5442,
or by email at MacmillanSpecialMarkets@macmillan.com.

First Edition: February 2020

10 9 8 7 6 5 4 3 2 1

An
Everyday Hero

★

Chapter 1

"Disorderly conduct. Public intoxication. Resisting arrest." Judge Duckett put down the paper, linked his hands, and stared over his reading glasses from his perch behind the bench with a combination of exasperation and fatherly disapproval.

Greer Hadley shifted in her sensible heels and smoothed the skirt of the light pink suit she'd borrowed from her mama for the occasion. "I'll give you the first two, Uncle Bill—" The judge cleared his throat and narrowed his eyes. "Excuse me—Judge Duckett—but I did not resist arrest."

"That you recall." Deputy Wayne Peeler drawled the words out in the most sarcastic, unprofessional manner possible.

She fisted her hands and took a deep breath. The impulse to punch Wayne in the face simmered below the surface like a volcano no longer at rest. But ten o'clock on a Monday morning during her arraignment was not the smartest time to lose her temper, and she'd promised herself not to add to her string of bad decisions.

She sweetened her voice and bared her teeth at Wayne in the facsimile of a smile. "I recall plenty, thank you very much."

Truth was she didn't recall the minute details, but the shock of Wayne's whispered offer on Saturday night to make her troubles go away for a price had done more to sober her up than the couple of hours spent in lockup waiting for her parents.

Dressed in his tan uniform, Wayne adjusted his heavy gun belt so often she imagined he got off every night by rubbing his gun. Giving him a badge had only empowered the part of him desperate for respect and approval. His nickname in high school, "the Weasel," had been well earned.

Unfortunately, she was the unreliable narrator of her life at the moment and no one would trust her recollections. Judge Duckett, her uncle Bill by marriage until he and her aunt Tonya had divorced, rustled papers from his desk.

The ethics of her former uncle acting as her judge were questionable, especially considering they had remained close even after he'd remarried, but if nepotism is what it took to make this nightmare go away, then she wouldn't be the one to lodge a complaint.

"A witness claimed you were sitting quietly at the end of the bar until a song played on the jukebox. What was the song?" Her uncle glanced at her over his glasses again, which made him look like a stern teacher.

"'Before He Cheats' by Carrie Underwood." She forced her chin up.

His mouth opened, closed, and he dropped his gaze back to the paper. A murmur broke out behind her.

She would *not* cry. She wouldn't. She blinked like her life depended on a tear not falling. Later, in the privacy of her childhood bedroom, she would bury her face in the eyelet-covered pillow and let loose.

Beau Williams, her cheating ex-boyfriend, was only partially to blame for her embarrassing behavior. It was a confluence of setbacks that had had her holding down the end of the bar. Hearing Carrie's revenge anthem had hit a nerve exposed by the shots of Jack. Rage had quickened the effects of the alcohol, and that's when things got fuzzy.

"Yes, well. That is a rather . . . Let's move on, shall we? The witness also claims after a heartfelt, albeit slurred speech about the vagaries of relationships and how the moral fiber of the Junior League of Madison was frayed, you fed five dollars into the jukebox and played the same song for over an hour. 'Crazy' by Patsy Cline, was it?"

Ugh. She didn't recall how much money she'd fed the machine, but it sounded like something she would do. "Crazy" was one of her favorite songs. A master class in conveying emotion through simple lyrics. She was just sorry she'd wasted five dollars on Beau. He didn't deserve her money, her heart, or Patsy.

"No one can fault my taste in the classics." Greer tried a smile, but her lips quivered and she pressed them together.

Her uncle continued to read from the witness statement, "You proceeded to throw two glasses on the floor, shattering them, and attempted to break a chair across the jukebox."

She swallowed hard. A vague picture of a frustratingly sturdy chair surfaced. The fact the chair remained intact while she was falling apart had sent her anger soaring higher and hotter. A glance from her uncle Bill over the paper had her giving him a nod. She couldn't deny it.

He continued, "A patron called 911. When Deputy Peeler

arrived, he pulled you away from the jukebox and forced you outside. That's where, he claims, you kicked him . . . well, you know where."

"Wayne dragged me down the stairs—"

"Deputy Peeler, if you please." Wayne sniffed loudly.

"As Deputy Peeler escorted me down the stairs, I lost my balance and fell. The heel of my shoe jabbed into his crotch. Sorry." Greer didn't make an attempt to mask her not-sorry voice with fake respect.

If she accused Wayne of misbehavior on the job, he would deny it and spin it somehow to make her look even more irresponsible. Lord knows, she'd embarrassed her parents enough for a lifetime. Anyway, seeing him rolling on the ground and cupping his crotch had been sweet payback.

"I sustained an injury where that spike you call a heel caught me." Wayne half turned toward her.

Instead of playing it smart and soothing his delicate male ego, she batted her eyes at him. "I'm sure that's left the ladies of Madison *real* upset."

Wayne took a step toward her. "You are such a—"

The gavel knocked against the bench and her uncle stood, looming over them. "I've heard enough, Deputy. Sit down."

Wayne turned on his heel and left Greer to face her uncle Bill. This was where she would promise such a thing would never happen again, and he would give her a stern warning before dismissing all charges.

"I'm striking the resisting arrest charge. It was an accident."

Greer forced herself not to look over her shoulder and stick her tongue out at Wayne. That left only two misdemeanors, which her uncle could expunge with a swipe of his pen.

He settled behind the bench and picked up his pen, his gaze on the papers. "You will pay for any damages."

"I've already reimbursed Becky." Technically, she'd had to use her parents' money, considering she'd crawled home from Nashville broke. "And apologized profusely. You can be assured there will not be a repeat performance. I've learned my lesson."

"Good. As for the other charges . . ."

Her deep breath cleansed a portion of the tension across her shoulders, and a smile born of relief appeared.

"You will perform fifty hours of community service."

Her smile froze on her face. It sounded like a lot, but she'd been stupid and immature and deserved punishment. "I understand. Clean roads are important."

"Litter pickup? Goodness no." He took his glasses off and smiled at her for the first time, but it wasn't the jolly-uncle smile she was familiar with. "You have talents that would be wasted on the side of the road picking up trash, Ms. Hadley. You will spend your fifty hours working at the Music Tree Foundation."

"I'm not familiar with it." She swallowed. The mention of music set her stomach roiling. "Highway 45 was in terrible shape on my drive in last week."

"The foundation is a nonprofit music program that focuses on helping military veterans and their families cope with the trauma they've endured serving our country. They're in need of volunteer songwriters and musicians."

"I can't write or play anymore." Her dream of hearing one of her songs on the radio had died. Not in a blaze of glory but from a slow, torturous starvation of hope. At thirty, she was resigned to finding a real job and cobbling together a normal life in the place she'd tried to leave behind.

"My decision is final. As far as I can determine, your brain—despite this lapse in judgment—is in fine working order. You can and will help these men and women heal through your gift of music. Unless you'd rather spend thirty days in county lockup?"

Would her uncle actually throw her in jail? For a *month*? "No, Your Honor, I don't want to go to county lockup."

"Good. Once you turn in your log with all your hours signed off by the foundation's manager, your record with this court will be cleared." He handed her file to a clerk. "Case closed. Next up is docket number fourteen."

She stood there until he met her gaze with his unflinching one. "Go home, Greer."

Her parents were waiting at the door to the courtroom. While they'd faced the horror of having to bail their only child out of jail stoically, her mother's embarrassment and disappointment were ripe and all-encompassing. Greer wilted and trailed her parents out of the courthouse.

She felt like a child. An incompetent, needy child living in her old bedroom and dependent on her parents for emotional and financial support. She thought she'd hit rock bottom many times over the years, but her situation now had revealed new lows.

The silence in the car built into a painful crescendo.

"The tiger lilies are lovely this year, don't you think?" Her mother's attempt at normalcy was strained but welcome.

Her father's hands squeaked along the steering wheel as an answer.

Greer huddled in the backseat and stared out the window, the clumps of flowers on the side of the road an orange blur. As a teenager, she'd chafed at her parents' protectiveness and had wanted nothing more than to escape to Nashville, where she'd been convinced glory and fame awaited. Now she was home and a disappointment not only to her parents but to herself. Even worse, she hadn't come up with a plan to turn her life around.

"Ira Jenkins is back in the hospital. I thought I'd run by and check on him. Since Sarah passed, he seems a shell of the man he once was." Her mother turned to face the backseat. "Would you like to come with me? I'm sure he'd be happy to see you."

"He won't remember me, Mama."

"I'm sure he will."

Greer scrunched farther down in the seat. The last thing she wanted was to make small talk with a man she hadn't seen in years.

"You'll have to get out eventually and face the music." Her mother's smile wavered and threatened to turn into tears. "So to speak."

Her mother was trying, which was more than could be said for Greer at the moment. Her parents deserved a better daughter. Someone successful they could brag on at the Wednesday-night potlucks at church. Not a daughter they had to bail out of jail.

"I will. I promise. Just not to see Mr. Jenkins." Greer leaned forward and squeezed her mother's hand over the seat, needing to give her something to hope for even if Greer wasn't sure what that might be.

Her father cleared his throat. "You need to think about the future."

He ignored her mother's whispered, "Not now, Frank."

"A job. Or back to school. We'll put you through nursing or accounting or something useful." He shifted to meet her gaze in the rearview mirror. "But you can't keep on like you're doing. You need a purpose."

"I'll start looking for a job tomorrow." School had never been her wheelhouse. She'd been sure she'd make it in Nashville and had never formulated a backup plan.

They pulled up to her childhood home, a two-story brick Colonial on the main street of Madison, Tennessee. Oaks had been planted down a middle island like a line of soldiers at attention. They had grown to shade both sides of the street. It was picturesque and cast the imagination back to a time when ladies lounged on porches with their iced tea and gossiped with their neighbors to escape the heat of summer. Air-conditioning had altered that way of life.

At one time, as a kid, she'd known every family up and down the street well enough to knock on their door for help or run through their backyard in epic games of tag. Now, though, the houses were being bought up by people who used Madison to escape the bustle of an expanding Nashville. They built pools in the backyards and fences and weren't outside except to walk their trendy dogs.

The march of progress through Madison added to her melancholy sadness. There was a reason not being able to go home again was a recurring theme in books and songs.

"We love you, Greer. You know that, don't you?" Her mother's voice was tight with emotion, but she didn't turn around, thank goodness.

Her mother never cried and if Greer witnessed tears, she would burst into sobs herself and embarrass everyone.

"I know. Thanks for everything. I'm going to do better. Be better." It seemed a wholly inadequate promise she wasn't even sure she could keep, but it was all she could manage. She ducked out of the car and skipped around to a side door of the house that was always unlocked.

Her room was both a haven and a mocking reminder of

the state of her life. Posters of album covers papered the wall behind her bed, the colors faded from the sun and the edges curling with age.

In high school, she'd gravitated toward indie folk artists and away from the commercially driven country-music machine located a few miles south. Joan Baez was flanked by Patty Griffin and Dolly Parton. Even though Dolly veered more country than Greer, no one could deny the legend's songwriting chops. The guitar Greer had hocked for rent money had borne Dolly's signature like a talisman. Sometimes Greer ached for her guitar like a missing limb.

The flashing glimpse of a woman in a pale pink suit stopped her in the middle of the floor. She turned to face the full-length mirror glued to the back of the closet door. God, it was like glimpsing her mom through a time warp.

Greer touched the delicate pearls that had been passed down to her on her eighteenth birthday. They were old-fashioned and traditional and stereotypical of a Southern "good girl." Not her style. She'd left them in her dresser drawer when she'd left home the day after high school graduation.

A tug of recognition of the women who had come before her had her clutching the strand in her hand as if something lost were now found. Was it her circumstances or her age growing her nostalgia like a tree setting roots?

She turned around to break the connection with the stranger in the mirror, stripped off the pink suit, and pulled on jeans and a cotton oxford. Her mother would appreciate seeing her in something besides the frayed shorts and grungy concert T-shirts she'd lounged around in the last week. She reached behind her neck for the clasp of the necklace, but her hands stilled, then dropped to her sides, leaving the pearls in place.

She stepped out of her room and was enveloped in silence. Her father had returned to his insurance office and her mother must have set off for her hospital visit. The house took on an expectant quality, as if waiting for its true owners to return. She was no longer a fundamental part of this world. Not unwelcome, perhaps, but a loose cog in her parents' lives.

She tiptoed downstairs to the kitchen and made herself a ham sandwich. May was too early for fresh tomatoes, but in another month or two her mother's garden would make tomato sandwiches an everyday treat.

Craving an escape, Greer grabbed a book and settled in her favorite window seat. The rest of the afternoon passed in the same expectant silence. The chime of the doorbell made her start and drop her book. If she pretended no one was home, maybe whoever was on the front porch would go away. The last thing she wanted was to face one of Madison's gossips masquerading as a do-gooder.

The creak of the door opening had her bolting to her feet.

"Greer? I know you're home. Are you decent?" Her uncle Bill's booming voice echoed in the two-story foyer.

She propped her shoulder in the doorway of the sunroom. "Letting yourself in people's houses is a good way of getting shot around here."

"While your mama would have liked to have shot me during the divorce with her sister, I hope we've made our peace." He closed the door behind him and Greer did what she'd wanted to do in the courtroom—she threw herself at him for a hug.

He lifted her off her feet and spun her once around. Her laugh hit her ears like a foreign language. It had been too long since she'd laughed from a place of happiness.

"You could have just come out to the house. You didn't have to get arrested to see me." Bill let her go, and she led him into the sunroom.

"Do you want something to drink?" Greer asked, already turning for the kitchen and the fresh brewed pitcher of sweet iced tea.

"No, thanks. Mary has fried chicken ready to go in the pan, so I can't stay long."

Bill had divorced her aunt Tonya more than a decade earlier and married the choir director of the biggest black church in town. A scandal had ensued not because he'd married a black woman, but because he, a long-standing deacon in the Church of Christ, had converted to a heathen Methodist.

"How is Mary?"

"Always singing." He shook his head, an indulgent smile on his face, as they settled into their seats.

His comment sprinkled salt on an open wound. She'd begged off going to church with her parents because of the questions she was sure to face and the hymns she couldn't bring herself to sing. Some of her earlier happiness at seeing him leaked out. "Good for her."

"I came to make sure you weren't mad at me."

"Why would I be mad?"

"I got the impression you expected me to dismiss the charges." His smile turned into a wince.

"I wouldn't have been upset if you had, but I get it. I was an idiot and deserve punishment." She picked at the fringe on a decades-old needlepoint pillow and cast him a pleading glance. "I'd rather pick up trash, though, if it's all the same to you."

"It's not the same to me." He crossed his long legs and tapped a finger on the cherry armrest of the antique chair that looked ready to surrender at any moment to his bulk. "Do you remember Amelia Shelton?"

"Mary's daughter? She was a couple of years ahead of me in school. We didn't hang out or anything, but she seemed nice." Greer couldn't remember the last time she'd seen Amelia. Greer's side of the family had skipped Bill and Mary's small wedding ceremony; the acrimony between him and her aunt Tonya hadn't faded at that point.

"Amelia is the founder and director of the Music Tree Foundation and is desperate for qualified volunteers. You've been playing and singing and writing music since you were knee high. It was meant to be."

"It's not meant to be. I've got to get a real job."

Her uncle made a scoffing sound. "You're too much like my Mary. You could never leave music behind."

"Music dumped me on the side of the road, gave me the finger, and peeled out." Greer shook her head and touched the string of pearls, her gaze on his polished black dress shoes. "I'm a mess, Uncle Bill. I have nothing to offer. In fact, I'll probably make things worse for whatever poor soul I get paired with."

She expected him to argue, but he seemed to be weighing the truth in her words like the scales of justice. His shrug wasn't in the least reassuring. "Amelia has done something really special with her foundation. It might do you a world of good to focus on someone besides yourself."

"Dang, that's harsh."

He patted her knee. "I've seen all kinds come through my courtroom. The ones who turn it around are the ones who quit feeling sorry for themselves."

"But—"

"But nothing. Beau is an asshole. Not the first or the last you're likely to encounter. Don't you deserve better than him?"

"Yes?" She wished she'd been able to put more conviction into the word.

Beau was successful, nice-looking—even though a bald spot was conquering his hair day by day—and respected in their town. They'd known each other since high school, but had only started dating in the last year.

He was solid and steady and comfortable. Three things lacking from her life. Catching him cheating with the president of the Junior League had been another seismic shift in her world, leaving her unsure and off balance.

"If you can't believe in yourself yet, then believe me. You are talented, Greer, and you have the ability to help people find their voice." He slipped a card out of his wallet. When she didn't reach for it, he waved it in her face until she took it.

A tree styled with musical symbols of all different colors decorated one side of the card. She ran her thumb over the raised black ink of Amelia's name and an address on the outskirts of Nashville. "I don't have much choice, do I?"

"Not if you want to stay in my—and the court's—good graces. She's expecting you tomorrow at three."

"No rest for the wicked, huh?" Her smile was born of sarcasm.

Bill rose and ruffled her hair like he had when she was little. "Not wicked. Lost."

Greer walked him out, brushed a kiss on his cheek, and murmured her thanks. She leaned on the porch rail and waved until he disappeared down the street.

I once was lost, and now I'm found. She'd sung "Amazing Grace" so many times that the lyrics had ceased to have an impact. But, standing on her childhood front porch, having come full circle, a shiver went down her spine, and goose bumps broke over her arms despite the heat that wavered over the pavement like a mirage. Her granny would have said that someone had walked over her grave. Maybe so. Or maybe change was a-coming whether she wanted to face up to it or not.

Chapter 2

The next afternoon, Greer pulled into the parking lot of the Music Tree Foundation. The building itself was a modest white house with a handicapped-accessible ramp outside and the look of a former doctor's office. The sign out front was branded with the same art as the business card in her back pocket. She parked and approached with the enthusiasm of a convict headed to the chair.

Amelia had been class salutatorian, a cheerleader, on the debate team, and had won scholarships for her community service. She and Greer had little in common.

Greer pushed the front door open. An electric-sounding chime announced her presence. An empty waiting room was on her right and a door-lined hallway stretched to the back of the house. The place smelled of new carpet and paint. The faint sounds of a guitar wavered in the background.

A woman stuck her head out of a room halfway down the hall, only her outline visible in the shadows. "Greer Hadley.

Right on time. Come down so we can chat." Amelia's voice gave away nothing about her opinion on the reason Greer was "volunteering."

Greer shuffled down the hall toward the opening, hesitating in front of a closed door when laughter emanated over a C chord. Stopping in the doorway of what appeared to be part storeroom and part office, she got her bearings.

Two guitars and a mandolin stood on stands. An electric keyboard was on its side and leaned against the wall. A fiddle lay across a card table stacked with papers and songbooks. Music stands huddled in one corner. Amelia sat on the edge of an office chair behind a desk, her chin propped up on her fist, a curious expression on her face.

"Come on in and sit. How long has it been?" Amelia's speaking voice was like warm butter. If memory served, her singing voice had been even richer.

"Since you graduated high school. You look great." Greer took a seat across from the desk, a feeling like she'd been called to the principal's office leaving her sitting up straight.

Amelia's natural curls were tight and glossy and held back by a brightly patterned head wrap. Caramel tones highlighted the ends of her black hair and lent a casual sophistication. Her sleeveless blouse showed off toned arms. She looked put together and successful. Greer squirmed.

"I'm thrilled you're helping us out. It's tough to get songwriters with your experience on board to volunteer." Amelia rolled her chair backward, pulled a manila folder from the top of a stack by the computer, and tucked herself back under the desk.

Greer held her hand up. "Whoa. I didn't exactly volunteer. I want to be up-front and tell you that I've left music and songwriting behind. It's gotten me nowhere and nothing."

Letting the silence build, Amelia narrowed her eyes and ran a finger over her bottom lip. Even though Amelia was a scant two years older than she, Greer felt at a distinct disadvantage in maturity.

"Yeah, Bill filled me in." Amelia tapped the eraser end of a pencil on the desktop. The rhythm was steady and hinted at impatience, although only kindness reflected in her voice. "I think you'll find your perspective on life altered as you volunteer here. All I ask is that you keep an open mind and give it your best."

"What if my best was ten years ago and I'm no more than mediocre now?" It was Greer's fear put into words to a woman she barely knew.

Amelia tilted her head. "I believe everyone's best is still ahead of them. I have to or I wouldn't be effective at running the foundation. Give it a chance."

"I haven't written or played music in months. What if I can't help anybody? What if I make things worse? Can I quit and tell Uncle Bill to give me litter pickup?"

Amelia's brown eyes flared like an oak tree bursting into flame. "No, you cannot quit. Your volunteer sheet for the court requires my signature, and you're going to have to earn your hours. Suck it up, Greer. Here's your first client."

Intimidated and fighting resentment, Greer sank down in her seat and took the folder Amelia held out. She skimmed the first page.

"This is a fifteen-year-old girl. I thought this program was for veterans?"

"It's for service members and their families. Ally's father died in combat four months ago."

A pang reverberated through Greer's belly. Imagining either of her parents gone made her feel sick. "That's terrible."

"Worse than getting cheated on by a self-centered jerk?" Amelia's smile held a dark humor.

"Most people think Beau is God's gift to Madison."

"You and I know the truth, don't we?" The pivot from adversary to comrade was disconcerting but Greer couldn't help but be grateful.

"We do. And you're right, losing a father at fifteen trumps getting cheated on at thirty." Sympathy rose up like the tide coming in. "When do I meet with her?"

Amelia checked the clock. "Any minute. She comes right after school. You can wait for her in room three if you want. That's just down the hall on the left. Did you bring your guitar?"

Heat rushed Greer's face. Her beloved Martin guitar had paid her rent for three months. She should have kept her guitar and given up three months earlier. "I didn't."

"Borrow what you need, then." Amelia gestured at her collection. "And stop by when the two of you are finished. I'll sign your sheet."

"How long are the sessions? An hour?"

"As long as you can manage. Good luck," Amelia said cryptically before swiveling her chair to face the computer monitor, the dismissal unmistakable.

Greer took the nearest guitar, not bothering to check its quality—did it really matter?—and continued down the hall until she came to room three. It was empty save for a squat rectangular table and two chairs. A plastic box in the middle of the table held sheets of music paper and pencils. The noteless lines used to hold anticipation of what she could create. Now, the empty lines mocked her.

Greer took the chair on the far side of the table, facing the door, and gripped the neck of the guitar. Instead of swinging it into her lap like she'd done a million times, she rested the body of the guitar on the floor between her knees. A discordant echo reverberated and hit her ear like fingernails down a chalkboard.

The scent of wood oil mingled with the metal of the strings. She ran her thumb across the calluses on her fingertips. They were softening. Given enough time they would be gone. Maybe she'd even forget how to play.

A rustle at the door drew her attention. A girl stepped through the door, kicked it shut behind her, dropped her backpack with a thud, and plopped in the seat across from Greer, lounging back and crossing her arms over her chest.

The girl's hair had been bleached and streaked with hot pink. Her roots and eyebrows betrayed her natural dark hue and complemented her olive complexion. Her only makeup was heavy black eyeliner and dark purple lipstick. Ripped jeans, a tight black midriff-bearing T-shirt, and black combat-style boots completed her ensemble. It was like the girl had studied a "How to be a Badass" pamphlet from the nineties.

"Who the hell are you? Where's the dude?" the girl asked between smacks of her gum. The faint scent of cigarette smoke made Greer's nose twitch. Playing in bars had sensitized her. She'd always hated the way her hair and clothes smelled the morning after a gig.

"I'm a new volunteer. My name is Greer." She kept her voice even and calm.

"Weird name."

It was an old family name, but Greer had a feeling Ally didn't care. "I assume you're Ally."

"You're old."

Ouch. But thirty *was* old compared with fifteen. There was a lot of life to be lived between the two. Greer made a show of reading the info sheet in the folder. "Funny, there's no mention of your sunny disposition."

The gum smacking ceased for a few heartbeats but restarted with more vigor. Ally barred her teeth in the way of a predator right before it pounces. "I guess Amelia didn't want to ruin the surprise." The girl struck a pose. "Surprise! What you see is what you get."

Even though Ally's mask of disdain didn't break, her waves of insecurity triggered Greer's Spidey sense. Yet if she called Ally on it, Greer would get bitten for sure. Greer might be old, but she still remembered being a teenager trying to fit in by not fitting in.

Keeping her sarcasm meter on high, Greer made a show of examining her fingernails. "Gee, I can't wait to get to know you better. You seem like a true delight."

"I don't want to be here. This songwriting therapy is dumb as hell."

Through the years working the bar and club circuit, Greer had learned how to read a crowd. Not that it took a dictionary to decipher Ally. She might as well have been lobbing rotten tomatoes over the table.

"You think I want to be here dealing with your shit?"

For a second, Ally's mask broke and revealed her surprise, but she spackled it back together with a saccharine smile and an eye roll. "Why are you here, then? Most of these mouth breathers are obsessed with pooping rainbows and making the world a better place."

"Court ordered me here."

A spark of interest had Ally sitting up a little straighter. "What'd you do?"

"Popped a cap in a mouthy fifteen-year-old."

Shock and awe widened Ally's eyes before logic had her making a scoffing sound. "Whatever. I bet you shoplifted at Walmart or something totally lame."

"I got wasted after I found out my boyfriend cheated on me and busted up a bar. What are you doing here? Your mama make you come?"

Ally averted her gaze.

Greer almost smiled. "You shoplifted from Walmart, didn't you, tough girl?"

"Shut up," Ally muttered.

While Greer had the upper hand, she plucked a sheet of paper out of the bin. "Now that we've got the warm, fuzzy ice breakers out of the way, why don't we fulfill our court requirements and write something?"

Greer half expected the girl to rip the paper up, but Ally only spun the paper around on the desk. "What am I supposed to do with this? I don't even know where notes go."

Greer flipped the paper over to the blank white side. "Then start with lyrics. Write whatever you're feeling. It doesn't have to rhyme or even make sense right now. The most important thing is the emotion behind the words."

Ally didn't move for too many agonizing ticks of the clock. Greer blanked her face like the piece of paper and returned Ally's stare. A challenge had been issued. Greer didn't dare break eye contact or show weakness. Losing a game of chicken to a fifteen-year-old girl would send her crashing through bedrock past rock bottom.

Ally's shoulders rounded and her gaze dropped. She took a pencil out of the box and huddled over the paper, her arm curved around the top as if Greer were planning to cheat off her. The victory had Greer wanting to fist pump, but she refrained. Instead she took a sheet of the music paper and doodled notes and chords along the bars with no reason or rhyme.

Ten minutes of silence passed, broken only by the faint scratching of lead and eraser on paper.

"Done." Ally put her pencil down as if she'd finished a timed test instead of an exercise in creativity.

"May I?" Greer pointed at the paper. Songwriting was a window into the soul and Greer never assumed another's work was for public consumption.

"Sure. Go right ahead." Ally's smirk was the definition of teenage obnoxiousness.

With trepidation, Greer picked up the paper and skimmed what Ally had written. When she was done, she looked over the top of the paper. "Impressive. I might have to notify the Guinness World Records department. I'm not sure the word 'fuck' has been used so many times in such a short amount of space."

"Are we done here or what?" Ally didn't wait for an answer but stood, swung her backpack over one shoulder, and left without a backward glance.

Indecision froze Greer in a half stand. She didn't really want to brazen out another half hour with Ally, but she hadn't fulfilled her court-ordered commitment, which was a serious problem. By the time she followed Ally out the door, the girl had vanished.

Somehow, Greer had to convince Amelia not to report her as deficient to the courts. Jail time would go on her record, and she'd never get a job. Next time—if there was a next time—she'd be sweetness to Ally's caustic attitude. She retraced her steps to knock on the jamb of Amelia's door, drawing the woman's attention away from her computer.

Amelia checked her watch, pushed a pair of cat's-eye reading glasses to the top of her head, and sat back with a smile. "I'm impressed."

Greer's excuses stuttered to a stop in her head. "Impressed? Ally stormed out after writing an expletive-laden diatribe."

"You actually got her to write something?"

"Yeah. But the session only lasted a half hour."

"Believe it or not, that's longer than her sessions usually last. Plus, you're not in tears."

Greer opened and closed her mouth. "She made a volunteer cry?"

"More than one, actually." Amelia held out her hand. "You want me to sign your sheet? I'll credit you a full hour."

"That'd be great." Greer unfolded the sheet from her back pocket and set it on the desk.

Amelia lowered her glasses and signed her name with a flourish. "I want you to meet with Ally again this Friday, same time. If it goes as well as today did, I'll put you down for twice a week thereafter."

"Are you sure? She didn't seem to like me very much."

"She doesn't like anyone very much right now. Not even herself. I don't know how but you've already gotten further than anyone else. All my regular volunteers have refused to work with her. And, bonus for me, you don't have a choice." Amelia tapped her steepled fingers together. "She needs help processing her grief. I don't know if music can do that for her, but I've got to believe it's worth a try."

Music had gotten Greer through hard times, but in the end, music had abandoned her. How could she wield music as a healing art when she had stopped believing in its magic?

The court decision gave her no choice but to return and

wrestle wits with a fifteen-year-old delinquent. "I'll be back on Friday."

"Hang on. You handled Ally so well, I have another difficult assignment for you to tackle. One a little closer to home." Amelia opened a desk drawer and pulled out a folder, laying a hand flat on top as if wanting to keep whatever was within it contained. "You remember Emmett Lawson?"

The name sent a jolt through Greer even though she hadn't seen him since graduation. "Of course."

"Mrs. Lawson canvassed Bill to get him in the program. His parents are worried sick about him." Amelia's voice dropped to a whisper that imparted both secrets and disquiet. "And for good reason."

Greer took a seat, perched on the edge of the visitor's chair. "I heard through Mama he'd been injured and got a slew of medals. Purple Heart. Silver Star. I didn't realize he was back in Madison."

Emmett Lawson had been an apple-pie, all-American boy in high school, and a literal All-American quarterback. Except he had forgone a football scholarship to Vanderbilt, instead attending West Point and accepting an officer's commission in the army. His return should have merited a hero's welcome, yet no one had even mentioned seeing him around Madison.

"It's complicated." Amelia kept her gaze averted and tapped her fingers on the file. "He refuses to leave the guest cabin out on his parents' horse farm. Do you know it?"

"I do." It had been the site of several high school parties. "Are you asking me to make a house call?"

Amelia heaved a sigh, her small smile doing nothing to banish the worry crinkling her eyes. "Exactly. See if you can encourage him to get some of his feelings out through music. Even better if you could coax him to come to us."

"I'm not a mental health professional. In fact, I'm probably in need of counseling myself or I wouldn't be in this situation." Greer gestured around the room.

"No one expects a miracle." An uncharacteristic hesitancy hitched Amelia's words. "You and Emmett were in the same class, weren't you?"

"Yeah, but we weren't good friends or anything. We didn't even hang out. He was a jock. I bounced between the music kids and the stoners. You should see if Misty Malone is available to pull him out of his shell. They were a hot-and-heavy item back then."

"He doesn't need an old flame turning up. He needs someone as stubborn as he is to annoy him. I think you'll do great."

Greer's huff landed somewhere between amusement and indignation. "Gee, thanks."

"That was a compliment. I thought for sure you'd bail on Ally after five minutes."

"When is Emmett expecting me?"

"He's not. And he most likely won't roll out the welcome mat. Believe me, I wouldn't ask you or anyone else to go out there if it wasn't for his mother calling in a favor. She's desperate."

Greer's curiosity trumped her natural inclination to stay out of it. "What happened to him?"

"Not sure. His parents didn't say, and I didn't get close enough to tell."

"You already tried to see him?"

"Yep." The word popped with plenty of sarcasm.

"Obviously, it didn't go well."

"Understatement."

"Why do you think things will go better with me?"

"Because you two are at least acquainted."

"I doubt he even remembers me from high school."

"Will you try? That way we can tell his mama we did all we could, and I can get my mom and Bill off my back." Amelia sent a side-eye glance in her direction. "Any hours you spend with Emmett will count double."

It was an offer she couldn't refuse. "Fine. I'll give it a shot."

A funny look passed over Amelia's face. She cleared her throat and turned back to the computer. "Let me know how it turns out."

Greer walked out with a brief backward glance. Amelia looked . . . troubled. But, as they didn't qualify as friends, Greer kept moving, slipping back into the small room she'd used with Ally to straighten up. She picked up Ally's expletive-laden lyrics to toss in the wastebasket.

She hesitated, this time reading past and around the curses. The lyrics were rough and meant to shock, but a compelling thread hid beneath them. A thread detailing a fight with anger and loneliness and questions for the universe.

Instead of wadding it up, she folded Ally's work and slipped it into her back pocket with her time sheet. Laughter and voices skated down the hall. A middle-aged man with a full gray-black beard and a belly that strained to split the buttons of his oxford stopped in the doorway.

"I'm sorry. I thought the room was available." His baritone brought to mind dark chocolate. Rich but with a bite.

Greer smiled. "It is. I was on my way out. I'm Greer, a new volunteer."

They exchanged a handshake. "I'm Richard."

"Volunteer or . . ." Greer wasn't sure what to call the people they were supposed to be helping. Certainly not patients.

"Volunteer. I heard you got assigned Ally. What did you do to piss off Amelia?"

"We have a family connection. Does everyone here know Ally?"

Richard slipped by her and laid a keyboard on the table. "Ally has rotated through all the volunteers. She's a nightmare. A lost cause. I don't know why Amelia keeps trying. The girl doesn't want to be here and as far as I can tell, she has no interest or talent in music or songwriting."

Greer fingered the paper in her back pocket. "Actually, I see some potential."

Richard was all wide-eyed skepticism. "Our time would be better spent working with people who want to be here. People who are actually in pain."

Greer murmured a polite good-bye even though she was feeling anything but. True, Ally's attitude made it difficult for anyone to harbor sympathy or pity for her situation. She had learned to push adults' buttons until anger and frustration drowned out any kinder tendencies. But the girl had lost her father. A devastating loss for anyone, much less a teenager. Greer had no doubt the girl was in real pain.

A twenty-something-year-old man with the upright, crisp bearing of a soldier met her in the hallway, a slight hitch in his gait the only tell that something was wrong. She raised a hand in greeting. He did the same, except where his hand should be was a stump. The legs sticking out of his cargo shorts were both metal rods. Her smile wavered not from disgust but the reality of what Richard had meant.

"Have fun," she said.

The man had soft eyes and a ready smile. "I will, ma'am."

Greer stepped outside and tipped her face to the sun. The heat scorched her tears away. That man didn't want her pity and neither did Ally. What would Emmett ask of her?

Chapter 3

Greer pumped the brakes as she approached the narrow lane that led off the main road to Emmett Lawson's cabin. A gate blocked the entrance and a fence stretched to either side. As if that wasn't enough to deter visitors, a No Trespassing sign swung in the slight breeze from the rusty top rail of the gate.

She tapped her thumbs on the steering wheel to the beat of the music on her radio, a catchy pop song with inane lyrics involving booty shaking. Without guilt, she could turn around and claim she couldn't reach Emmett.

Except Amelia's offer of double hours was too much to resist. A summer stroll through the woods would net her at least an hour. She parked on the side of the two-lane country road, half blocking one lane. Not that she was worried about causing a traffic jam. She looked in either direction. Nothing but bees traveled across the road.

Greer fanned herself with her straw cowboy hat and pulled at the lock and chain on the gate, hoping they were just for show, but the chain had been looped twice and the lock was heavy duty. The cabin was through the woods, but she couldn't remember how far back. She popped onto her toes but spotted no evidence of human habitation. Emmett was a man who didn't want to be bothered.

Curiosity arched like a cat in her psyche. In high school, Emmett had strode through the school like a god, worshiped by girls and boys alike. Even Greer hadn't been immune. She'd spent most of World History staring at the back of his head and imagining what it would be like to be the focus of his blistering blue eyes and brilliant smile.

Not that boys like Emmett noticed girls like her. It was a universal law, like gravity or inertia. She'd existed on the fringes, artsy and weird, like a distant planet in his orbit. Her friends had been in music and theater. Emmett had been the quarterback dominating the football field while she'd been under the bleachers looking for trouble.

Yet, he hadn't been a self-centered asshole. He'd been friendly and outgoing and well-liked by everyone, even her. What had happened?

She swung a leg over the fence. Splintered wood caught her along her inner thigh. Stuck with one leg on either side, she heaved herself all the way over and hopped while examining the deep scratch. At least she'd have proof for Amelia that she'd tried to see Emmett.

The wedge heels on her sandals sank into the soft ground. She kicked them off and tossed them on the other side of the fence by her front tire. Pine needles pricked her soles but it wasn't unpleasant. It had been years since she'd felt the ground under her bare feet. Between the shade and the piney scent of the trees, the stroll was almost pleasant.

The trees ended in an abrupt line and spit her out into the blinding heat of the sun. Her hat did little to protect her. The cabin was nestled in a slight dip between rolling hills. It was a slicker, modern version of an old-timey cabin. Half the cabin was made with traditional-looking chinked logs, the other half with white-washed wooden boards. The wraparound porch and red metal roof added to the charm. It was picturesque.

Yet, the approach revealed an unkempt underbelly to the place. Grass grew knee-high on either side of the lane leading to the house but shorter between the tire tracks. Clumps of orange-and-black tiger lilies and black-eyed Susans poked out of the grass as if the landscaping had been abandoned. The bushes in front of the cabin had sent runners off in every direction. Chaos had gained the upper hand.

A shadow shifted on the front porch, but all she could hear was the ebb and flow of insects and birds. The movement materialized into a man. Emmett. She halted thirty feet from the porch steps and squinted against the sun knowing Emmett could see her perfectly as she fought the sun and lost.

"Hi!" Out of nerves, she waved like a deranged beauty queen in a parade. When he didn't respond, she dropped her hand and smoothed her skirt.

"Get gone." His voice rumbled like a rusty gate that hadn't been opened in a long time.

"I'm not sure you remember me, but—"

"I said, go!"

"I just want to—"

The report of a gun had her yelping, covering her ears, and crouching down.

"You have one more chance to skedaddle. Now go."

She rose. Her legs wobbled like noodles. While she couldn't

see him, the barrel of a shotgun glinted where it stuck out from the porch rails, except it was pointed at the sky and not at her. While her body had turned to mush, her head whirred. Was she going to run for home like a scared rabbit or stay like an idiot?

"You shoot that gun one more time and I'm going to tell your mama." Her voice ended on a squeak.

Nothing moved. Even the critters around them had fallen silent. Or maybe she couldn't hear them because her heart was trying to beat some sense into her. The flight portion of her fight-or-flight response was winning.

"Are you seriously threatening to rat me out to my mama? Maybe you won't be alive to talk." Although his words contained a threat, something about his voice had lightened, as if she had surprised him.

She squared herself with the shadow of Emmett and crossed her arms over her chest, her gaze stuck on the gun. If it swung toward her, she would make a dive for the tall grass. "I know your mama, and she'd come out here and jerk a knot in your tail if I told her about this."

"For the love of God, I'm not going to shoot you." He cracked the barrel and set the gun out of sight. Although it was still on Greer's mind as she shuffled forward.

"I'm Greer—"

"Greer Hadley. I know who you are. I'm not having sex with you so go on home."

Instinct had Greer gasping and clutching her great-grandmother's pearls. She didn't think she was still capable of being shocked. She was wrong. "I'm not—how could you think—? Oh my God, you are a pig."

"Am I? Well, I'm sick of you girls traipsing out here like I need a reminder of my glory days. The sign on the gate says no trespassing. I meant it."

"Maybe you need to replace it with 'Trespassers Will Be Shot.' There's got to be a law against shooting at innocent visitors."

"You weren't in any danger. I know my way around a gun."

"Common human decency should have kicked in before you fired." She took her hat off and fanned herself. The heat from the sun mixed with the shot of adrenaline made her stomach climb up her throat. She shuffled toward the porch steps.

"I told you to leave." Had some of her panic transferred to him? It sure sounded like it.

"Don't worry, I can't be gone soon enough, but I need to sit down in the shade for a second before I'm sick." She wobbled on the edge of fainting.

"You're sick?"

"Your little stunt scared the shit out of me, Emmett. Give me a minute of peace to cool off, would you?"

He retreated to the house before she got a good look at him, but she didn't care. She plopped down on the top step of his porch, the shade a blessing. A row of three ceiling fans broke the stagnant air around her, and she dropped her head between her knees, her hat tumbling down the stairs.

"Here." He nudged an icy glass against her upper arm.

"Thanks." She drank deeply, finishing half of the tea in one go. She glanced over, her gaze bouncing off his legs, her breath catching in her throat.

One calf was ropy muscles covered in dark blond hair. The other was a dark metal imitation. Scuffed gray athletic shoes were on his feet. A black sleeve covered the knee of his amputated leg and disappeared into the leg of slouchy cargo shorts a size too big.

She shifted until her back was against the porch and finger-combed her sweaty hair out of her face. Forcing her gaze off his legs, she took in the rest of him. While the boy who had ruled the halls of Madison High School was recognizable, the man who had taken his place exuded a bitter darkness that boy had seemed immune to. But no one was immune to tragedies. They struck with no consideration of good or evil.

Instead of calming, her stomach turned even more rambunctious. "How've you been, Emmett?" The question popped out before she could put a lid on the knee-jerk politeness. Obviously, things had not gone well for him.

"Fine. Peachy. Never been better. Is that why you've come all the way out here? You're not here to fuck me out of my *mood*?" Every word dripped with sarcasm.

So much sarcasm, in fact, that Greer recognized the ploy from her own personal library of reactions. Hit before someone could exploit your weaknesses, or even worse, offer a mealy-mouthed side of sympathy.

"You kiss your mama with that mouth?" Greer asked with the tartness of lemonade even as she took another sip of sweet tea.

His lips twitched, slight but unmistakable. She'd chosen wisely. Coddling was not what Emmett needed. She wasn't actually sure what a man like Emmett needed, but a good kick in the butt after his reckless, insane greeting was more than deserved.

"Twice on Sundays," he said in a voice laced with amusement before his mouth settled into a harsh line. "What are you doing here, Greer?"

"I can't believe you even remember me." Besides their limited interaction in class, her dominant memory of Emmett was from their senior year, in a busy hallway between classes. He'd swooped in and told off a guy who'd been bothering her for weeks. Did he even remember, or was she one of hundreds of misfits he'd rescued back then?

"Why wouldn't I? We were in the same grade. You sat behind me in World History."

"That's right, I did." She kept her voice vague as if just remembering the fact. Lord, she hoped he had no inkling that she'd imagined what his hair would feel like under her fingers. A bout of embarrassment had her flapping her shirt. "Am I to understand women have been coming out here to . . . you know, *offer* themselves to you?"

"A couple. I guess they want to save me."

"I don't know that you need saving, but you could surely use a shower."

He barked a laugh, but she was serious. His hair was longer than she'd ever seen it—ragged and choppy with a slight curl where the ends hit the collar of his T-shirt. It was also darker, but she wasn't sure if that was from the years gone by or the lack of shampoo.

"Why are you here, Greer?" he asked again, sounding exhausted.

"I volunteer for Amelia's Music Tree Foundation. Are you familiar?"

He mumbled another curse and ran a hand down his face. "I told Amelia I wasn't interested."

"Did you greet her in the same charming manner as you welcomed me?"

"Something similar." Emmett's smile held no humor.

Amelia was going to get an earful. Her caginess about Emmett the day before was making more sense. She'd better sign off on a dozen service hours after putting Greer's life in danger.

"You should be honored we agreed to make a house call," Greer said with a faked lightness.

"I didn't ask for your help."

"No, but your mama did. Don't you want to make her happy?"

"I'm not ten years old; I'm a grown man. I don't live my life to make my parents happy. Or proud." His declaration unearthed another streak of bitterness.

"From what I heard, you came home a hero, so I'm sure you've made your family proud. Your mama is worried about you out here all alone is all."

"A *hero*? You're just like Mama and them. You don't understand shit. Go on, and don't come back." His about-face was ruined by a slightly unbalanced totter on his artificial leg. The screen door banged shut followed by the slam of a solid door in red to match the roof.

The tension retreated with him like a black cloud. She rose and descended the steps, scooping her hat up and putting it back on her head, the straw like hot needles against her scalp. Shuffling backward from the house, she took in the bees circling the lips of the beer bottles set up in a triangle and the half-empty Jack Daniel's next to a rocking chair.

As she turned, a twitch at the window curtains registered. Forcing herself not to look back, she stalked toward her car, only slowing when the protection of the trees swept around her. Sweat slid down her back and itched her scalp.

She made it back over the gate without adding to her injuries, retrieved her shoes, and sat in the blessed coolness of her AC for a few minutes. She couldn't imagine Emmett sitting down to talk out his issues, much less putting his feelings to paper. Too much roiled under the surface. She'd done her duty by Amelia and the foundation.

Yet, a different duty tugged at her conscience. Duty to a boy who'd been kind to her for no reason. Duty to a man who'd sacrificed more than a leg for his country.

She stopped at the crossroads. Right would take her home, where she had nothing waiting on her but the palpable worry emanating from her loving, hovering parents and an uncertain future. Left would take her around the perimeter of the Lawson's horse farm to the main house. What did she owe Emmett? What did she owe herself?

Before she could delve into the whys and wherefores, she turned left. The Lawson's house was antebellum in style with white columns out front. Emmett's mother had hosted teas and ladies' get-togethers at the house when life was slower and socializing had nothing to do with electronics. Greer had never been invited inside.

A horse barn stretched out to the right and the fences were well maintained this close to the working fields. The Lawsons specialized in training Tennessee walking horses and dressage horses, not racing.

Greer parked out front and wished for a ponytail holder and a stick of deodorant. She had never seen Mrs. Lawson without perfectly coiffed hair and makeup and dressed in chic, age-appropriate clothes.

Greer tugged on the hem of her skirt. Her wardrobe consisted of clothes appropriate for bars and performing, not calling on one of the oldest, most respected families in Madison. At least she'd put on her pearls that morning. She stepped onto the porch and raised her hand to knock when raised voices on the other side made her hesitate.

She couldn't make out the words, but a man and woman were arguing. Mr. and Mrs. Lawson presumably, although she'd never seen either of them say a harsh word to or about the other in public. They were admired and lauded. Mr. Lawson was a deacon and Mrs. Lawson headed up the charitable acts society at their church.

She swallowed and considered her options. If she retreated, she wouldn't come back. Her guilt over not being able to help Emmett would eventually fade and life would go on. She wouldn't fool herself into believing otherwise.

Couples fought all the time. They could be arguing over dinner plans or what color to paint their living room. She rapped on the door and the voices cut off. She rocked in her sandals and half turned to look back at her car and the road beyond, feeling awkward and wishing for an easy out.

The door cracked open and revealed a sliver of Mrs. Lawson. She was in jeans and an untucked, oversize T-shirt with the farm logo on the pocket. Her hair was in a messy updo and her face was makeup free.

While it had been years since Greer's parents had guilted her into attending church with them and she'd seen Mrs. Lawson, she did not look like the same woman who lived in Greer's memories. The skin at her eyes had thinned and sagged and the lines around her mouth had deepened. Her state of dishevelment wouldn't have been surprising with anyone else, but Greer had never seen Mrs. Lawson looking less than perfect.

"Mrs. Lawson." Greer pasted on a smile she'd learned to wear when the spotlight was too bright and her stage fright crept up to sabotage her.

"Why, Greer Hadley. I heard you moved back in with your parents." Although no judgment marred the words, the way Mrs. Lawson refused to meet Greer's eye told her enough about what else she'd heard.

"I have, yes. Just until I get on my feet."

"What can I do for you, dear?" While her small smile contained a welcome, she didn't swing the door wide and invite Greer inside.

Sweat prickled the back of her neck as she searched for a space between polite and intrusive. "I've come from seeing Emmett and was hoping you had a moment to chat."

Mrs. Lawson touched her bloodless lips with blue-veined hands. "Oh my. Did he do something . . . impetuous?"

"I should have called first." Greer forced a reassuring smile. Mr. Lawson was nowhere in sight over Mrs. Lawson's shoulder.

"I'm so sorry. He's having a difficult time at the moment." Worry was writ in large print across Mrs. Lawson's face. "What did he do?"

In the little time Greer had spent with Emmett, she could sense the two things he couldn't bear was to be a burden and to be pitied. No wonder he had sought out the solitude of the cabin. But if Mrs. Lawson was aware Emmett was scaring people off by shooting at them, she might have a stroke.

"Nothing you need to apologize for. I'm working with the Music Tree Foundation, and Amelia had asked me to stop by to see him."

Mrs. Lawson's mouth formed an O before she nodded and fully opened the door to finally invite Greer inside. "Can I get you something to drink?"

"No thanks. I had tea at Emmett's."

"Did you? I didn't think he let visitors get that close." The laugh Mrs. Lawson attempted cracked.

The Lawson house was more than 150 years old. The wood emitted a scent that whispered of ladies in hoop skirts and men on horseback. Mrs. Lawson led the way into a living room, throwing Greer into another time altogether. The mid-century furniture and accents of yellow flashed a picture of the ladies from town gathering for afternoon drinks and cigarettes before anyone knew they caused cancer.

The furniture was delicate and the dust motes plentiful. Greer sank to the edge of a couch covered in a floral tapestry. Mrs. Lawson took a green velour armchair across from a low coffee table. The magazines stacked on top were months out of date. She fiddled with her wedding band. It was loose.

"What's happened to Emmett, Mrs. Lawson?" Greer didn't mean to launch a direct assault, but Mrs. Lawson didn't deflect the seriousness of the question.

"War happened."

"His left leg?"

"Amputated right below the knee. He feels the loss keenly— you'll recall what an athlete he was—but his problems go deeper and darker than the physical. I don't know what to do."

"Can you get him out of the cabin?"

"I've tried, but he refuses."

"What about food? He must have to go to the grocery on occasion." *And the liquor store*, she wanted to add, but didn't.

"I take him groceries every week and the occasional home-cooked meal. He's already lost too much weight." Mrs. Lawson pulled a tissue out of her pocket and blew her nose. Grief had stripped away any social affectations.

Greer could only imagine how difficult it was for Mrs. Lawson to see her only child suffer, but enabling his behavior wasn't doing him any favors. He required a reason to rejoin the living and food seemed a fundamental need. "If you want my advice, I would stop food deliveries immediately. Lure him here with a dinner invite when you know he's good and hungry. He'll come out before he starves."

Mrs. Lawson looked away but nodded. "I'll stop. I'm desperate enough to try anything to reach him. Anything to get him home. That's why I reached out to your uncle Bill."

Home. Even though Emmett was physically back, Greer understood what Mrs. Lawson meant. "I didn't realize he was musically inclined."

"Oh, but he was. He loved the guitar in high school. Spent hours in his room. If he hadn't been such a good football player—and of course, his father encouraged sports over music—Emmett might have joined the band."

Greer blinked and worked on squaring her memories with the new information. "Does he still play?"

Mrs. Lawson shook her head. "I'm not sure. Wait here a moment."

She scurried away, the creak of the old wooden stairs and ceiling tracing her footsteps. The noise increased to bumps and bangs.

"You've come from seeing Emmett?" The male voice swung her attention from the ceiling to the doorway.

She shot to her feet. "Mr. Lawson. Nice to see you, sir."

He made a brushing motion as if her greeting were an annoying no-see-um. "How was he?"

How to answer? Truthfully or politely? "He was fine."

Mr. Lawson retained a military bearing along with a buzz cut and clipped manner of speaking. Emmett had his build, but had inherited his smile and sense of humor from his mother. Greer had always found Mr. Lawson intimidating.

"He still out there running everyone off with a gun and drinking himself to an early grave?"

"He wasn't drunk." For some reason she couldn't fathom, considering Emmett had been rude and scared the bejeezus out of her, she didn't mention the gun or the bottles lined up like a squadron on his porch.

"Small mercy. I would appreciate if you wouldn't go gossiping around town about our situation."

"Of course not. I'd like to try to help Emmett. I'm volunteering with the Music Tree Foundation."

He snorted. "Volunteering? Is that what you kids are calling court-ordered service these days?"

Anger went off in her chest like a sparkler. "Your son needs help, and it doesn't seem to me that anyone else is breaking his door down."

Footsteps sounded on the stairs. Greer held Mr. Lawson's stony stare for as long as she could, grateful for Mrs. Lawson's interruption. "Is everything all right?"

"No, it's not, Judy, and there's no use in pretending it is." He never took his eyes off Greer. Was he worried she would steal the silver? "Your parents are good people, but considering Emmett's situation, the last thing he needs is a drunk influencing him."

The sparkler of anger turned into a Roman candle. "I'm not a drunk, Mr. Lawson. It was one night of poor decisions. Decisions I'm atoning for now."

Mrs. Lawson held a dust-covered guitar in her hands. "Greer is trying to help Emmett, dear."

"We don't need her kind of help."

"You should be grateful I'm not calling the police and filing a report against *him*."

"I'm going to march out there and order him to move back

here. That's all there is to it." Remnants of his life as a soldier clipped his words and squared his shoulders.

"That is a terrible idea, sir." Greer wished she were taller and more intimidating. "Let me try to—"

"You will leave him alone." His voice tolerated no dissent.

A kernel of gumption sprouted in her heart. The last decade stumping and failing in Nashville had left her confidence and conviction battered. Success had never even grazed her fingertips. She'd stopped fighting for her dreams because her dreams had been dismantled piece by piece, year by year, until they were rubble.

Where did the sudden urge to fight for Emmett come from? The defeat reflected in his eyes and the set of his shoulders had been only too familiar. As much love and worry as his parents carried for him—and she recognized Mr. Lawson's anger was born of love—they didn't understand him. She did.

Emmett was a wounded animal burrowed in a hole. He wouldn't be ordered out by Mr. Lawson or coddled out by Mrs. Lawson either. He had to be lured out, maybe even bullied out. She would probably fail—again—but dammit, she would try.

"I'll do what I believe is right, Mr. Lawson." She took a step forward. "Now if you'll excuse me."

Mr. Lawson hesitated a beat longer than was polite before he cleared the doorway. Greer walked away as if she were leaving the stage after a poorly attended set. Head high and an unbothered expression on her face.

She stepped outside. The humidity made a deep breath impossible. As she reached the bottom of the porch steps, Mrs. Lawson pushed through the screen door. "Greer! Hold up a second, would you?"

Greer turned and looked beyond Mrs. Lawson, where the

long shadow of her husband haunted the hall. "I'm sorry if I upset you or your husband. I can assure you, it wasn't my intention."

Mrs. Lawson whispered, "Everything seems to upset Henry these days. He loves Emmett. Wanted to give him a hero's welcome home—newspaper article, a party, school visits—but Emmett refused."

"Expectations can be more dangerous and disappointing than reality."

"Yes, they can." Mrs. Lawson touched Greer's wrist. "You seem very wise for one so young, my dear."

Greer was taken aback by the observation. Compared to her high school friends who were married with mortgages, Greer had been left behind. Her drunken exhibition at Becky's had only cemented her state of immaturity.

Doubt inserted itself like a splinter. Her life was in shambles. Why did she think she could help a man as broken and hurting as Emmett Lawson?

"Here." Mrs. Lawson pushed the guitar into Greer's chest.

She held her hands up. "What am I supposed to do with Emmett's guitar?"

"Take it to him. See if it will make a difference." Mrs. Lawson was starved for hope. All Greer had to offer were crumbs.

"Mr. Lawson doesn't want me to interfere, and Emmett told me point-blank to never come back."

"I'm sure he did." Mrs. Lawson's blue eyes cut as deeply as her son's. "But you wouldn't be here right now if you weren't going back."

Mrs. Lawson was right. Greer would try again. Not right away, but soon. She'd give him time to get comfortable in his solitude, before she shattered it again. In the meantime, she'd research issues returning veterans faced. Especially ones who had been wounded.

Greer wrapped her hand around the neck of the guitar, the weight like an anchor. "I'll give it another try. As long as he doesn't threaten to shoot at me again."

Tears shined behind Mrs. Lawson's smile. "Thank you."

Disappointment was inevitable, but Greer was too far down the road to do a U-turn now. "I'm not a therapist or even a good example of a successful, functioning member of society. Keep your expectations low."

Mrs. Lawson's laugh was weak but natural. "Will you let me know how you make out?"

"Sure thing." Greer gave a little wave as she drove off, letting her smile and shoulders slump as soon as she was out of sight. What had she gotten herself into?

Chapter 4

The next two sessions with Ally at the Music Tree Foundation passed in silence. Not a comfortable, friendly silence or even a silence born of them working on lyrics, but an oppressive, stalking silence like that of a prisoner awaiting execution. It was exhausting.

Greer wanted to coax Ally to open up and talk to her, but she had no experience with teenagers, beyond what she herself had experienced in high school, and had no idea how to breech the wall of resentment and cocky bitchiness Ally had erected.

Greer fantasized about quitting and letting someone else deal with Ally, but according to Amelia, Greer was the last resort. If she walked out, Amelia wouldn't sign off on her service hours, and Ally would be expelled from the program and referred back to the juvenile court system for a more severe punishment.

Unable to throw Ally back into the system, Greer girded herself for another soul-withering session of silence before stepping inside the Music Tree Foundation. Singing echoed from down the hall. The harmonizing between Amelia's rich alto and the husky baritone drew Greer closer like the Pied Piper.

She pressed her ear against the door and closed her eyes. It was an old mountain song about a young man dying and leaving his true love behind. The writer's name had been lost to the mostly illiterate musicians handing it down through the generations.

"Eavesdropping? Is that what you're stooping to now?" The slice of Ally's voice was a jagged line of darkness into the light the music cast.

Greer popped her eyes open long enough to say, "Shut up and listen," then she closed her eyes again and retreated into the magic Amelia and the man were creating in such a mundane setting.

Greer didn't notice Ally move, but when the song ended and Greer returned to the narrow hallway smelling of fresh paint, Ally had positioned herself like Greer's mirror image. Silence again beset them, but it was unburdened. Words weren't necessary when sharing music.

It had been a long time since music had cast magic for Greer, but in the silence, she remembered how it used to be. Before music had transformed from a joy into a grueling job.

Greer nudged her chin back toward their workroom, and Ally followed her inside without complaint. As the spell from the song faded, Greer whispered, "Did you feel it?"

A hesitancy and unsureness stripped away Ally's usual indifference. "I think so."

"What did the music make you feel?" Greer pitched her voice low as if the music hung in the room like spirits that could be frightened away.

"Kind of sad."

"Me too. I felt like crying, but at the same time, I didn't want it to end."

"It was more than just the words that made it sad, though, wasn't it?" Ally's gaze darted to Greer's face and back down.

It was as if Greer had sighted a rare bird. She forced a non-chalant lilt into her voice. "The minor key gives it a melancholy feel. The best songwriters wield power over people's emotions. The choice of key makes the difference between a happy pop song and an FU breakup song and a melancholy ballad."

"Who wrote that song?"

"No one knows. Was it a woman who lost her lover too young? Or a man who knew he was dying? Or was it made it up by a musician with a vivid imagination one winter when there was nothing else to do?"

"What do you think?"

"I like to imagine a woman, alone on some mountaintop, writing that song to honor her lost love."

"That's super-depressing."

"Life can be depressing. And unfair. And just plain sucky."

While Ally didn't answer, her eye roll seemed to signal her agreement. An opening yawned. Greer wanted to know more about her father's death and what had driven her to shoplift. But the opening felt too much like a trap. Like Emmett, Ally would protect her truths at all costs.

What better way to earn trust than to give trust? "Do you want to know how I ended up here?" Greer asked.

"Thought you busted up a bar after getting cheated on?"

"Beau cheating on me was the last, pathetic straw. Want to hear the rest of the story?"

"Whatever." Ally shrugged her adolescent haughtiness back on like a grungy concert T-shirt.

"I spent a decade trying to *make it* in Nashville." Greer wasn't sure what making it even looked like anymore. "Ten years of my life gone by with nothing to show for it. I came crawling home with even less than I left with."

"How long had you been dating the cheater?"

"Around six months. I went to high school with him, but we had lost touch over the years."

"Is he hot?"

"He's nice-looking in a buttoned-up, preppy kind of way, I guess. But hot? Nah." They shared a smile. "I suppose Beau reminded me of who I used to be."

Ally abandoned her indifference, sitting forward with wide eyes. "How'd you find out he was cheating on you?"

"I went by his place as a surprise and caught him with his pants down. Literally."

Ally's chair creaked. "That wasn't cool of him. At all."

"No, it wasn't." But had it been cool of her to string Beau along because he was stable and comfortable? She ignored the niggle of guilt. "Long story short, I moved back in with my parents, drank too much one night, and got arrested for disorderly conduct and resisting arrest."

"And you chose to volunteer here because you're a musician?"

"I'm not a musician anymore. My uncle was the sentencing judge and Amelia is his stepdaughter. I'd have rather picked up trash on the side of the road, but I can't complain about the air-conditioning."

"I'm just glad you're not a self-righteous do-gooder like Amelia and the women from Fort Knox."

"What women from Fort Knox?" Greer kept the rampant curiosity off her face and out of her voice, afraid Ally would scurry behind her walls. When the girl only tapped a pencil on the table, Greer said, "I'm definitely not a do-gooder. In fact, I hit the policeman who was trying to arrest me in the nuts. Accidentally, I think. Although it might have been a Freudian slip."

Ally's lips twitched. Could it possibly be the start of a smile? "I think those can only be slips of the tongue, not knees."

"I actually jabbed him with my foot, which happened to be in a spiked high heel. He went down like a sacked quarterback."

"Sounds awesome." While Ally wasn't smiling, her eyes twinkled and hinted at who she might have been before tragedy.

"It was pretty hilarious until they threw me in county lockup." Greer gave an exaggerated shudder, but she didn't need to pretend to be disgusted. "A bunch of rough, rowdy, mostly drunk women. One toilet. I had sobered up enough at that point to recognize I was in a heap of trouble."

"What'd you do?"

"Called my parents."

"Were they pissed?"

"Honestly, it would have been easier if they had been. They were sad and disappointed. Not like I can blame them."

"Sounds like how my mom looked when she got to the mall after I was caught."

"The mall and not Walmart?"

Ally crossed her arms and leaned her chair back on two legs. "I do have my standards."

"What'd you lift?"

The chair banged back to the floor, and Ally chewed on her thumbnail. The black polish was chipped and the nail was bitten down to the quick. She could whip from bravado to jittery tension faster than a hiccup. "A Coach purse."

"Fancy, but I don't think it would have matched your boots."

"It wasn't for me."

"For your mom?"

"She deserved something nice." Defiance hardened Ally's features. "My only regret is that I got caught."

At fifteen, behind Greer's façade of coolness, she had been naive and dreamy and protected from life's travails. She wouldn't have understood someone like Ally. At thirty, however, Greer could relate a little too well.

"I regret embarrassing myself, but mostly I regret embarrassing my parents." Strangely, it didn't feel weird at all to be unloading her truths to a fifteen-year-old. "They had to sit behind me in court while I was sentenced. How did your mom react?"

Another shrug that seemed exclusive to teenagers. "She's worried I'm turning into a delinquent."

"Are you?" Greer kept the question light on judgment.

"Nashville sucks. I hate it," Ally said through clenched teeth.

"As Nashville recently kicked me to the curb like it was trash day, I can't disagree. Is it school or your neighborhood or what?"

"It's everything. Mom says we're settling down here and not moving again. She hated the moving."

"You didn't mind base hopping?" Greer asked.

"No. It was cool. Dad made it fun. Took us out to explore. We would try all the restaurants and do the touristy stuff no one ever does when they live in a town." Ally picked at her nails, leaving flecks of black on the white tabletop. "I miss him."

Greer couldn't imagine losing a parent so young. What would she have done without her mom and dad and a soft place to land? "I'm sorry about your dad."

Ally's gaze flicked up, then back down to concentrate on denuding her nails. "I'm sorry about your *life*."

An unexpected dark humor arrowed out of Ally and hit

Greer right in the funny bone. Her laugh echoed against the concrete walls. "Yeah, my life is a freaking mess. I'm not sure what wisdom I'm supposed to impart to your impressionable little mind except to serve as a cautionary tale."

"I don't know. As grown-ups go, you're not a complete moron. At least you don't treat me like I'm mentally impaired."

"Surely your mom—"

"Not Mom. The principal, the kids, those bitches from Fort Knox."

"What did those women want?"

"I guess to make themselves feel good that their husbands and their kids' dads are still alive."

Their visits were probably more altruistic than Ally was giving them credit for. Yet, feelings were feelings and something the women had said or did triggered Ally's bitterness. Or perhaps it was simple jealousy. They still had husbands and their kids still had fathers.

"Do you have family in Nashville?"

"No family anywhere. Dad was in foster care before he joined up, and Mom left home at sixteen. They didn't want her. My dad used to say they had each other and that's all they needed." Ally rubbed her nose but didn't look up.

"What's your mom doing now?"

"She needs to find a job to save up some money to change things. Doesn't matter what."

"Change things how?"

"She wants to go back to school. Nursing. Problem is she never graduated high school and needs her GED first."

"Community centers or libraries sometimes offer classes to help adults get their GED. Has she looked into it?"

Ally shrugged and Greer veered the conversation in a different direction.

"What was your dad like?"

"Normal, I guess. Kind of embarrassing sometimes. He used to sing as loud as he could in the car. Or dance in public." A natural but deeply buried sweetness and humor seemed to bubble up with her words, and her lips twitched into an almost-smile. "He worked a lot. And when he deployed, he was gone for months and months."

"That had to be rough."

"Yeah, but we lived on base and all the kids had a parent gone at some time or another. It made it easier knowing you weren't alone."

Alone. Ally got an A-plus in pushing people away, but was she waiting for someone to stick around? Greer wasn't known for her sticking ability. She wasn't even sure what her future held after satisfying her service hours. Maybe she'd take off and start over in a new city.

A knock made them both turn toward the door. Amelia stuck her head in. "Time's up, ladies. Richard needs the room."

Instead of each second of their session ticking off like kicks to the head, the time had sped by. More questions lined up in Greer's mind, but Ally was up, her backpack swinging over a shoulder, and out the door in record time.

"See you next week!" Greer called down the hall.

Ally flipped a bird over her head but didn't turn around for a reaction. The door banged closed. Greer couldn't help but smile and raised her eyebrows at Amelia. "Classy girl."

Amelia laughed and backed into her office. "I have to say, I'm impressed."

"Impressed that she basically told me to eff off?" Greer followed and propped her shoulder against the doorframe.

"Impressed you've stuck it out. And did I actually hear talking? Was that you or her?"

"Both of us. It's referred to as a conversation."

"That's really great progress." Amelia met Greer's sarcasm with sincerity.

"Besides the epic failure of our first session, I haven't gotten her to write music, though. Isn't that kind of the point?"

"The point of the music is to help process the anxiety or depression or PTSD they're experiencing. The music is merely a tool to get them to a healthier place. A powerful tool, in my opinion, but there are other ways."

"I'm not sure what's going on with Ally." A burgeoning worry for the girl had grown through the session. "She's definitely not happy. It's her dad's death, but also the change in her circumstances. I don't think she fits in at her new school."

"I don't think she *tries* to fit in."

"Maybe so, but what wisdom can I offer? I've never gone out of my way to fit in either."

"Fitting in is overrated. You made a name for yourself in Madison through your music. You were unique but not in a destructive way. Maybe you can help her find a constructive path." Amelia sat behind her desk and shuffled folders until she landed on one in particular. "Where do you stand with Emmett Lawson?"

"I think it's best to stand out of range of his shotgun. Thanks for the heads-up." Greer narrowed her eyes at Amelia, who had the grace to grimace.

"I swear if I truly thought he was a danger, I wouldn't have suggested you go, but he's all bluster." Amelia sat, heaved a sigh, and slumped back in the chair. "I hate to give up on anyone, but he needs something we can't provide."

Amelia spoke from a place of logic. A song wouldn't fix Emmett's issues. It wouldn't even plug the holes. But there was the matter of his guitar. Greer was toting it around and building up the courage to face him again, but had chickened out every time she'd driven by the locked gate and No Trespassing sign. After all, if she couldn't even handle an angsty teenager, how did she expect to handle a man with very grown-up problems— and a gun?

Yet, her session with Ally had given her a new confidence. "Double hours still apply, right?"

"I'll consider it hazard pay."

"Let me give it one more shot." She huffed a laugh to cover her spate of nerves. "Not literally, I hope."

As she was leaving, Greer stopped halfway down the hall before returning to pop her head around Amelia's door. "Just in case . . . if something happens to me, you know where to look."

Chapter 5

Emmett Lawson rocked in a chair on his front porch and tapped the barrel of his shotgun against his leg. Not his flesh and blood one, but the other one. The length of carbon fiber that was a poor substitute for what he'd lost.

Yet, he felt petty and ungrateful for voicing a complaint. He'd seen men at Walter Reed worse off by a country mile. Men who'd lost both legs or hands or all of the above. As his buddy Terrance had pointed out, at least he still had the ability to jerk off, thank the Lord. A small smile surfaced before disappearing once more into the darkness of his thoughts.

He eeny-meeny-miney-mo'ed the five shots of Jack he had lined up on the porch rail even though they were identical. An empty shot glass rolled at his feet. He landed on the middle shot and knocked it back. The burn took his mind off the phantom tingling in his lost foot and got him one shot closer to passing out, which was his ultimate goal.

Even though his mom and dad were only a mile away as the

crow flew, he missed his other family—the army. Instead of pity, they gave him shit. Instead of tiptoeing around his feelings, they stomped all over them. It had been comforting to still be treated like an army captain and not an invalid. Even at Walter Reed, the mood veered more toward kick-ass rather than downtrodden.

Now his only company was the occasional horse that wandered to the fence that separated the cabin from the Lawson horse farm. A pretty tan-colored mare had drawn him over one afternoon, her belly round with a foal. He'd only had a sad, shrunken apple to offer, but she'd taken it from his hand with a gentle nip and good-natured chuffs.

He missed the freedom of galloping a horse, the wind and pound of hoofs blocking out the world, but the thought of scrambling into the saddle and the awkwardness that would ensue was unbearable. The horse represented yet another loss, and he ignored the mare when she'd returned a few days later. Eventually, she'd given up on him too.

If it were only the horses. When he'd first returned home to Madison, the looks and whispers full of pity from the townspeople made him sick to his stomach. He felt like he'd let people down by getting his fucking leg blown off. On the opposite end of the spectrum, his dad wanted to hold him up like some goddamn hero. He wasn't, no matter what the army tried to say. Good men had died under his command. Men who had deserved a hero's welcome home instead of a flag-draped casket.

Clink. Clink. Clink. The dull sound didn't harmonize with the birds singing or the bugs humming around the blooming blue hydrangeas lining his porch. It was unnatural. The bushes were growing out of control, but Emmett preferred leaving the landscaping and grass untamed. Maybe he'd let them devour the cabin along with him.

Besides a daily text from his mom, his parents had left him alone for the past week. He got the feeling the text was so that he could assure them he hadn't eaten the end of his shotgun. While he couldn't quantify the heavy feelings that squatted on his chest, he wasn't ready to die. He didn't deserve the peace that came with death.

Movement at the edge of the woods stilled his rocking. He brought the gun up and laid it on the porch rail to steady it in case he needed to scare off another do-gooder. He squinted, the lowering sun behind the person and in his eyes.

It was a woman for sure. No mistaking the sway of hips and long legs. Rays of light glinted off the woman's chestnut hair. "Ah, hell," he muttered.

It was Greer Hadley again. Was his warning shot and general air of assholery not enough to scare her off forever? She had something in her hand. A gun? Was she going to challenge him to a duel? A smile tugged at his mouth, but he squashed it. Laughter was off-limits.

He grabbed his binoculars and let out another curse. Even worse than a gun, she carried a guitar. His focused eyes drifted to Greer's legs. She was in another skirt, but this one wasn't as tight as the last one she'd worn. The breeze whipped the hem around her thighs. He pressed the binoculars tighter against his face and took in the length of her legs. Long and lean and sexy as hell. Ironic he was a leg man when he didn't have two of his own.

If he'd had his service rifle from the army, he could have shot the guitar out of her hand, but he wouldn't risk hurting her by using his shotgun. It had been his great-grandfather's and was known more for its deafening report than its accuracy.

The lethargy that had kept him rocking and staring off in

the distance most of the day drained out of him. His foot tapped faster the closer she got until he couldn't stand it any longer and popped up to meet her at the bottom of the steps.

He didn't even care if she noticed his awkward descent, always leading with his intact right foot. In fact, he hoped she commented on it so he could meet her pity with fury. Anger was the only thing that made him feel alive.

"What's that?" he asked, even though he recognized every curve and nick of his old guitar. It had been his solace and his secret in high school.

"Your mama asked me to drop her by. The poor thing was in pitiful shape, though. I cleaned her up, restrung, and tuned her." She swung the guitar up and strummed a C chord.

The sweetness of the sound was exactly why he'd left the guitar behind, along with everything else that reminded him of his life before. "I don't want it. Pawn it and give the money to my mom. Or keep the money yourself. I won't tell." Mostly because he barely talked to his parents and when he did it wasn't about anything deeper than the weather or food. "Or, hell, give it to me, and I'll use it as a garden planter."

"Are you insane?" The way she ran her hand over the curve of the guitar sent awareness zipping through his body. "This is a Martin."

"Yeah, I know. I saved up an entire year to buy it." He turned to tackle the stairs again. "I don't care what you do with it."

He didn't want the damn thing sitting around the cabin mocking him. She grabbed his shoulder, and he twisted around. Shock that she would touch him at all mixed with the realization he hadn't so much as shaken another person's hand for months.

"Your mama wouldn't forgive me if I didn't make sure you

got her." She shoved the guitar at his chest and his hands came up automatically to take it.

Anger so familiar as to be a comfort licked like the start of a wildfire. "Fine. Tell her you gave it to me, and then tell her what I did with it."

He tightened his hands on the neck and raised the guitar over his head like a rock god ready to shock and awe his audience of one. Splintering the guitar into pieces would hurt, but he craved the pain. It would distract from the deeper regrets that tormented him.

He tensed his arms to bring the guitar down. She slammed into him like a linebacker. His weight shifted unexpectedly onto his artificial leg. His balance was already shitty and the two shots of Jack didn't help his reflexes.

He let go of the guitar to catch his balance, but he was a goner. His shoulder took the brunt of the fall, but his head smacked something hard and sharp. He rolled to his back, his ears ringing. He touched his temple at his hairline and his fingers came away bloody.

Greer was on the ground too but didn't spare a glance toward him. She cradled the guitar like she'd rescued a child from a speeding car. She ran her hands over the wood, her voice breathless. "Thank the Lord, I think she's okay."

"What about me? You cracked my head open." His voice descended into tantrum levels.

Her mouth pulled down and her eyes crinkled. Good, she should be worried. After setting his guitar down like it was a Fabergé egg, she crawled over to him. The closer she got the more her expression resembled suppressed humor and not worry. "Awww . . . did Humpty Dumpty take a fall?"

"I could have a concussion." He pushed himself up on his elbows.

"It's barely a scratch, you big baby. I *know* you've been hurt worse." Her gaze skated down to his leg and back up, but it held neither pity nor awkwardness. She shook her head and tutted. "What were you thinking? If you had smashed the guitar, I would have given you more than a bump on the head. Your guitar deserves better."

Maybe it did. But he wasn't equipped to care for anyone or anything—not even himself. "I may be down a leg, but I'm pretty sure I could take you."

"Ha! Haven't you heard that I'm a terror to the balls of Madison's men?"

"Did Beau finally grow a pair for you to keep in your pocket?"

Her face changed in a heartbeat. The sass and playfulness gone, hurt and sadness in their place. "I figured word had gotten around to everyone. Even you. Beau and I broke up."

His foot did not taste good. If he ever left the cabin or not let all his calls go to voicemail, he might have heard the gossip, but he hadn't. "I'm sorry. I didn't know."

She sat back on her knees, her skirt exposing several inches of her thighs. "It's all right. I mean, all right you mentioned it. Not that what he did was all right."

In high school, Greer had been cute in an awkward, gawky way. Until she got onstage. Onstage, she'd transformed and commanded everyone's attention with a confidence she'd grown into.

He forced his gaze off her legs. He shouldn't be noticing her legs or the curves of her hips and waist and definitely not the way the pink V-neck stretched across breasts that for sure weren't there in high school.

"How did Beau screw up?"

"Why do you assume it was him and not me?"

His gaze zipped down her legs and back up. "Because he'd be an idiot to break up with you."

She looked away and smoothed her hair behind her ear as if embarrassed, but the corner of her mouth ticked up for a millisecond before firming. "I caught him coitus interruptus with Marcy Sims."

He winced. "Oh man. Awkward."

She shrugged. "I should have expected it. My weekends were busy with gigs, and I worked as a bartender during the week. I guess I should have made an effort to come home more often."

"Hold up. Are you actually blaming yourself for his wandering dick? He should have manned up and broken up with you before screwing around. Which reinforces my theory that he had no balls to begin with."

A smile banished her sadness. "Who am I to argue?"

A fire ant bit him on the finger. "Fire ants are going to feast on us if we keep sitting here. Come on."

He got to his feet with minimal stumbling and held out a hand. She looked up at him, her head cocked. Was she deciding whether he was trustworthy or not? Based on their most recent interactions, he could make an educated guess on which side of that equation he would fall.

She surprised him by slipping her hand into his and allowing him to haul her up. The top of her head was at eye level. Taller than he remembered. Prettier eyes too. Hazel that veered toward green. Her thick hair waved to her shoulder blades. He let go of her hand with a palpable reluctance.

"Take the Martin with you when you go." His harsh tone was an attempt to cover his sudden awareness of her.

"Nope." She scooped the guitar up and clomped up his porch steps. She stopped at the rail, where four shots remained lined up for his obliteration.

She tossed him a look he interpreted as judgmental, but instead of chastising him, she picked up a shot and killed it. Then, without an invitation, she opened his screen door and disappeared inside the cabin.

He stared, torn between outrage and admiration. His life had taken on a rhythm since being discharged from the service, driven by the rise and fall of the sun and the spinning of the earth. It was natural and predictable and . . . boring.

Greer Hadley was not boring. He was on a roller coaster chugging slowly to the top of the first rise. Anticipation and fear and an out-of-control adrenaline rush lurked. It was not a comfortable feeling. But it was exciting.

He tackled the stairs, one at a time, and banged into the house. It was a mess. His dirty clothes were piled in front of the small laundry area, cordoned off by accordion-style doors. His clean clothes filled one of the overstuffed armchairs. Folding seemed like a waste of his time. He was too busy staring at nothing and drinking.

Empty beer and whiskey bottles decorated the mantel, mimicking the way his mother used candles to decorate for the holidays. A yellow jacket buzzed around the lips, on the hunt for something sweet.

His diet relied heavily on frozen pizza, chips, and Little Debbie snack cakes. Basically, anything that didn't require cooking. He would eat the fruit and sometimes the vegetables his mother included with the occasional grocery run she made for him, and once a week or so, she would send over a casserole, which was welcome, but he was surviving fine.

"What a dump," Greer said.

"I wasn't expecting company." His face heated. Dammit, why was he embarrassed when she was the one who'd barged in?

Her gaze traveled down his body and back up. "You cleaned yourself up since last we met, so that's a start."

A supernova went off in his chest. He didn't need to look in a mirror to know his cheeks had gone splotchy. The curse of his fair skin. After her last visit and the poke about his appearance, he had been taking regular showers. Honestly, he'd forgotten how nice it was to be clean.

She laid his guitar across the mound of clean clothes and wandered to the wall that separated the living area from the galley-style kitchen. Crossing her arms and tilting her head, she studied the hole he'd put through the wall with his fist. He rubbed his still-sore knuckles even though it had been a week since the incident. An empty picture frame hung askew, providing a border for the jagged hole in the wall like it wasn't an accident and rather part of an avant-garde art show. Broken glass crunched under her flip-flops.

"What were you going for here?" She took a step back and held her hands up as if framing a scene. Humor played at the corners of her mouth and her arching brows. "Commentary on the rotten core of our pillars of society—I assume this is a load-bearing wall—or an expression of the beauty of rage?"

He needed to fix the wall before his parents noticed. They would for sure haul him off to the VA for the counseling he'd avoided thus far. He hadn't worked up the courage to leave the cabin to face people who would remember him as the football star or the soldier. He didn't know who he was now.

She squatted down to pick up the picture he'd punched out

of its frame, shaking shards of glass off it. Wearing his football uniform, he stood tall and proud and smiling before his last high school football game. A bittersweet moment frozen in time. The confidence and optimism of someone on the verge of setting off in the world shone from his toothy smile. The boy in the picture was a stranger.

Greer ran her finger over his innocent, smiling face. No doubt, she either pitied the man he'd become or wished for the old one back. He plucked the picture out of her hand, crumpled it in his fist, and tossed it over his shoulder. Later he'd rip it into pieces and flush it down to the septic tank, where it belonged.

"You're welcome to leave. Unless you want to clean up for me." The bite in his voice veered unattractively toward peevish.

Her lip curled. "I'm not your maid."

"You're not my therapist either."

"That's not why I'm here."

"Why are you here, Greer? 'Cuz I sure didn't invite you."

Her mouth opened and closed, then she shook her head. "I don't know. You were nice to me once, and I thought I could return the favor. That's dumb, I guess, considering the situations aren't even comparable."

He racked his brain. He remembered her, of course, but they hadn't run in the same circles. "What are you talking about?"

"You don't even remember." She barked a laugh.

"I'm sorry, but I don't."

"It's so weird."

"What? Me?"

"No, that an incident can make such a big impression on one person and not at all on another." She chuffed and shook her head. "You remember Wayne Peeler?"

"The Weasel?"

"He was harassing me in the hall one day before World History. I'm adept at handling handsy assholes nowadays—bartending and playing gigs bring out all kinds—but back then I didn't know what to do. I froze. You grabbed the back of his collar, shoved him into the lockers, and whispered something in his ear, I don't know what you said, but I'm pretty sure he tinkled in his pants. He left me alone after that."

Emmett vaguely remembered the incident, but not what he'd whispered. Probably an R-rated threat of an ass whooping. He'd held enough power and cache at the school to make threats stick like tar even if he lacked the feathers to actually follow through on a beat-down.

"Glad I stuck up for you back then, but you don't owe me anything, if that's what this is about." He waved his hand between them.

"Did you know Wayne is a deputy now?"

"I'd heard something to that effect. Has he let the power go to his head?"

"Straight to the little head between his legs," she said darkly.

He tensed. "What's that supposed to mean? What happened?"

"You didn't hear?"

"I don't get out much." He didn't bother to check his sarcasm. "Tell me."

She tilted her head and narrowed her eyes. "Nope. You're going to have to get the story from someone else, which means having a conversation with an actual human. And it's a good story. Let me know what the rumors are, and I'll fill you in on what *really* happened. Toodleloo."

She waved her fingers and stepped around him. She moved faster than he could and had skipped down the steps before he made it onto the porch. She turned around and walked backward, holding up one of his shot glasses.

"Here's to you. Here's to me. May we never disagree. But if we do, then screw you. Here's to me." She tossed the shot back, dropped the glass at her feet, and quick-stepped toward the tree line. He watched until she disappeared.

Only when his cheeks grew sore did he realize he'd been smiling the whole time. He cleared his throat and set his mouth in a line even though there was no one to judge him. The sun had fallen below the tree line, casting dusky fingers over the field. Lightning bugs blinked and drifted into the treetops. He retreated to the house when the mosquitos began to feast, leaving the remainder of the whiskey shots untouched.

No one had been in the cabin since he'd moved in. Two weeks at the big house was all he'd been able to stomach. His nightmares had awakened his parents and they kept trying to get him to talk, talk, talk. Which was the last thing he'd felt like doing since coming home. He craved silence and solitude and . . . nothingness.

Except, with Greer come and gone, restlessness had moved in and made itself at home. He paced, and then for lack of anything else to do, performed some of the PT exercises they'd given him at Walter Reed. He hadn't seen the point in keeping up with them when his future consisted of the rocking chair on the porch of the cabin. Rocking the years away had seemed a good, solid plan at the time. Now, he wasn't so confident.

He grabbed a dustpan and broom and cleaned up the broken glass. He looked around for the wadded photo. It was nowhere, not even under the couch or the antique buffet. While he was in this rare mood, he folded his laundry, put it away, and loaded the dirty clothes into the washer.

For the first time in a long time, his mind and body were tired. The spate of activity had worn him out. He collapsed on the couch and eased his artificial leg off. As much as he hated looking at his stump—it for sure wouldn't win any beauty pageants—a physical relief accompanied the freedom from the prosthetic.

The oddity of not seeing his leg still struck him on occasion. It was a truth learned as a child: certain things belonged in pairs—shoes, hands, eyes, and legs. He flipped the lights off, laid back on the couch, and pulled a blanket over his legs so his mind wouldn't struggle with the incongruity and his heart didn't have to deal with the loss.

Greer danced behind his closed eyes like a shadow boxer. She'd left the damn guitar. Tomorrow he'd use it as target practice and hang the remnants in the water oak at the edge of the road so she'd see it when she came back. God, he could just imagine the tongue lashing she would dispense. He smiled to himself in the dark.

Even though he was tired, he couldn't sleep with his thoughts riding a merry-go-round pushed by Greer. He reached for his cell phone, the screen light making him squint. He hesitated, weighing the implications of reaching out, but he wasn't a cat. Curiosity wouldn't kill him. Hopefully.

He hit his parents' phone number and prayed his mother picked up. Not surprisingly, his prayers once again went unanswered.

"Hello." His father's gravelly voice brought forth memories of watching him in the ring training yearlings.

Emmett's hand tightened on the phone. "Hey, Dad. I wanted—"

"What's wrong? Do you need help? I can be there in ten minutes." It sounded like he was already on the move.

Emmett sat up. "No. I don't need help. Jesus. I'm fine. I'm on the hunt for information."

"About what? The therapist your mother mentioned?"

"Can we occasionally talk about something besides my fucking leg, please?" His voice broke like glass, leaving jagged edges ready to cut.

"Don't talk like that."

Emmett wasn't sure if his father was referring to his cursing or the blow-off. Not that he planned to ask. It was easier if no one looked behind the curtain. The view was sure to be a wasteland. He wanted his parents to stay safely tucked away in the little room he'd designated for them. One where they still thought of their son as a hero.

"I didn't call to argue. Can you put Mom on?"

Her voice came on immediately. "Emmett, sweetheart, what do you need?" The eagerness in her voice churned guilt in his chest.

"What have you heard about Greer Hadley?"

"She came by here and I gave her your guitar. A nice girl." A few beats of silence. "Did she drop it off?"

Was Greer a nice girl? He rather hoped not. "Yeah, she dropped it off."

"You should start playing again. You loved it so in high school." There was a hope in her voice he couldn't quite squash.

"Maybe. Right now, though, I'm more interested in Greer. What's the scuttlebutt around Madison?"

"Oh. Well, as to that . . ." She cleared her throat.

Emmett swung his foot to the floor and leaned forward. Like

any good Southerner he could sense juicy gossip like a dog could sniff out fresh-cooked bacon. "What'd she do?"

"It's not really for me to say."

"She told me she caught Beau cheating on her with Marcy Sims."

"Goodness me. I didn't realize Beau and Marcy were fooling around. Greer has been through some hard times, but she has a good heart."

His mother was either too much of a lady to gossip or wasn't in the loop. Her voice dropped to a whisper. "Is there anything you need? Anything I can do for you?"

While he cringed in anticipation of her coddling and pity, he wasn't immune to her desperation. When he was a kid, he'd loved sitting in her lap and even having her cut up his peanut butter and jelly into perfect triangles. His lunches had been envied by all.

"I've been craving one of your casseroles. In fact, I'm running low on staples too."

"I'll make you a big pot of hoppin' John. Enough to—" Silence crackled over the phone. "Actually, I'm volunteering tomorrow and won't have time. I forgot."

"As soon as you can manage would be fine. Could you put Dad back on now?"

"What is it, son?" his dad asked.

Son. Biologically, it was a certainty. They shared too many physical traits for Emmett to think he was the spawn of the mailman, but he'd fallen well short of the legacy his ancestors had blazed in military service, from the Revolution to the Civil War and through the post 9-11 conflicts around the world.

However, now was not the time to delve into their complicated family history. "What's Greer Hadley's story?"

"She's a troublemaker. I told your mother not to give her your guitar. Did she upset you? Do I need to have a word with her father at church on Sunday?"

"No! I just want to know what she's been up to lately."

"She got drunk and tore up Becky's place down on Highway 45. Deputy Peeler tried to arrest her, and instead of going quietly, she kicked him . . . well, down there. Wayne ended up in the ER, and Greer got sentenced to work volunteer hours at that foundation Bill Duckett's stepdaughter started. Nepotism at its finest."

Emmett was torn between shock and laughter. Laughter won out.

"It's not funny," his dad said. "She had to move home because she couldn't make it in Nashville—not that anyone is surprised—and now she's stirring up trouble in Madison. I don't want you seeing her again."

His dad's holier-than-thou, deacon-of-the-church attitude smothered Emmett's amusement. "First off, I'm a grown man. Next, unless Wayne Peeler has had a personality transplant, he's still a little prick who probably deserved to suffer permanent damage to his balls. And, lastly, Greer is a talented musician and the Music Tree Foundation is lucky to have her, no matter how she ended up there."

"She's a mess, Emmett, and will pull you down with her."

"News flash, Dad, I'm an even bigger mess than she is. Tell Mom I'm looking forward to the hoppin' John." He disconnected and tossed his phone, not caring where it landed.

Exhaustion blanketed him like the darkness, stifling and oppressive. He flopped back on the couch and closed his eyes. It was the first night in a long time he wasn't going to sleep with the help of alcohol numbing his senses.

His brain sputtered like an old truck with a drained battery. His thoughts circled Greer and his parents until he fell into dreams that thankfully didn't tread old, nightmarish ground.

Chapter 6

Greer walked through the foundation's doors with a smidgeon more confidence than she usually carried. Her last session with Ally had felt like a turning point. The question was whether or not she could strengthen the tentative connection. A lot could happen in a teenager's life over a weekend.

As Greer strode down the hall, Amelia's voice rang out from her office. "Greer! Do you have a second?"

Greer backtracked and took a seat. "What's up?"

"I got an interesting call this morning from Mr. Lawson. You ruffled his feathers."

"By trying to help his son?" She clenched her teeth.

"You didn't tell me you planned to talk to the Lawsons."

"I didn't think it was a big deal. I know them from church."

"Mr. Lawson said you took Emmett's guitar." While Amelia's voice didn't reflect any judgment, the accusation hung in the room.

"I didn't steal it, if that's what Mr. Lawson implied. Emmett's mama asked me to give it to him." Greer slid down in the chair and crossed her arms. The defiance rushing her body should have been dammed by her age. "So I ran it by his place."

Amelia leaned forward, propping her chin in her palm. "How did your visit go? Any progress?"

Greer shrugged before saying, "He didn't threaten to shoot at me this time, which I'm counting as a win."

It didn't seem right to talk about the lined-up shots of whiskey, punched-out picture, and general chaos.

"Based on your . . . reason for joining the program, Mr. Lawson is worried your influence on Emmett won't be . . . positive." Amelia spoke as if she were picking her way across a cottonmouth-infested stream, and ended with a sigh. "He asked me to pull you from Emmett's case."

"That old coot." She popped up and paced. "It's not like anyone else is banging down Emmett's door with offers to help. His dad wants to believe Emmett will be back to normal—whatever that is—and holding down the front pew at church in a couple of weeks."

"You don't agree?"

"The more time Emmett spends at that cabin alone, the harder it will be to get him out. I may not have been an A student, but I understand inertia." She threw up her hands and sprawled back in the chair. "But whatever. Emmett is not my problem anymore, apparently. He can pickle himself in Jack and rot out there for all I care."

Her conscience niggled with the lie. She didn't *not* care, but she was juggling her own problems like a drunk clown on a unicycle.

"You're ready to write him off?" Amelia asked.

"What else can I do? You're taking me off his case, right?"

"I said Mr. Lawson wants you off Emmet's case."

"You want me to go against the wishes of his father?"

"Emmett is a grown man."

"You should know that Emmett doesn't want me to come back either. He doesn't want anyone around to watch."

"Watch what?"

"His self-destruction."

Amelia's sigh made Greer feel younger than the years between them. "It's entirely up to you. I can take him off your docket. You'll still have Ally, and two veterans will be starting in the program next week. I'll assign you one or both of them. They're excited about music and won't shoot at you. No doubt, it'll be easier."

"Sounds good. I need easy. My life is already too complicated. I've got my own future to figure out, including finding a job that actually pays money. Emmett needs more than a music volunteer; he needs a PhD psychologist. I can't help him." Every single excuse was valid. Then why did Greer feel like a disappointment? It was a feeling she had become intimately familiar with.

"I'll make the additions to your schedule." Amelia half turned, effectively dismissing her.

Greer headed to the room to wait on Ally, but was too upset to sit and paced instead. Mr. Lawson's interference was both infuriating and embarrassing. Any confidence she had entered the foundation with had been wiped away by Mr. Clean.

"Worried I wasn't going to show?" Ally slumped her way into the room and to the chair across from the table.

Greer took a deep breath and tried to focus on Ally. Thick liner only emphasized the dark circles hanging under her eyes. Her clothes were wrinkled as if she'd slept in them the night before, and her roots were noticeable, which added to her haggard appearance. A general air of not giving a damn reminded Greer of her younger self, but it had always been a front. Greer had cared what people thought of her too much. Considering how Mr. Lawson's poor opinion burned, she still cared too much. Was the affectation a defense mechanism for Ally too?

Greer sat down. "I'm worried about someone else in the program. Believe it or not, he's way more screwed up than you. You're a teacher's pet in comparison."

"Oh yeah? How so?"

What was protocol in terms of volunteer-client privilege? Music therapy certainly wasn't brain surgery. "He's a friend of mine from high school. Lost a leg in combat. Drinks too much. I went to visit him and he tried to scare me away with a gun. On top of that, his dad is convinced I'm a terrible influence and wants me removed as his volunteer. What do I do?"

Ally's eyes flared with surprise. "You want to know what I think?"

"Sure. Why not?" Just because Greer sought advice from a fifteen-year-old girl didn't mean she had to take it, but she was glad she asked.

Ally sat a little straighter. Hints of the girl she had been before tragedy banished her smirking indifference. "Did he wave the gun around or actually fire it?"

"Into the air to scare me off. He'd never hurt me. The question is, should I back off like his dad wants or make myself a huge pain in the ass?"

"Like you do with me?" The smile that came to Ally's face was teasing but not mean.

"Is that a vote for back off?"

"No. You should keep at him. You're good at being super-humanly annoying."

"Gee, thanks." Greer had trouble summoning even a whiff of pretend outrage. Inside, she buzzed with the realization that no matter how bitchy Ally got or how hard she pushed Greer away, really, really, *really* deep down, Ally didn't want Greer to give up on her either.

"Enough about other clients. How about we explore old-timey bluegrass and mountain music? A history lesson, if you will."

Interest flashed over Ally's face before she reassumed her expression of apathy. "Whatever."

The giveaway was the pencil Ally tapped on the table. Impatient. Not to leave but to hear the music. Interpreting Ally's moods and words and gestures was like learning a foreign language, but Greer was slowly becoming fluent.

The hour passed with astonishing speed, considering how time had defied the laws of science during their sessions of silence. From the magic of the Internet, Greer played grainy recordings from the early days of bluegrass to modern takes on the same songs to current music on the radio that tipped a hat to its roots.

"What do you think?" Greer asked as casually as possible.

"The songs on the radio right now are so shallow compared to the older stuff. Those songs are haunting." Ally had taken up two pencils and used them like drumsticks on the table.

"Consider what the early settlers had to endure. It was a hard life. Most of them were poor and illiterate. What did they have as an outlet? Music was a way to deal with their sorrows."

"Where did they get instruments?"

"Some were passed down from their ancestors as family treasures. Some people became skilled enough to make their own. But, regardless, the most important instrument is a voice, and everyone has one of those."

"Not everyone can sing." Ally looked up through her lashes.

"Not everyone can sing *well*. What about you? Do you like to sing?" Greer tried to look casual, but found herself leaning over the table. It was dangerous to give Ally a nudge when they walked a tightrope between trust and failure.

"I'm okay." A half smirk indicated Ally was better than okay. At least in her own mind.

Greer checked the time. Richard would be knocking soon. "How about we try to write a song next time? A real song."

"Are you serious?" Ally asked as if Greer had suggested they hold up a liquor store together.

"Sure. It can be about whatever you want. A hanging or a highwayman. Lost loves are always good. Why don't you work on some lyrics over the weekend?" Greer kept her voice super-chill. The moment was a springboard into new territory, and the possibility of falling on her face was better than average.

"Should the lyrics rhyme like a poem?"

"There are no rules. They can rhyme but don't have to. It can be complicated or simple. What's important is that it has a rhythm."

"What kind of rhythm? Like this?" Ally used the pencils to tap out a simple one-two march.

"More like a heartbeat. Something internal. Rappers call it flow."

"You listen to rap?" Ally's incredulity made Greer smile.

"I listen to anything if it's good. Classical. Pop. Country. R and B. And yes, rap."

"What if I suck at writing?" Ally's attention was on the still-drumming pencils, the cadence picking up in speed and intensity.

"You'll for sure suck. No doubt about your massive level of suckage."

Ally's gaze bounced up, her face a mask of shock. Then, she laughed, the noise bouncing around the room like bubbles at a kid's birthday party. "You are *really* bad at this encouraging thing."

The effervescence infected Greer and made her smile. "I'm encouraging you not to get discouraged. The magic of songwriting happens when you put the lyrics to music and make everything fit together. Most of the time it's painstaking, frustrating work."

"But not always?"

"There are rare instances when songs seem to manifest fully formed. It's special when that happens. A moment to be savored."

A knock preceded Richard's head popping through the crack. "Almost done?"

"Yep. The room is all yours." Greer grabbed her bag and followed Ally out the front door. "Do you want to grab a quick bite before you head home? My treat."

As soon as the offer was out, Greer worried she'd overstepped some unwritten rule about fraternizing outside of the foundation. She hadn't exactly studied the fine print.

"Thanks, but I can't. Mom is waiting for me at home." A shadow passed over Ally's face even though she stood in sunshine.

It was only four. "Did she find a job?"

"Sure."

"Doing what?" As soon as the question was out, Greer knew she'd set off a trip wire.

"I gotta go." Ally turned and walked away.

Nothing of the girl who had laughed earlier remained. Ally picked her way through a straggly copse of pines and disappeared behind the office building next door.

Anger at herself warred with worry for Ally. Maybe things were fine at home. Normal. Even if things weren't fine and normal, was it any of Greer's business? Where was the line?

Emmett was another problem niggling her conscience. Greer was no longer on his case. Emmett and Mr. Lawson would be relieved. She would stay away and let sleeping dogs lie.

Trouble was, Greer was prone to cross lines and wake up dogs.

Chapter 7

Greer sat cross-legged on her bed and painted the nail on her index finger a sparkly purple. Her mama wouldn't approve. A subdued light pink would have been a classier choice. She'd never gone for safe, though. She'd taken risks, assured by the books and movies she'd ingested that risk equaled reward. Except it hadn't. Risk equaled loss.

She hesitated with the brush trembling over her next nail. If she toed the line and played by the rules, would her life's trajectory change for the better? She scrubbed the purple polish off with an acetone-soaked cotton ball, leaving a clean slate.

It was Saturday. In Nashville she would have been in full-hustle mode. Busking on the streets for the tourists during the day. Playing dive bars in the evening. Bartending until two in the morning. Contrary to the image of a dissolute musician, partying all night and getting up late the next day, Greer had worked until her fingers bled—sometimes literally.

The first couple of weeks at home in Madison with nothing to do but sleep, read, and let her parents take care of her had been heavenly. But boredom and uselessness had moved home with her. She needed a job. A real job that paid steady money.

A knock accompanied the squeak of her door. Her mama stood with their cordless phone, her hand over the mouthpiece, and whispered, "A call for you. A man."

Beau had been blocked from her cell. He had some nerve calling their house phone. "Tell Beau to go to—"

"Doesn't sound like Beau." Her mama's cheeks flushed.

"Who is it, then?"

Her mother shrugged and held the phone out. As if poking a toe in water whose temperature was unknown, she took the phone and waited until her mother backed out of the room. "Hello?"

"That took long enough." The growly impatience on the other end marked Emmett like a fingerprint.

"Terribly sorry to inconvenience you, *sir*." Her response had more layers—of irony and sarcasm—than her mother's famous coconut cake.

"You should be. I'm a busy man." The unexpected humor in his voice bordered on charming.

"Shooting whiskey—and at trespassers—must be terribly time-consuming. How do you fit in the required rocking on the porch?"

"I have a tight schedule. In fact, I have a thousand more rocks to get in before noon."

"You're crazy." She was glad he couldn't see her smile.

"Not yet, but headed in that direction."

She wasn't sure if he was joking or serious. "I guess you heard."

"About your breakdown at Becky's? Yep. Got the story from my dad."

A flush heated her body. No doubt Mr. Lawson put the worst possible spin on her actions. She wasn't proud of herself, but she was atoning for her mistakes. Or at least trying to. "No, about your big-shot daddy calling Amelia at the foundation and complaining about me."

"He didn't." Anger morphed the denial into a statement.

"Apparently I'm not the sort of person he thinks you should be hanging out with." Silence from the other end had her hastening to add, "Not that what we were doing was hanging out."

"Of course not." Hesitation hitched his next words. "What would you call it?"

"Court-ordered volunteer hours for me; a pity party for you."

"Ouch." A pause. "I'm craving cake now."

A laugh spurted out despite her best efforts. "You have a kitchen."

"Yeah, but not the ability to use it or the fixings for cake. I've been surviving on frozen pizzas."

"Poor baby."

"I sense your sympathy is insincere."

"Very."

"I lost a leg fighting for the red, white, and blue, for God's sake. Don't I deserve a rum cake?"

"I imagine a pity party would be better served by a fruitcake. One that's been frozen since Christmas." She bit the inside of her cheek to stem another laugh.

"That's just plain mean."

"I'm not here to coddle you."

"Cobbler? I would love warm cobbler. Blackberry or peach. And ice cream."

"You're talking like I'm actually going to bring you something."

"You owe me. I found out what you did to poor old Wayne. Is the damage permanent?"

"I'm not planning on finding out. Aren't you afraid I might do the same to you if you make me mad?"

"Should I be afraid of you?" His voice had lost some of its tease.

"Probably. I'm a terrible influence or haven't you heard?"

"Perfect. Good influences never got me anywhere." After a few heartbeats of silence, he said, "A six-month-old half-thawed fruitcake doesn't sound half bad. What's wrong with me?"

"More things than I have time to list over the phone." She gnawed on her bottom lip. She had almost convinced herself to play it safe. Almost. "I'll bring the cake if you'll provide the drinks for your next pity party."

"I got drinks covered. When?"

"It's a surprise party."

"What if I'm busy?"

Their laughter joined in a pleasant harmony.

"I'll expect all the gory details about what went down at Becky's," he said.

"I'll expect your guitar to be in one piece."

"Bring your guitar. We can duel after gorging ourselves on whiskey and old, dry fruitcake." He disconnected.

Smiling, she tossed the phone on the bed and picked up the purple nail polish.

Fifteen minutes later, she skipped down the stairs, waving her drying nails and holding the phone under her arm. She found her mama in the kitchen wearing a blue flower-printed apron and kneading bread. An old Mason jar filled with bread starter sat on the counter. The smell of sour yeastiness brought her back to being eight years old and long summer days of running through sprinklers.

Greer hung the phone up and peered over her mama's shoulder as she worked the dough. Her hands held strength but the years had thinned her skin and knobbed her knuckles. Time had flowed along while Greer thrashed against the tide.

"Are you and Daddy taking a trip this summer?" Greer asked.

Her mama's millisecond glance contained years of worry. "Not this summer."

Because of Greer. Her mother wouldn't admit it, but Greer knew she'd disrupted their lives. "You don't have to stick around because of me. I can watch the house. No wild parties, I promise." She held up three fingers in the Girl Scout oath.

"Not this summer." Her mother scattered flour over the ball of dough, plopped it in a bowl, and covered it with plastic wrap to rise. "Who was that on the phone?"

"Emmett Lawson." Greer couldn't quite stifle a smile.

Her mama, as sharp as always, narrowed her eyes on Greer. "I didn't realize you were friends."

"We're not. Emmett is part of my volunteer work at the foundation."

"Nothing romantic, then?"

"Romantic?" Greer's heart set up an allegro tempo in her chest. "What gave you that idea?"

"I don't know. You seem different. I haven't seen you grin like that in a long time."

Greer wiped the smile off her face, but her mama was right. Greer felt different. Lighter. As if she'd hauled herself a few rungs up from rock bottom. "It has nothing to do with Emmett.

He's a cranky you-know-what. Like the world's most annoying brother. Like—" She took a breath to come up with another convincing denial, but her mother's swerve saved her.

"Poor Henry and Judy," her mother said in a tutting voice.

"Why do you feel sorry for *him*?" Mr. Lawson had revealed himself to be a judgmental bully who deserved to walk the aisle and confess his sins in front of the congregation.

"To have their only boy come back so changed. Emmett used to be such a nice boy."

"He's still nice." Why did Greer feel the need to defend Emmett? Especially with a lie. The man was a sarcastic asshole on legs—or leg. "What do people expect from a man coming back from a war we can't win missing a leg?"

"Emmett won't let his parents help him. Henry's heart is broken."

"I wasn't aware he possessed one," Greer muttered.

Either her mama didn't hear or chose not to acknowledge her bad manners. "You know your father and I are here for you. Whatever you need. I'm glad you came home to us."

Not caring about the flour dotting her mama's apron, Greer hugged her. As depressing as it was to have to move home, she had a soft place to land. And based on the worry and love in Mrs. Lawson's face as she'd pushed the guitar at Greer, so did Emmett.

Greer pulled away and turned to the rack of cookbooks next to the refrigerator. "I'm going to look for a job."

"That's wonderful. Doing what?"

"I don't know yet. I'm not qualified to do much except bartend." She pulled a dog-eared church cookbook from the shelf.

"You'll figure it out and land on your feet. You always do."

Did she? She'd gotten knocked down so many times, she felt like she was crawling to some imaginary finish line.

Wiping her hands on a white dish towel, her mother came up beside her. "Are you looking for a particular recipe?"

"How do I make a rum cake?"

Twilight was falling by the time Greer parked on the side of the road next to the padlocked gate. The afternoon spent cooking with her mama had forged new ground. Greer kept catching glances of the woman she aspired to be as if she were playing hide-and-seek. Someone like her mama—steady, calm, yet fierce about the things and people she cared about.

Which might explain why she was climbing over Emmett's locked gate. Wearing shorts, a T-shirt, and flip-flops, she strolled through the trees, holding the rum cake. A thrum of energy filled her. Like the humming crickets and flashing lightning bugs, her circadian rhythm skewed toward night.

As she cleared the trees, she could see a light on in the cabin. Not that she worried Emmett might be out. The closer she got, the faster the butterflies reproduced in her stomach. As many times as she reminded herself she was visiting out of a sense of duty, there was more to it. A more she couldn't define.

Before she made it to the bottom of the porch steps, the front door swung open and Emmett stepped out.

She struck a pose and presented the cake. "Surprise!"

"I can't believe you actually brought cake. Are we going to crack a tooth on it?"

She tramped up the steps, stopped with only the cake plate separating them, and smiled into his eyes—a dark, rich blue and currently twinkling. "You're lucky my dad polished off the fruitcake in February. This is Miss Lilith's famous rum cake." Miss Lilith had a well-earned reputation of being the best cook in their church. "I hope I did her recipe justice."

Emmet hummed and took the plate from her. "This looks amazing. Come on in."

She followed him into the kitchen. He uncovered the cake, leaned over, and took a deep breath with his eyes closed. "You didn't skimp on the rum."

"I knew you weren't a teetotaler."

He pulled down two plates and cut generous slices out of the Bundt cake. "Speaking of, I promised to provide the drinks. What's your poison?"

"Milk, if you've got any."

He took a half gallon out of the fridge, removed the cap, and sniffed, making a pained face. "It's gone bad. Mom didn't bring me any groceries this week."

"Really?" Greer was surprised, but pleased Mrs. Lawson had held out. She tried to sound casual. "Guess you'll have to hit the grocery tomorrow to restock."

"Nah. I'll call Mom and have her make a run. She should have already done it." Emmett took their slices into the living area and set the plates on the side table.

"She's a busy lady and not at your beck and call." Greer plopped into an armchair that had previously been obscured by a mountain of clothes, while Emmett sat on the couch.

He narrowed his eyes on her, a bite of cake on his fork. "I can smell your disapproval through the rum."

"You're a grown man who is making his mother run his errands."

"I'm not making her. She offered and I accepted." He took another bite.

"You should be doing your own shopping."

"Really? And is that what you're doing? Are you shopping and cooking for your parents?"

She hadn't expected him to flip the script. "That's different."

"Whatever you say." He took the last bite and rose. "Want more?"

"No, thanks." Greer poked at the moist cake on her plate, her appetite diminished with the realization the high road she'd been trotting down had taken a dip.

She had moved home and fallen into the same patterns as if she were a teenager and not an adult. It had been comforting, but now she could see the danger of getting too comfortable with the situation.

He came back with another slice and devoured it in a half-dozen bites. When he was finished he stacked their plates on the side table and sat back, rubbing his hands down his thighs. He wore loose khaki pants that covered his artificial leg.

"You didn't bring your guitar," he said.

"No."

"Why not?"

She went for total nonchalance, crossing her legs and smiling. "I sold my Martin a few months ago for rent money." Her chin wobbled, ruining the affect she was going for, and she looked away to hide the sudden threat of tears.

"I'm sorry." In contrast to her forced smile, he was somber, from his voice to the way he leaned forward to squeeze her hand.

"If I'd given up sooner, I might still have her with me. I met Dolly Parton backstage at the Opry when I was twenty-two and she signed it. And the leather strap was tooled with flowers. It was beautiful. Sometimes it feels like I lost a limb." The words were out before they registered. His hand jerked away from hers, but she grabbed his wrist and held fast. "That was a stupid thing to say. I'm sorry."

Their gazes held, his blank for a few blinks before his eyes crinkled and a laugh rumbled out. "It's actually refreshing for someone to forget about my leg."

"Obviously, hocking my guitar is nothing like what you've gone through. *Are* going through. I'm seriously an idiot." The Jaws of Life were going to be required to pry her foot out of her mouth.

"Don't worry about it. I can't imagine what it took to part with your guitar when you're a musician." If he wanted to stay off the topic of his leg and her slip of the tongue, she would oblige, even though talking about her Martin was depressing.

"I still have the guitar my parents bought me twenty years ago," she said.

Only when his fingers moved to stroke down her wrist did she realize she still had hold of him. Her grip loosened and their hands separated slowly, remaining in contact until their fingertips parted.

"It's good enough to perform with?" he asked.

"I'm not performing ever again."

"You've got to be kidding me." Disbelief transmitted in his voice and half smile.

"I'm not kidding. I'm done. I haven't had the desire to play since I left Nashville, and I've been perfectly happy." She couldn't meet his eyes when she made the declaration. While it wasn't definitely a lie, neither was it true. Her feelings were too complicated for simple categorization.

He made a scoffing sound and sat back, shaking his head.

"And everyone thinks I'm the one who's screwed up and hiding from life."

"You are."

"I know I am, but so are you."

Just because his comeback was juvenile didn't make it any less true. She was hiding. From her mistakes, her fears, and most especially, the future.

She popped up. "At least I'm trying to move forward."

"Seems to me like you're treading safe waters. I can't believe you're never going to play again. That's a waste of your talent. What turned you into such a coward?"

Anger rose to meet his accusation. "What turned you into such an asshole?"

"Seems like you can't handle tough love when it's turned on you, huh?"

"Why am I even here?" She didn't expect or want him to answer. "You better ration the cake. If your mom doesn't run out here with your Pop-Tarts and pizza rolls, you might starve."

She stalked through the door and jogged down the steps and toward the tree line, knowing he couldn't keep up. She glanced over her shoulder once she'd reached the overhang of branches and slowed. Outlined by the cabin lights, he stood on the porch, his shoulder propped against the top pillar, his hands tucked into his pockets.

She tore her gaze away from him and moved deeper into the copse. Had she run because she was mad at his assumptions or because she feared he was right about everything? Was she truly moving forward?

An urgency she hadn't felt in a long time swirled her thoughts around. She still wasn't sure what her next step was, but she would make it soon.

Chapter 8

Greer stopped by Amelia's office on her way down the hall to grab an instrument for her session with Ally. Amelia wasn't there, and Greer stepped softly as if she were doing something wrong. She bypassed the mandolin and headed toward the guitar as if it were putting out a homing signal.

A tenor's voice wavered down the hall but grew faint when Greer closed the door to her soundproof workroom. Besides strumming a few tuning chords on Emmett's guitar, she hadn't played since her disastrous night at the Bluebird Café. Her fingers stiffened as if she were experiencing an allergic reaction to the strings. The sting of humiliation hadn't dimmed over the weeks gone by, when she'd blown her last, best opportunity to catch a record executive's ear in spectacular fashion.

Greer checked her phone. Ally was late. Their last conversation scrolled through her memory. Had Greer been too pushy and curious about Ally's mom? Getting information out of a teenager was like interrogating a spy. They were born knowing how to resist.

Just as Greer was ready to give up, Ally sidled in the door, looking even more mulish than usual. Greer bit back a needling comment about the time. She wasn't Ally's mother or even her friend. It didn't matter; Greer would still get credit on her volunteer sheet for the court.

Ally dropped her backpack and slumped into the chair as if her spine were taffy. The kick she gave her pack sent it spinning three feet away.

"What a ray of sunshine." Greer attempted to defuse the brewing conniption fit with a smile.

Ally shot her a look dripping with antipathy, but at least she had acknowledged Greer's existence. "I had a bad day."

To Greer's reckoning, Ally was entitled. The girl was having a rough year.

"Want to talk about it?" Greer asked with no expectation of being taken up on the offer.

At Ally's not-unexpected silence, Greer pulled a pencil and blank music sheets out of the plastic bin, ready to move on to business.

"It's this girl at school. Caroline." Ally's words came in a rush. She grabbed a pencil and picked at the eraser. "She's a total bitch."

"I had a couple of run-ins at school with mean girls myself."

"You did? Please." Ally's epic eye roll would have won the gold at the Olympics.

"Hey, I wasn't always a broke, out-of-work, former musician fulfilling court-ordered volunteer hours. I had an awkward phase." Her self-deprecating, yet depressingly true, admission got a brief smile out of Ally.

"Yeah, but look at you. You're . . . pretty or whatever."

"You're pretty too." Greer swallowed the "if" hovering on her tongue. While Greer thought the eyeliner and dark purple lipstick didn't suit Ally, their boldness reflected the turmoil she battled.

Ally made a scoffing sound. "You're not going to tell me to lay off the makeup and grow my hair out?"

"I'm super-jealous of your hair, actually. It's edgy, which is always good for a musician." Ally ran her hand over her hair and shot a suspicious look in Greer's direction.

While Greer might have let it grow an inch longer and revert back to its natural dark brown, her envy was real. Having her longish, naturally curly hair in Tennessee meant braids and ponytails at least six months out of the year.

"What's mean-girl Caroline been doing?" Greer asked.

Ally flicked the eraser she'd picked off across the room. "You've got to promise not to tell anyone."

Greer hesitated to make such a promise. If whatever was happening was a threat to Ally's safety, she'd have to go to Amelia or Ally's mother. A broken promise would sever the friendship they were knitting together session by session, yet what choice did she have?

"I promise." Greer held Ally's gaze until the girl gave a nod.

"She's posting stuff online about me that's not true."

"Take it to the principal."

"Yeah, turning narc wouldn't make things worse at all." Ally's sarcasm registered at radioactive.

Greer was beginning to really appreciate the kid's attitude. "You're right. Bad advice. Have you confronted her? Asked her to stop?"

"The account is anonymous."

"How can you be sure it's her?"

"We were the only two left in the bathroom this afternoon, and she said something that ended up being posted ten minutes later word for word." Ally picked up another pencil and worked on decapitating its eraser.

"Is it sexual stuff she's posting?"

"Mostly. Some if it's about my dad, though."

"What about him?"

Ally dropped her chin to her chest, but not before Greer noted the slight wobble. "Stuff about how he probably got himself killed on purpose because he was embarrassed to have me for a daughter."

The words rattled around Greer's head. In the space between shock and understanding, rage bloomed. How could someone exhibit such cruelty at such a young age?

Greer took several deep breaths, attempting to extinguish an eruption. She didn't want her anger to scare Ally or make her clam up. "Does your mom know what's going on?"

"She's got enough to deal with."

Greer held back questions. Things obviously weren't good at home or school for Ally. "None of the stuff this Caroline girl is spreading about your dad is true."

"It might be. I don't know. Mom talks about him like he's still alive, but I was there when his casket was unloaded. No one told me how he died. Was it quick or did he suffer? Was he a coward or a hero? I deserve to know, don't you think?"

Greer swallowed past a lump in her throat. Her mind went straight to Emmett. The questions he'd posed had made her uncomfortable which in turn had caused her to lash out at him when it was really herself she was upset with. It hadn't been fair, but then, when was life ever fair? What if Emmett had been the one to return in a casket? What if she'd never gotten the chance to know the grumpy, funny, frustrating man he'd become?

Ally's dad wouldn't see her graduate high school or get married or be able to hold his grandkids. It wasn't fair. The adults around her probably thought they were doing the right thing in protecting her, but she deserved the truth. Even more, she was strong enough to handle it.

"I do think you deserve to know. Can't you ask your mom?" Greer knew the suggestion was inadequate before it was even out of her mouth, but what options were there?

"Yeah, sure." Ally's response was as noncommittal as they came.

"All right, let's leave the questions about your dad for a second and focus on Caroline. What can you do to stop her?"

"It's too late. Even if she stopped posting today, thanks to her lies, everyone at school thinks I'm a slutty troublemaker. Girls don't want anything to do with me, and the guys—" A disgusted grunt came from her throat.

"What are the guys doing?" A chill passed through Greer.

"They either think it's hilarious to say gross stuff to me in the halls or they ignore me altogether."

Greer sat back and chewed on her thumbnail. How could she keep this to herself? It was harassment. What could she do to help without breaking her promise? "Have you thought about changing schools?"

"It's the only public school close by. We can't afford private school." She flicked the pencil. It flew end over end, landing on the floor. "I'm used to being the new kid. I know the drill, but this place is different. Harder."

Greer didn't know what Ally had been like before, but her

father's death had changed her. Perhaps it was a combination of the place and the person being too different to fit together.

"You need to talk to your mom, Ally. About all of this. Your dad, Caroline, the way you feel. I'm sure she wants to help you." Except Greer wasn't sure.

"School will be out for summer soon and I won't have to think about it for a while." Ally pointed at the guitar. "I thought we were here to work on music. I can't be late getting home."

Greer wanted to say more—wanted to *do* more—to help, but the boundaries of their relationship were indistinct and her inexperience with kids and the complexity of Ally's problems left her floundering.

Greer pushed back from the table and pulled the guitar into her chest, her hands instinctively falling into their assigned places. A rush of heat had her body tingling and her heart racing. Prickles of sweat popped up along the back of her neck.

As if the room had stretched, she heard Ally from a distance say, "I've always wanted to play the guitar. I took piano when we were stationed in North Carolina when I was little, but we left the piano behind when we moved to Kentucky."

Greer's stomach clawed to escape. Even though there was only an audience of one, her fingers fumbled to find the strings to play a proper chord.

"What's wrong? You look ready to hurl." Ally herself looked both concerned and freaked out.

Grown-ups weren't supposed to have breakdowns. Especially in front of a kid who had her own overflowing Dumpster of worries to deal with. Greer forced a smile. *Fake it until you make it.*

"I haven't played for a while. Before this dry spell, I can't remember a day I went without playing since I was ten and my mom and dad got me a guitar for Christmas."

"Why'd you stop? Was it because you got arrested?"

"I stopped because"—she swallowed and tried to assemble a reason that didn't make her sound crazy—"it got too hard."

It had been hard long before she stopped, though. Music had become a mocking reminder of her failures. By the end, her songs had deserted her, and the silence in her head was a physical ache.

"I'm sorry." Sincerity laced Ally's voice. She understood loss.

Greer wanted to kick her own butt. She had lost something she loved. Something she could revive if she wasn't such a coward. Ally had lost *someone* she loved. Her dad was gone forever.

"Nothing to be sorry for. I'll get over my fears. Eventually." Greer put the guitar down, but still it called to her like a mocking siren. She ignored it. "Let's start with lyrics. Were you able to get anything down on paper? And it's okay if you weren't, by the way. It's not—"

Ally rummaged in her backpack, pulled out a stack of papers, and dropped them on the table. The top sheet was covered in words and scribbles and doodles of flowers in the margins. Greer flipped through the pages with her thumb. They were all similarly filled.

"Wow. Writer's block is not an issue."

Ally popped up and meandered along the walls of the small room as if she were a wild animal desperate to escape a cage before being tortured. Greer couldn't argue the fact that watching someone read and pass judgment on your writing was a form of torture.

"They all suck. In fact, give the pages back and I'll burn them," Ally said, making a grab for the stack.

Greer pulled the papers out of Ally's reach. "Not a chance. Yes, they probably suck, but that doesn't mean we can't transform them into awesome. That's the thing about words—people too, if you want to get philosophical: letting go of the bad can open us to be even better." If only Greer could edit out the bad decisions she'd made.

Greer skimmed the top page. It was a story about a boy walking away and not looking back at the girl who loved him, leaving her with a broken heart. Songwriting was intensely personal. Whether the pain lived in Ally or whether she'd channeled her dad's death, Greer had enough respect for the process not to ask.

The subject had been done a million times over, but Ally's turn of phrase was unique and begged to be spoken or sung aloud, yet it lacked a complexity Greer knew Ally possessed.

"Rhyming is overrated." Greer underlined the last words in a handful of the lines. She gestured Ally over and turned the paper so Ally could see. "These are good, but a listener will check out if the cadence is too repetitive."

"I need to know the rules, I guess." Ally's shoulders fell into a slump as she sank down on the edge of her seat.

"First rule: there are no rules. In fact, the best songwriters break the rules. Your homework for our next session is to listen to songs you like and figure out why. Then, listen to songs you hate and figure out why. Can you do that?"

"Lay around and listen to music? I think I can manage it." Ally's sudden smirk made Greer wonder how her mother had survived her teenage years without having a chronic case of whiplash.

"You have to *really* listen. Study them. I want a list of specifics."

"What do you mean?"

"I mean, you must become a student. Is a song's chorus repeated too many times? Is the imagery conveyed too on the nose? Is the actual music complex enough to support the lyrics or vice versa? Dig deep."

"Okay. But how am I supposed to compose music without an instrument?"

"You have an instrument."

"No, I don't. I told you we left the piano behind when we moved."

Now it was Greer's turn to smirk. "Your voice, dummy."

"I don't want to sing in front of people."

"You don't have to. You can compose all by your lonesome in your room."

"Like how?"

"I don't know, you sort of get lost in your head until you stumble into the music."

Ally shook her head. "That makes no sense."

How could she describe the feeling? Greer took two pencils and tapped out a slow three-quarters-time rhythm on the desk, letting her body sway to the beat. "First, find a beat."

Ally picked up two pencils and joined the rhythm.

"Good," Greer said. "Then close your eyes and let your mind wander."

Greer followed her own instructions, expecting to find a barren wasteland. Instead, a simple melody wavered in the void, and she hummed a few bars before incorporating Ally's first lines. She opened her eyes.

Ally's mouth was open, her eyes wide, making her look younger and vulnerable. "You made what I wrote sound good."

"Your lyrics *are* good." Greer waved the piece of paper. "A universal story of lost love. Powerful stuff."

A knock interrupted them. Time was up.

Anxiety strummed through Ally as surely as if an out-of-tune chord were playing. She shoved the stack of songs into her backpack and swung it over one shoulder. "Gotta go."

"I can give you a lift and get you home that much faster." Greer rose.

"No, thanks." Ally ducked past Richard. By the time Greer gathered her bag and the guitar, the tinkle of the front door chimes were fading.

Amelia tapped on her laptop, her cat's-eye glasses emphasizing a boho-chic look that could have graced the cover of a magazine. Greer dropped her time sheet on the desk and returned the guitar to its stand, running her fingers down the strings in a regretful caress. Was this how a man suffering from impotence felt?

"Things are going well with Ally." Amelia stated it as fact as she signed her name with a flourish. "How did things go with your new assignments?"

Greer had met earlier in the week with two new veterans. After dealing with Ally and Emmett, she had anticipated a battle to get them to participate. Instead, they'd been eager to learn and write. She had enjoyed both sessions, but the spark Ally brought hadn't been there. The push-pull she shared with Ally was challenging, which made the time they spent together engaging, frustrating, and inspiring.

"What's the story with Ally's mom?" Greer tucked the time sheet into her bag. Now that she'd added the two new veterans, hours were adding up more quickly than she'd anticipated.

Amelia sat back and pushed her glasses to the top of her head. "What's wrong?"

"Nothing in particular." Greer poked her toe at the edge of a faded rug. "This looks like the rug Uncle Bill and Aunt Tonya had in their dining room when I was a kid."

"Bill gave it to me when I started the foundation. He's been good to me."

Greer and Amelia had one thing in common: they both loved Bill Duckett. Not even her aunt Tonya's resentment and anger toward him after the divorce had dimmed Greer's worship of him. He'd always had time for Greer, and she'd loved visiting him in his chambers and trying on his long, dark robes.

Amelia put her glasses back on and turned her attention to the computer screen. "Anything else you need?"

"No. I'll see you next week."

Before Greer made the turn into the hall, Amelia called her name. She did an about-face.

"I've been doing this long enough to trust my instincts. I'd advise you to do the same," Amelia said. In her eyes were stories—tragic and uplifting—of men and women who had come and gone through the foundation's doors.

Greer nodded and headed out. Her stint at the foundation was supposed to be a simple exercise in addition. One hour after another would add up to fulfill the court requirements.

It was unsettling to think the work she was doing with Ally and the others meant more than the paper she got signed every week. She didn't want it to mean more. She didn't want to worry and wonder what Ally was doing outside the meager two hours a week they shared.

But it was too late. She already cared.

Chapter 9

Drawn by the rumbling thunder, Emmett stepped onto the porch. Dark clouds lined the horizon like ink blots engulfing the setting sun. The stagnant air was so dense he felt like he could break it in two with his bare hands. The coming storm would do the job. The lights in the cabin flickered before going out.

As a child he'd held an unnatural fear of storms and the tornados they could spawn. The edge of Madison had been hit when he was eight, and he'd never forgotten walking a formerly quaint neighborhood street where only sticks and stones remained. The utter destruction had stalked his imagination and nightmares for years.

Only when he'd faced the destruction of war had he let go of his fear of storms. There was a purity in the force of nature that man's crude bumbling desecrated. Nature was neither good nor evil, only powerful. Men at war, on the other hand, were rarely good and mostly evil.

He'd joined the army with the notion he was making the world a better place, keeping the ones he loved safe, making a difference. Had he made a difference? The lives of the family whose house had been destroyed in a drone strike he'd witnessed had been changed forever.

Statistics were kept on civilian casualties, but reports never detailed the horror of a young girl screaming for her father or the boy lying in the street covered in burns, his mother weeping over his body. The report on the ambush that had ultimately taken his leg and the life of his sergeant hadn't described his unbelievable pain and the way his sergeant had choked on his own blood at the end. Emmett couldn't scrub the details out of his head.

Since then, storms no longer scared him. If a tornado bore down on him, he wouldn't cower but meet the onslaught and beg to be taken. Perhaps then he would find peace.

Lightning flashed and thunder followed a few seconds later. The storm was still miles away, but an electric feeling vibrated the air. Chaos was coming.

His weather radio blared from inside, but he ignored it and walked down the porch steps to welcome the onslaught. The wind went from zero to sixty faster than a Mustang. The tops of the trees bowed in supplication.

A streak along the ground caught his eyes. He squinted. It was coming straight for him. Not a dog. He hoped to God it wasn't a skunk or a rabid raccoon. Lightning rent the fabric of the sky. The animal cowered in the middle of the path. A black-and-white kitten.

A raindrop hit Emmett, trailing down his cheek like a tear. He raised his face as the rain poured out and obscured the landscape. Emmett looked to where the kitten had been but it had vanished.

He backed under the cover of the porch and shook his head like a dog. The temperature had dropped. He was rain-soaked and refreshed. The wind howled and blew gusts of rain in all directions as a premature dusk gripped the land.

The heart of the storm was right on top of him now. Adrenaline streaked through him like a flash of lightning, leaving his nerve endings sizzling. There were some things he missed about serving. The fear-excitement cocktail served on a daily basis was one.

The kitten reappeared five feet in front of him, bedraggled and terrified. It disappeared into the dank muddy underworld beneath the porch. It would be safe enough.

He plopped in a rocking chair and enjoyed Mother Nature's wrath. His leg throbbed. He'd been up and moving more lately. His stump was sore, his thigh muscle ached, and the burning in his phantom limb ramped to uncomfortable levels.

Too soon, the harsh leading edge of the storm gave way to a windy rain. No tornado would spirit him off to Oz tonight. His adrenaline ebbed, and he closed his eyes, listening to the pelt of rain on the roof of the cabin and the rustle of the wind in the trees.

In the relative calm, a plaintive cry came from under him. Over and over the kitten howled. Was it injured or merely scared? He wished it would shut up and go away. There was nothing he could do to help the thing. Keeping himself fed had become an issue lately. His mom still hadn't dropped by his requested groceries and even more tragic, no casseroles.

The kitten's ceaseless cries shredded any peace he'd managed to garner from the storm. Emmett stomped inside, ignoring the pain in his stump at every step. He left his rain-soaked clothes on the floor outside the laundry and pulled on a T-shirt and shorts. After easing off his prosthetic, he laid on the couch, wired and restless, but without power, he had nothing to fill the silence.

The kitten's howl reached through the floor and grabbed him around the neck. He muffled his ears with a pillow, but the faint sound poked at him like a claw. He sat up and threw the pillow across the room, knocking a lamp to the floor.

"Goddammit!" His holler echoed through the room.

Leaving his prosthetic behind, he hopped up and out the door, tucking a flashlight into his waistband. Using the hand-rail like a crutch, he jumped each step on his one leg. At the bottom, he laid on his side in the stew of grass and mud, clicked the flashlight on, and shone it under the porch.

Eyes reflected back at him in the farthest corner. Of course. Was he going after a kitten? The crying revved up like a children's toy on repeat. Was it his imagination or did the kitten sound weaker? He sat up and rested his arms over his good knee. The kitten would live and run back into the woods in the morning.

Except it had probably been dumped by some jerk who couldn't be bothered to take care of his damn animals. Dumped to die a long painful death by starvation or even worse, as prey to a coyote or fox. It was helpless.

Emmett shimmied under the porch, cursing himself every inch of the way. Cobwebs made him shudder, and the smell of damp earth and decay ignited flight instincts. The feeling of being trapped in a grave pressed in as he drew within reach of the kitten.

He slowed his movements, afraid to spook the little thing, but it didn't move, either too terrified or too tired to fight him. He wrapped his hand around its body, each rib defined. It trembled but didn't bite or scratch him. Life or death, the kitten had accepted its fate.

A surge of protectiveness welled in Emmett's chest. There were too many he hadn't been able to save, but he could do something for this pitiful creature, even if it was only to offer it a dry place to spend the night.

It took longer to work his way out from under the porch with one leg for leverage and a handful of kitten he didn't want to crush. Finally he rolled out onto his back and stared up at the black sky, the rain too soft now to wash away only God knew what coated him.

He staggered to his foot. His shoulder pitched into the porch, a protruding nail ripping through thin cotton to bare skin. Exhaustion overcame him like a tsunami. He crawled up the porch steps and collapsed on the damp wood. The clean smell of cedar was a comfort after the funk of moist earth under the porch.

The kitten tucked itself in the crook of his neck and under his chin, the vibration of its purr like an offering. He would rest for a few minutes before fetching something for the kitten to eat and drink. His eyes closed and he sank into blackness.

Pressure along his side brought him out of his coma-like sleep. He blinked against the weak light. Gray clouds blocked the sun, leaving him in deep shadow on the porch. In the army, if you didn't learn to catch sleep in uncomfortable positions and places, then you didn't sleep at all. A clean porch under an overhang was luxurious. Except he must be out of practice because his body was hating him this morning.

Another nudge against his hip had him raising his head and squinting at the person looming over him.

"You gave me a scare." His father's face took shape.

Frown lines and the bags under his eyes were made more pronounced by gravity. Always trim and athletic, Emmett's father had seemed to defy the march of time. His hair had remained blondish-brown with no gray, and more important, it simply *remained*. But in the moment, Emmett could catalog the years gone by in wrinkles and worry.

"Morning." Emmett's voice was hoarse.

"Do you need aspirin and water? Feel up to eating?" His dad held up a bag.

Emmett's stomach growled. If his nose wasn't deceiving him, country ham and biscuits awaited. He'd skipped dinner the night before. He sat up and rubbed his face. His stubble was turning into a beard. "I'm starving, actually. I didn't eat anything last night."

"Did you drink your dinner?"

For a moment, Emmett didn't catch his father's meaning, but when he did, embarrassment flushed through him. He'd never broken house rules as a teenager—no drinking, no drugs, no sex—so having his father suspect he was hungover summoned a teenage-like shame.

"I haven't been drinking." The defensiveness was misplaced. He had spent more nights than was healthy hanging out with Jack Daniel's.

His father merely cast a look at the half-empty bottle of whiskey and row of shot glasses on the table by the rocking chair.

"I was actually . . ." He checked all around them, but there was no sign of the kitten. "I was out in the storm because I thought I saw something."

His dad kept a cat in the horse barn to keep the mouse problem under control, but it had never been a pet. Admitting he'd crawled through cobwebs and mud to rescue a kitten who'd since returned his kindness by running off was not an option. Anyway, based on the weird look his dad was giving him, he might not believe the truth.

"Power back on?" Emmett asked.

"Came back early this morning. Why don't you get cleaned up while I brew some coffee." His dad hesitated before offering a hand up. The last time his dad had shown up unannounced to offer help, Emmett had yelled at him to mind his own damn business and get the hell away.

As there was no graceful way to rise to his one leg, he clasped his dad's hand. With the strength of a longtime horse trainer, he hauled Emmett up with little effort and held on to Emmett's hand longer than was necessary or comfortable.

How long had it been since he'd held his dad's hand? He'd shaken it on many occasions. After his last high school football game. At graduation, both high school and college. At his officer's induction. But a time had once existed when he'd slipped his hand into his dad's for comfort and protection. Crossing the street or walking into school the first day of kindergarten.

His dad let go, clearing his throat and leading the way into the cabin. Emmett hopped behind him like a defective toy soldier. He grabbed his prosthetic and retreated to the bathroom. The pity on his dad's face was what he had been trying to avoid since coming home.

He flipped the water on to heat and examined the beast staring back at him from the mirror. His mud-caked hair was three shades darker, and his face had chunks of dirt stuck to it. His sleeve was ripped where he'd caught his arm on the nail, but blood mixed with grime and disguised the extent of the injury.

He might have laughed at himself, except his dad had looked him over as if his appearance wasn't a shock. Like he spent his days and nights drinking and wallowing around in mud only to sleep on his porch. Could he blame his dad? Emmett had shut his parents out. No doubt their imaginations elicited the worst-case scenarios.

He sat on the edge of the tub and swung his legs around to stand under the hot spray. Brown rivulets of grime ran down his body. He shampooed three times before he felt human again and paid careful attention to cleaning his stump and the gash on his arm.

Using a set of the many crutches he kept stashed around the cabin, he slipped into the bedroom. No clean underwear. A fact he wouldn't mention to his dad. Commando, he pulled on his usual uniform of loose-fitting khakis and a T-shirt.

He attached his prosthetic and pulled his pant leg down to disguise it as usual. Walking out to join his dad in the kitchen with his prosthetic camouflaged lent a sense of normalcy he desperately needed.

His dad stared out the narrow window over the sink and sipped a mug of black coffee. Emmett poured himself the same and leaned his hip against the counter. His dad had maintained the same military-style haircut since Emmett could remember. He had also retained a stern demeanor that Emmett associated with drill sergeants even though his dad had been in Army Special Forces.

"I knew men who came home broken, Emmett. Good men.

Back then we didn't talk about it. We were expected to suck it up and deal with it."

Emmett tamped down an instinctive defensiveness only his dad could arouse. None of the impatience of their recent clashes laced his dad's voice, though, and Emmett forced himself to ask, "Did you suck it up?"

The intensity his dad focused out the window made Emmet wonder if the Second Coming was taking place in the overgrown field. Finally, his dad said, "I had friends who turned to alcohol and drugs. Some ended up homeless or dead. They eventually disappeared."

His dad had never discussed his time in the army beyond platitudes about the glory and honor of serving his country. A display case of his medals took their rightful place next to a case of Emmett's great-grandfather's World War II medals and his grandfather's Vietnam medals. His dad had engaged in obscure, ambiguous conflicts around the world. Had he made hard decisions that cost lives? Did he carry regrets?

Emmett wasn't brave enough to ask. Instead, he said, "I'm not an alcoholic." *Yet.* The word hung in the air between them. He had tramped too far down that road to be comfortable with the denial. "I wasn't drunk last night."

His dad's gaze flitted toward him but settled to stare out the window. He didn't believe Emmett, and honestly, given his recent history, Emmett wouldn't have believed the pronouncement either.

His dad continued on as if Emmett hadn't spoken. "There was little help available back then, but there is now. Here's a pamphlet from a center in Arizona."

His dad pulled a full-color shiny pamphlet from his back

pocket and held it out. Emmett took it and skimmed its pages. It was a rehab facility. Private and discreet. A well of bitterness soured any warm, fuzzy feelings Emmett had developed over the last half hour. Of course it wouldn't do for Madison to gossip about the Lawson boy's "problem."

Emmett tossed the pamphlet on the counter. "That's not the kind of help I need."

"What do you need, son?" His dad finally shifted to face off with him. "You've got a lot of life ahead of you. What are you going to do with it? Waste it out here? Aren't you lonely?"

He hadn't considered his state of loneliness until Greer and a damn kitten had reminded him what it was to care about something other than his own sorry self. And now he'd pissed Greer off so badly, she might never speak to him again, and the kitten had probably realized Emmett couldn't take care of himself, much less it.

"I'm figuring things out," he finally said.

"I could use some help on the farm. I've got more horses than I can train at the moment, and a mare close to foaling."

Emmett had gotten a business degree with the thought he'd maybe one day come home and take over, but that seemed a lifetime ago and impossible now. "I'm not as good with horses as you are."

His dad made a scoffing sound. "I wasn't either at your age. Too impatient, I suppose. Patience comes with age and experience. You're a Lawson; horses are in your blood."

Emmett couldn't deny it. He'd loved the horses for as long as he could remember. They had moved back to Madison after his dad had retired from the army when Emmett was in middle school. His grandfather had been getting on in years and his dad was a man of duty, first to his country and then to his own father.

"Did you ever resent having to give up your army career to take over the farm?" Emmett asked.

"I accepted God's will."

Emmett envied his dad's blind faith in a deity he no longer bought into. "But was running the farm what you wanted?"

His dad sighed. "It wasn't about what I wanted. It was what God willed. Someday you'll learn to listen."

Emmett ran a hand through his hair. "I don't believe in God, Dad. Not after what I've seen." His stomach churning, he dumped the too-strong coffee in the sink and retreated to the porch to take up his customary spot in a rocking chair.

His dad followed him out. "I saw plenty of bad too."

"I only heard about the courageous fight and the glory of serving your country. Your biggest worry was earning medals to hang in the Lawson family collection." The first thing his dad had done was ask for Emmett's medals so they could be included.

Every time Emmett looked at the case he saw the sergeant who'd died under his command in the reflection. He would never receive a parade in his honor, and his wife and child had been left with only a folded flag. It could have been Emmett. Some nights he was convinced it *should* have been him. The vagaries of fate had left him doubting the balance of justice.

His dad slapped the column of the porch stairs. "It wasn't my place to burden anyone else with my issues."

"My issues are a burden to you? I'm sure it's difficult to explain me away to all your church friends. You're welcome to pretend I don't exist." He jabbed and sliced with his words, wanting to hurt his dad. Hurt him enough so he'd leave Emmett alone.

His dad's face reflected a mortal blow, and remorse came back to inflict its own wound on Emmett. He'd grown up an obedient son and a good soldier, but the habit of following orders had died alongside his men. He refused to apologize.

The reality was Emmett was never going to live up to the Lawson ideal. After all, he'd had the bad grace to get his leg blown off and his mind scrambled.

His dad rocked on his feet as if he wasn't sure which direction to head. Fully confront Emmett or retreat? He chose to retreat, clomping down the steps and walking away.

Emmett stood on the porch and watched the sun chase the clouds.

He'd gotten what he wanted. He was alone. Strangely, relief didn't surface. An icky feeling crept through him like a virus attacking healthy cells. The crystal of the wind chimes sent a shaft of light to wink off the bottle of Jack at his elbow.

If his dad's accusations weren't so fresh, he might give in to the temptation. But he was self-aware and disciplined enough to recognize the danger looming down the path he was treading.

A soft mewl had him cocking his ear. It came again from the far side of the porch. He looked over the rail but didn't see the kitten. No way was he crawling under again. Instead, he foraged his kitchen for something suitable for a cat to eat. His fridge was a wasteland, so he grabbed the bag of ham biscuits and filled a plastic container with water.

He limped down the porch stairs and crumbled half a biscuit and part of the ham next to the water on the sun-warmed grass. He sat on the bottom step, still and silent.

The soft crunch of grass and leaves alerted him to the kitten's approach from under the porch. It moved with caution, but as soon as it fell into the food, it ate with gusto. Once the kitten was halfway through, Emmett reached out and stroked it behind the ears.

Like a rusty motor turning over, its purr was audible. It was skinny and dirty and flea-bitten. It had probably never been given a reason to trust people, yet here it was letting Emmett offer aid and affection.

Lethargic after its first good meal in forever, the kitten didn't protest when Emmett took it inside, determined it was a female, and gave her a bath, drowning as many fleas as possible. What the kitten needed was a flea treatment and a trip to the vet.

He spent the afternoon in a quandary. He hadn't left the cabin in three months. Grass had grown halfway up the hubcaps on his truck. As much as he'd railed against his dad, too many of his questions had burrowed in his psyche. What was he going to do with the rest of his life?

He was only thirty, even if some days, his experiences left him feeling ancient. Unless he planned on ending it all—which, out of bravery or cowardice, one he'd never seriously considered— he couldn't hunker down at the cabin forever.

He grabbed his keys from the front table and tucked the kitten in the pocket of his cargo pants. The truck interior was hot enough to slow-cook barbecue. He turned the key but instead of rumbling to life, the engine emitted a series of clicks.

He wiped his sweaty forehead with the sleeve of his T-shirt and tried again. *Click.* He cursed loud enough to scare a bird out of the hydrangea bush a few feet away. The battery was dead. There was a poetic analogy somewhere in the situation, but he chose not to examine it.

Tommy Thompson, his center for two years on the football team, had taken over Thompson and Sons garage after his father had passed and would drop everything to help Emmett. At one time they'd been good friends.

The kitten popped her head out of his pocket but didn't try

to escape. She seemed to enjoy the ride in his pants. Taking cover in the shade, he scrolled the numbers in his phone. His finger hovered. The moment took on an importance far beyond a dead battery.

He'd tried to separate himself from the living, but somehow life had found a way to claw him back into the fold. Finally, he tapped the number and waited.

Chapter 10

Greer knocked on the front door of Becky's Bar and Grill. No windows disrupted the sea of gray-painted concrete blocks. Becky's black SUV was parked around the side in the shade of a water oak. She was probably in the kitchen or office.

Bars had been Greer's stomping ground for years, and the layouts were all similar. She understood how much work it took to successfully run a bar and how difficult it was to find good, reliable help. After busting up the joint, Greer wasn't sure whether she qualified as either, but desperate times and all that.

Smoothing down her oxford shirt and making sure it was neatly tucked into her jeans, she knocked on the solid metal door next to a Dumpster around back. Sweat, both the nerves and Tennessee-heat-induced variety, trickled down her back. The smell of old food and skunked beer emanating from the Dumpster reminded her of all-night parties after gigs when she was young and pursuing the goal of living life to the fullest. Her stomach tried to turn itself inside out.

She raised her hand to knock again, but before her knuckles made contact, the door swung open.

Becky poked her head out, squinting. The hallway behind her was dim and windowless. "Hey, Greer. I thought we were all settled up. What can I do for you?"

"Actually, I'm here to see if I can do something for you." When Becky's eyes remained scrunched in confusion, Greer pasted on a smile and said, "I need a job."

"Well now. That is a surprise. Come on in." She pushed the door fully open and Greer stepped inside. Although the hum of an AC unit reverberated down the stark concrete-block hallway, the circulating air was humid and stale with the smell of old cigarettes.

Becky led the way into a small office. A laptop was open on a desk covered with papers. A chair with ripped vinyl sat against the wall. Greer shifted on her feet. While she'd made an atonement tour right after the "incident," she felt as if her misdeeds followed her like a black cloud. Not bad luck, but bad decisions. A string of them going back to turning up her nose at attending the community college in Madison to move to Nashville.

"First, let me apologize once again for my behavior. I'm not sure what got into me," Greer said.

"About six shots of Patrón, according to your tab." Becky's sarcastic smirk and raised eyebrows settled Greer's nerves. Sarcasm, she could handle.

"I will never touch the stuff again. *Blech.*"

"That's what they all say." Becky's laugh betrayed her love affair with smoking. As her laugh faded, she linked her hands over the papers on her desk. "Sit down. Let's talk."

Greer sat, the split vinyl biting into the back of her legs through the denim of her jeans. "I'm an experienced bartender and waitress, and I know how difficult it can be to find good people."

"Are you good people?" Becky was in her fifties and had grown up in a trailer park on the edge of Madison. Although she'd never been invited into the women's church circles, she had gained a reputation as a sharp businesswoman, but even more so as a kind person.

"I'm trying to be good people." Greer held her stare, unblinking, until her eyes burned.

Finally, Becky said, "I could use some weekend help behind the bar. My regular bartender, Edgar, has a new baby at home and his schedule has gotten more difficult to manage."

"Weekends are good. Perfect, actually. I'm volunteering during the week as part of my plea agreement."

"Doing what?"

"Working with veterans and their families using songwriting as therapy. It's been really great." Greer forced a confident smile even though her difficulties with Emmett and Ally bothered her like a swarm of no-see-ums.

If Becky thought she couldn't even handle a volunteer gig, no way would she trust Greer in the bar. And Greer needed this job for her sanity as much as for the money.

"You can mix drinks?"

"Even the fancy ones. I supported myself for years bartending."

"I thought you were a musician?"

"Music didn't pay the rent."

Becky gave an understanding harrumph. "Can you be here at three on Friday?"

"I can. Yes." This time she didn't have to force a smile. This was the start of her reinvention.

"Great. Now, skedaddle, I've got some distributors' butts to chew." She turned away and picked up the receiver of an old-fashioned avocado-green phone.

Considering Becky was now her boss, Greer did as she was told and skedaddled out the side door. Her step lighter than it had been for months, she did a little jig to her car. Her phone vibrated, putting a halt to her impromptu performance.

She fished it out of her back pocket. Emmett's name flashed. She tensed. Their last words had been harsh, and she wasn't in the mood to apologize. But what if he needed help? Now didn't seem the time to piss off the universe.

"Have you fallen and can't get up?" she asked, half needling and half worried.

"Har-har. Thanks for asking, but I'm fine."

The hand clutching the phone eased. Her relief was like taking an antacid, and her insides returned to their previously scheduled activities. "I'm glad."

"I'm . . . sorry."

Surprised he was the first to offer an olive branch, she slipped into the shade of a tree and flapped her shirt. The night's storm had only ratcheted up the humidity. The air was stagnant and the temperature registered barely below that of the surface of the sun. "That must have cost you to admit."

"Actually, no. Our fight's been eating at me. I'm just glad to have the excuse to call you and tell you."

"Excuse? Is your apology not the reason for your call?"

"No. I . . . uh . . . actually do need help." The words came like each one hurt.

Part of her wanted to tease him about needing her, but she was afraid it would send him back into his hidey-hole. "Tell me what you need."

A pause. "I was a total jerk. It's that easy for you to forgive me?"

"I wasn't exactly sweetness and light. I should be more understanding of your . . . situation."

"No." He barked the word, then continued on in a softer tone, "No, I like the fact you don't pussyfoot around my bullshit."

The silence between them felt both fragile and unbreakable. She injected her voice with a dark humor she knew he'd appreciate. "You said pussy*foot*."

She was rewarded with one of his rare laughs. "Are you busy? Could you come out to the cabin?"

"I'm available. I just finished up at Becky's Bar."

"Lord, you didn't trash the place again, did you?" An answering tease roughened his voice.

"A few broken glasses does not qualify as trashing it. Actually, you're speaking to Becky's new weekend bartender." Only when she said it aloud did she recognize how pathetic her pride sounded. A weekend bartender in a podunk town like Madison wasn't anything to brag about. She braced for his ridicule.

"Congrats, Greer. I'm proud of you for putting yourself out there."

She blinked back a sudden sting of tears. "I have you to thank, you know."

"Me?"

"The other night, you were right about more than I wanted to admit at the time. I owe you an apology too. I'm sorry I got defensive and stormed out."

"Wow. We're both acting all mature and adult-like. This is weird."

A laugh sputtered out of her. "I know. Call the papers. What can I help with?"

"My truck battery is dead, and I have a somewhat urgent errand."

"Did you run out of Hot Pockets?"

"A week ago, as a matter of fact, but that's not what I need you for. Any chance you can give me a ride?"

"Sure. Of course. I'm on my way."

"See you soon." He disconnected, and she stared at the blank screen for a few seconds as bubbles of happiness fizzed inside of her.

She got moving toward Emmett, her car AC drowning out the radio. He was leaving his fortress of solitude. Whether she had anything to do with his change of heart or not, at least he had called her. Reality was, he had probably pissed off the rest of Madison and had no one else to call, but the moment felt significant.

When she pulled off the road next to the locked gate, he stepped out from behind a pine tree before she even turned her engine off. He arced one leg over the fence and wobbled. She knew better than to jump out and take his arm. That was the kind of help he couldn't tolerate.

Instead, she clutched her steering wheel as if that would help steady him and watched his struggle through the corner of her eye. He got his other leg over without toppling and checked a bulge in the side pocket of his cargo pants. She caught her breath when the bulge moved and a little black face poked out. He opened the passenger door and slipped inside.

"Is that a cat in your pocket or are you just happy to see me?" she asked.

Another of his rumbly laughs filled the car. This one applied a shock straight to her heart, making it skip faster. He pulled the kitten out and set it on his lap. It was painfully skinny. "My friend here needs a trip to the vet. Does Harry take walk-ins?"

"Harry retired last year, and Ryan Humphries bought his practice. I'm sure he'd make the time for you."

"He'll do." He buckled himself into the passenger seat. The kitten climbed up his shirt to perch on his shoulder.

Greer couldn't move.

The kitten's purr could be heard over the AC noise as it bumped its head against his chin, seeking attention. He rubbed a finger along its cheek. Greer swallowed. In the small confines of her car, she was aware of him in ways she hadn't thought about—hadn't let herself think about.

His knees almost bumped the console, his shoulders were wider than the seat, and his elbow encroached onto her side of the armrest. She'd been thinking of him as her obligation. Her project.

But he was also a man. A handsome man with cool, complicated blue eyes shadowed with troubles and cheekbones that cut too sharply in his face. He needed as much care and tenderness as the kitten.

"Why are you looking at me like that?" His tone veered toward suspicious.

"Nothing. I'm not . . . What?" She clamped her mouth closed to stop her babbling.

He quirked an eyebrow. She forced her focus away from him but was clumsy on the turn, jouncing them into the washed-out groove on the shoulder. The kitten meowed in protest. Once on the road toward town, she searched for an innocuous subject. "Have you picked a name?"

"I'm not keeping her."

She took her foot off the gas and glanced over. He stared out the window, his arms crossed. The ball of fur kneading his neck and leaving little red marks dented his aloof, tough-guy image.

"Why not?" She concentrated on not running a stop sign or getting pulled over. With her luck, it would be Wayne.

"I can't take care of a cat."

"Why not?" she asked again like an annoying toddler.

"Because . . ." He shook his head and shrugged.

"Great answer. Real insightful."

He shifted, his elbow bumping hers. "You know why I can't keep her."

"Actually, I don't know."

"I can barely take care of myself."

"You can take care of yourself just fine. You have *chosen* to neglect yourself as some sort of punishment."

His arm tensed against hers. "What are you talking about?"

"At a wild guess, I would suspect you're punishing yourself for surviving. If the ghosts of your guys that didn't make it home could haunt you, I'd bet they'd kick you where the sun don't shine."

He muffled a curse with his hand, a bark of laughter escaping. "I don't think you understand how therapy works."

"I'm not your therapist."

"You're my music therapist, aren't you?"

"I assumed I was fired. Something to do with my ass, your good foot, and a shotgun?"

"I thought we'd moved past that little incident."

"Doesn't mean I can't tease you about it." She flipped her hair over her shoulder and tossed him a smile. A funny expression she couldn't decipher put a crinkle between his eyes. It was like she was sitting behind him in World History again, filled with a nervous excitement that he might finally notice her. She cleared her throat. "How does therapy work anyway?"

"You talk. They listen then nod as if they fucking understand then spout some platitudes." The bitterness was like a wound that wouldn't scab.

"Didn't work so well for you, huh?" She turned into the veterinarian office parking lot and took a space as close to the front as possible without seeming obvious.

"I'm not talking to a stranger about my problems."

"How about a friend?" With the delicacy of snipping the wire to an unexploded bomb, she asked, "Or your father?"

"Are you kidding me?" He climbed out of her car and shut the door on their conversation.

The tension from the car followed him like a dog and clipped his voice at the receptionist's desk. "Can Ryan work me in? I have a stray kitten that needs a once-over."

The receptionist was young and pretty and so blithely happy about everything from the weather to typing Emmett's information into the computer, Greer was jealous. Had she ever been in possession of such starry-eyed optimism?

Maybe right after she'd moved to Nashville and assumed success was one gig away. The years had ground her hope to dust like a pestle to mortar.

Emmett pulled the kitten from his side pocket and put her on his shoulder. She seemed happy to set her claws in his cotton shirt and burrow into his neck. He walked over to a corkboard covered in flyers for animals to give away. The majority were cats.

"Should I put something up for her?" He nodded toward the kitten.

"You're serious about giving her away?"

"Yes." The way the word lilted into an almost-question made

her wonder if he wasn't already growing attached. "What would I do with a cat?"

Love it. She bit the inside of her cheek and merely shrugged. Was he so damaged he couldn't love anything or anyone—even himself? As if already wanting to distance himself, he plucked the kitten off his shoulder and handed it to her.

Greer ignored him while they waited. A help wanted flyer took up the middle of the corkboard. The vet clinic was looking for another receptionist and animal tech. Was she qualified? She tucked the idea away to mull over it.

Ryan Humphries strode out of a windowless door, a huge smile on his blandly handsome face. While he was the same age as Greer and Emmett, he had the well-fed, contented look of an older man. The solid frame that had made him a high school All-Tennessee tight end had expanded, yet he still carried himself as if he were ready to jog onto the field and take up his stance.

"It's great to see you, man." Ryan went in for a hug.

Emmett stood with his arms at his sides as if enduring the affection. After one bone-rattling pat on his shoulder from Ryan, Emmett raised a hand, not to return the sentiment, but to put space between them.

"You look"—Ryan's gaze dropped to Emmett's legs and his smile faltered, but didn't disappear—"great. Really great."

Greer barked a laugh, drawing both men's attention. Emmett's tight lips morphed into a half smile when his gaze clashed with hers. He was in desperate need of a haircut, a week of sleep, and a month's worth of hearty meals.

"Greer Hadley?" Ryan's gaze zipped down her body and back up, the slight gleam veering less toward "old friend" friendly than "how *you* doin'" friendly. "Heard you were back. Heard about Beau too. Rotten situation."

She sidled closer to Emmett. "How's Jessica?"

"No idea. Divorce was final three months ago." He held up his left hand. Where a ring used to reside was a fading white strip of skin. "She couldn't get out of Madison fast enough."

"I'm sorry. I hadn't heard," Greer said.

"Thank God there were no kids to complicate things." He made a sweeping gesture with his hand. "Come on back, and I'll take a look at your kitten."

She hoped she was misreading the vibes Ryan was putting out. Not even if Elvis in his bad-boy "Jailhouse Rock" days was resurrected and wanted to sweep her off to Graceland would she consider a relationship with a man at the moment—undead or real.

If it were possible, Emmett's frown had grown more pronounced and was aimed squarely at Ryan's back. She elbowed him and mouthed *what's wrong* as they followed Ryan into an exam room. He only narrowed his eyes at her.

She set the kitten on the silver metal table. Ryan's exam was deft and gentle and made her think he actually knew what he was doing.

"What's her name?" Ryan glanced up at Greer as he set the kitten down. It crouched closer to Emmett, who unfolded his arms from across his chest to stroke the kitten's head.

"Don't ask me." She thumbed toward Emmett. "She's his kitten."

"Not mine. She's a stray. I'm thinking some asshole dumped her out at the road leading to the cabin. I'm not keeping her. In fact, if I cover her workup and shots, maybe you could send her to a shelter or something." He tucked the kitten closer.

Ryan propped his hip against a storage unit topped with a laptop. "Shots or not, the county shelter will euthanize her by the end of the day if she shows up looking like that."

"What's wrong with her?" Emmett's hand closed around the kitten as if Ryan were threatening to do the deed himself.

"She's too skinny and fleabitten. They're already overrun with ferals and strays. If you're going to keep her, I'd suggest a blood screening, a flea bath, and vaccinations. If you're not, I wouldn't waste the money on the long shot she'll get adopted at the shelter."

Emmett turned to Greer. "You can take her, can't you?"

"Mama's allergic."

If for one second she thought Emmett would actually send the kitten to the county shelter, she would have taken the kitten anyway, but too much of the old Emmett lived in him, whether he wanted to admit it or not. He was honor-bound to do the right thing.

Emmett muttered a curse, then held the cat out, its paws dangling over either side of his palm. "Fine. Give her the works—blood screening, bath, shots."

Ryan's lips twitched as if he too had foreseen the inevitability of the decision. "I'll be back."

Once they were alone, Greer asked, "What are you going to name her?"

"Cat."

"*Cat?* That's pitiful."

"Yet wholly accurate."

"How about Tanya? Or Reba?" She caught his eye roll and paced. Who would Emmett have idolized? "Stevie? Bonnie?"

"As in Bonnie Raitt?" His eyebrows perked, and Greer pounced.

"She's an incredible songwriter and guitarist."

"Yeah. I suppose Bonnie would be fine." He whispered the name as if testing it: "Bonnie."

She turned away and pretended to examine a mundane

watercolor print to hide her smile. While she hadn't made any strides with him in terms of actual music, he was shuffling toward the land of the living, but one wrong move would send him scurrying back to his solitude.

Ryan returned with Bonnie, freshly washed with a shaved place on her front leg and a small bandage. Bedraggled and resentful, she was handed over to Emmett, who tucked her back into his pocket. Without a meow of protest, she burrowed out of sight, knowing she was safe.

While the two men shook hands, Ryan said, "We have a flag football league on Saturday morning down at the park. You should come out. It would be like old times."

"No, thanks."

"Come on, man. You'll know most of the guys. They'd be excited to see you on the field again." Ryan's smile was cajoling. "We need a decent quarterback."

"I said no." Emmett sounded like a drill sergeant. He didn't break eye contact with Ryan or try to diffuse the tension through politeness.

Ryan's throat worked with a swallow, and he stepped back and held his hands up as if Emmett needed talking off a ledge. "No problem. Offer remains open anytime, though. I'll see you two around town." His gaze lingered on Greer, and although he wasn't being creepy or pushy, she felt uncomfortable nonetheless and discarded the idea of applying for the receptionist job.

She wasn't being fair. Ryan was a nice guy with a good career. Except she couldn't summon an iota of attraction. In fact, she couldn't remember the last time she'd been truly attracted to a man. Her relationship with Beau had been based on the familiar comfort of an old couch. Which was probably why he had cheated.

"Come on. I'm hungry." Greer tugged on the side of Emmett's T-shirt. It stretched taut before Emmett allowed Greer to lead him out of the exam room and to the receptionist's counter to pay. Ryan didn't follow them.

After Emmett handed over his credit card, Greer stepped into the sweltering afternoon sun. The air was thick, but a gusting breeze heralded the approach of a late-afternoon thunderstorm. She unlocked her car and climbed behind the wheel. It took extra maneuvering for Emmett to fold his body into the compact seat, his artificial leg and pocket of kitten adding to the complications.

She cranked the AC, but it didn't have time to cool the interior before she parked on Oak Street in front of the Downtown Café.

"What are you doing?" he asked.

"I told you. I'm hungry and you're buying me a chicken salad sandwich and a side of cobbler." She cracked her door open. The temperature of the air outside was dropping fast.

"I am, am I?" He didn't sound angry, yet he made no move to get out.

"Yep. And if you don't come on now, we're going to get soaked." A fat droplet splatted on the windshield. More followed, picking up pace.

She hopped out and squealed as the sky opened, making a run for the overhang on the front of the café. Emmett came around the front of her car in an awkward run-walk. Her first instinct was to turn and pretend something else caught her eye, but Emmett was too sharp and would notice the pity look-away. She held his gaze as he came up to stand inches away from her, water dripping from his hair and trailing down his cheeks.

Only then did she look away, but not out of pity and not

because of his leg. While he was too lean for his six-two frame, the muscles of his chest were defined through the cling of his damp T-shirt.

Her breathing picked up its cadence and her voice turned breathy. "How's Bonnie?"

"Peachy." He patted the bulging cargo pocket. "Speaking of, I hope that's the cobbler of the day."

"Keep her stashed. She'd probably violate the diner's health code." She backed into the door of the café.

Emmett's gaze darted across the row of booths against the window, his slight smile morphing into a look that could only be described as murderous.

Chapter 11

*G*reer. Thank God, I've finally run into you." Beau's voice
gripped the laws of time and gravity, leaving her reeling.
She grabbed for the nearest stable object, which happened to be
Emmett's arm.

"Do you want to leave?" Emmett whispered, his lips barely
moving.

What she wanted was for Emmett to put his army training
to good use and teach Beau a lesson. "No. I can't avoid him forever. Madison is too small."

"You got that right." His forearm flexed within her grasp,
reassuringly strong and solid. "I'm here if you need backup."

Thank you, she mouthed before reluctantly letting him go
and turning to face her ex.

Beau Williams was handsome in an "I'd rather not get my
hair mussed" kind of way. Facing him now, especially in close
proximity to Emmett, she couldn't remember what had attracted her in the first place.

A high-strung, workaholic real estate agent, he was the stark opposite of the easygoing, undependable musicians she'd hung out with in Nashville. As the music scene had lost its shine, Greer had bumped into Beau one night. She'd run toward someone familiar and safe. And boring.

As if looking through the wrong end of a pair of binoculars, she felt like she was examining her life and loves from a great distance. Standing next to bigger-than-life Emmett, she realized her relationship with Beau seemed small and insignificant. A mere blip.

"Did you want to talk to me about something in particular, Beau?" Bypassing the wait to be seated sign, she slipped into an unoccupied booth. Emmett scooched onto the opposite bench, his legs bumping hers. One flesh and blood, one hard and mechanical.

Beau made a move to sit next to Emmett, but he spread his legs and propped his elbows on the table to block him. She'd never been so grateful for manspreading in her life.

"Could we speak outside? In private?" If Beau had had a hat, it would be in hand. His earnestness had been another appealing trait, but it hadn't translated into honesty or trustworthiness.

"Sorry, but I'm hungry and Emmett owes me cobbler."

Beau started and stared. "Emmett Lawson. I didn't even recognize you. You look . . . different." His gaze dropped as if he could see through the table.

Why did people have to make such a big deal about his leg? Neither his heart nor his brain had been damaged. He might have come home changed from his experiences, but he was still a man.

"You look different too, Beau." Emmett lounged in the booth, but his leg was like a strung bow against hers under the table. "Sorry about your hair."

Emmett hit a bull's-eye. Beau's hand flew to the back of his head where a bald spot was forming like the swirled eye of a hurricane. In another decade, he would look just like his daddy—potbellied with only a monk's tonsure left.

"I can wait until you're done. Can we meet?"

"What makes you think I'll be done with Emmett anytime soon?" She sugared her voice with innuendo. Emmett's brows flew up and his cheeks turned ruddy, but he didn't disabuse Beau of the notion.

"Because . . . well, you know." Beau's gaze darted between them. "I need to explain what happened."

"I got the birds and the bees talk from my mama years ago, but thanks." She shot him a smile that qualified as more of a baring of her teeth. If he thought she was too polite to start a scene, he must not have heard about her drunken tantrum at Becky's.

Beau glanced around the restaurant. It was early yet for the dinner crowd, and the tables and booths within earshot were empty. He dropped his voice to a whisper anyway. "I'm sorry. It was a mistake. A huge one. Now that you're back in Madison, things will be easier between us. I got lonely, is all."

"I trusted you." She had no anger left for Beau, only disappointment. Not only in him, but in her own judgment.

"I'll make it up to you."

"It's too late for that. I'm not interested." She studied the menu—as if she needed to look at it, she always got the same thing—and ignored Beau.

"But Greer—"

"Dude, she's not interested in getting back with you. Get out of here before I officially lose my temper." Emmett made to get up, but he lost his balance on his rise and grabbed the corner of the table.

"I'm not fighting you, Emmett. You're . . . disabled. It wouldn't be fair." Although Beau said it kindly, a seismic shift occurred in Emmett.

She shot out of the booth and notched herself into Emmett's side. Pressing a hand into his chest, she maintained enough pressure to keep him from launching at Beau. The last thing any of them needed was Emmett to get in a fight with Beau and the police showing up. Her parents had endured enough talk about her already.

"Don't forget about Bonnie," she whispered close to his ear.

His hand went to his cargo pocket, and like a pressure cooker valve released, his body lost most of its tension.

"Get out of here, Beau. We're done." Greer kept her voice low but firm.

"But—"

Emmett moved with reflexes honed on the battlefield. Beau's shirt was in his hand, and he pulled the smaller man within inches of his face. "Quit arguing and get out before I ram my disabled foot up your ass."

Emmett shoved Beau away. Beau stumbled backward into the corner of a table. Both he and the table clattered to the floor. Silence blanketed the restaurant. A man in a white cook's uniform and a waitress ran out of the kitchen. Two old men stood up from their booth in the corner and a family of four stared from a table in the middle.

Beau clambered up and righted the table, seemingly as

anxious as she was to avoid more gossip. Lord knows, their issues had provided the town with enough to keep it fed and watered until fall.

With the fake smile still on her face, she tugged Emmett's arm. "Let's go. I've lost my appetite."

She was surprised when he followed her out the door without protest. The rain had stopped. Steam rose from the streets, negating the brief drop in humidity and temperature. They didn't speak until she was driving, the AC working overtime to cut the heat.

Emmett took Bonnie out of his pocket and plopped her on his shoulder. The kitten seemed to enjoy being high enough to see out the windows, her curiosity tempered with a need to remain close to him.

"This is the opposite way as my place." He crossed his arms and his voice reflected a general disgruntlement.

"We're going to the store."

"No, we aren't."

"I'm the one behind the wheel, Mr. Tough Guy, and I say we are."

His lip twitch gave him away. *"Mr. Tough Guy?"*

"All I need is for your little display of muscled aggression to get tongues wagging again."

"Trust me, I wasn't nearly as aggressive as I wanted to be. Not my fault the man is clumsy. I barely shoved him."

She suspected he was looking out the passenger window to avoid eye contact. Emmett had lashed out physically because of Beau's well-intentioned albeit tone-deaf observation.

"He did kind of deserve it," she said.

"Hell yes, he did." Emmett shifted, his profile hard, his

cheekbones stark in his face. "Now that we're in agreement, can you take me home?"

"No. You need cat food and litter and a box for Bonnie, and since Beau interrupted our meal, I'm going to grab something easy to cook for us. Do you like spaghetti?"

His silence had her shoulders rolling inward and her hands tightening on the steering wheel. Was she overstepping? Which part of her announcement would he argue with—keeping the kitten or fixing him dinner?

"Who in their right mind doesn't like spaghetti?" he asked with a marked incredulity.

His easy acquiescence drew a laugh born from relief out of her. The big-box store parking lot wasn't packed, but the chances of running into someone one or both of them were acquainted with approached 100 percent.

Sweat broke over his forehead before she'd even turned the car off. "I can't go in there."

"Afraid of slashing prices?" Her joke fell flat. She cleared her throat. "The longer you stay away, the harder it will be to face people."

His glare held red shades of a rageful storm. "You're one to talk."

"What do you mean? I've been to the store plenty since I've been home."

"When's the last time you played the guitar or sang?"

"That's different." Now it was her turn to stare out the window and avoid eye contract.

"I remember a girl whose life's blood was music."

"I call bullshit. You barely noticed me."

"You got up onstage at the talent show our sophomore year

and shocked everyone. That song you sang. I don't remember how it went, but I remember how I felt in that moment."

She had shocked him back then? His words in the here and now left her astounded, consternated, flabbergasted. There wasn't a single word to sum up her surprise. "You remember my song?"

"I remember how cute you looked in that denim skirt and tank top. You'd plaited your hair—it was longer then—and it hung over your shoulder while you played. You closed your eyes when you sang as if none of us were there. It—*you*—were amazing. Something I'll never forget."

"But . . . I didn't even win. Dan McGee won for playing 'Stairway to Heaven.'" Her body felt tingly as if it had fallen asleep and was just now waking.

"He won because he was on the football team and everyone knew the song."

The talent show had been her coming out. It had been the first time she'd played outside of her bedroom. Back then, the excitement vibrating her body as she stepped into the bright circle of light on the stage had outpaced the nerves.

Restless teenagers had made up the crowd, but when the first note left her fingertips, she had closed her eyes and imagined herself onstage at the Grand Ole Opry. The song had been one of her first attempts at songwriting. Simple, perhaps, but written from a place of purity that had gotten tainted over the last decade.

"Was I actually good back then?" The question was more immediate and one he couldn't answer. She'd lost all confidence in herself, personally and professionally.

"You were fantastic." He cocked his head and snared her gaze with his. "Why did you give it up?"

"Give it up? Nashville chewed me up and spit me out."

"Music exists outside of Nashville, Greer. You don't need an adoring crowd or a record deal to write and perform."

She sighed and slumped in her seat. "The constant string of rejections from labels and crowds got too hard to handle. The people in bars were more interested in getting drunk or hooking up than listening to me play."

"I get that rejection can be tough, but you can't give up."

"I ran out of money."

"I'll give you a loan and you can—"

"Stop it." She barked the words and closed her eyes. "My last gig was at the Bluebird. Tough to get and a place where singers get discovered. I knew that. I was ready."

"What happened?"

"I stepped up to the mic and panicked. It was like an evil witch had stolen my voice. My fingers forgot what to do on the strings. I bombed. It was a nightmare. I packed up and left Nashville that night."

He muffled a curse in his hand. "You drove home only to catch Beau in bed with Marcie."

"The universe kicked me while I was down, that's for sure." Greer hadn't confessed the entire sorry tale to anyone. Not even her mother.

People entering and exiting the store flashed in her rearview mirror. One young mother pushed a screaming toddler in a cart. An older couple walked hand in hand, laughing together. Life teemed around her and Emmett, yet it felt like just the two of them against a world that considered them damaged goods.

"You're better off without Beau. How did you end up with him anyway? He was uninteresting at best in high school and it doesn't seem like much has changed."

"I guess he was my anchor to Madison. To home." The older she got, the more she appreciated the uncomplicated safety of her hometown.

"An anchor weighs you down. Keeps you in one place. Why would you want to be with someone like that? You should be with someone who encourages you to fly." He gave her knee a brotherly pat and opened the door. "I'm starved and if you're serious about the spaghetti, let's get this ordeal over with."

Unaware of the crater his words had left in her chest, he maneuvered out of the car. The simple wisdom from a not-so-simple man jump-started her heart like a pacemaker. He stood outside the car, holding the kitten to his chest with one hand and petting her, before tucking her into his pocket.

He turned and ducked his head to see her through the windshield. "You coming or are you afraid to be seen out in public with me?"

Pasting on a smile, she joined him, and they weaved their way through cars and pickups to the entrance. "To be honest, I'm a little afraid of running into your dad."

"Why?" At her silence, he grabbed her wrist and pulled her to a stop on the sidewalk, close enough to the sliding doors to feel a burst of cool air every time someone entered.

"I find him more than a little intimidating."

"You must need volunteer hours bad to put up with me."

She looked up at him and grinned. "Maybe I'm the one who needs therapy since hanging out with you is a form of self-torture."

He searched her face but didn't return her smile. In fact, he was as serious as she'd ever seen him, even when he'd fired his warning shot.

She dropped her smile. "That was a joke, by the way. Self-torture would be to get back together with Beau. Don't get a big head, but hanging out with you is easy. I don't have to put on a face, if that makes sense."

His hand loosened and trailed over her hand. "Yeah. It does actually. I don't put on a face with you either."

"I didn't think you bothered to put on a face with anyone."

"I try with Mom and Dad. Especially Mom, so she won't worry."

"News flash: she's super-worried."

The ghost of a smile crossed his face and reminded her of the carefree, confident Emmett of the past. Yet, she liked the darker, more complicated Emmett of now even better.

"Come on before Bonnie uses my pocket as a litter box." He nudged his head toward the entrance.

She grabbed a cart and wheeled it up and down the aisles, packing it full of simple dinner ingredients and healthy snacks.

"I don't need to stock up for the apocalypse," Emmett grumbled, yet dropped in three boxes of macaroni and cheese.

Once she was satisfied, they meandered to pet supplies and picked up a box, litter, and kitten food. Although he tried to be smooth, she noticed the cat toy he slipped under a bag of rice. Bonnie had never been in danger of being abandoned in a shelter.

They pushed the cart side by side to the checkout, their elbows bumping. Only the slight hitch to his gait reminded her of his injury.

"How's little Bonnie Raitt doing?" she asked.

He stuck his hand into his pocket. "Curled up into a ball. At least she hasn't pooped in my pocket."

"My stars, if it isn't the two lost souls of Madison." The female voice was only too familiar. And loud.

Greer turned. Better to face her adversary than leave her back exposed. "Hello, Ms. Justine."

Look up "busybody" and Justine Danvers's portrait would be printed in all its glory, toothy grin included at no extra charge. She'd been left a widow by her wealthy husband in her early thirties and had never remarried, but not for a lack of trying. Boredom, loneliness, and a natural affinity for gossip had combined in a perfect storm.

While from a distance Greer felt sorry for her, getting up close and personal was dangerous. What kept Justine content was knowing everything good, bad, and salacious about the people of Madison.

"Greer. I spoke with your dear mama at church last Sunday. Why haven't you attended since you've been home? I assure you that no one blames you for what happened with poor old Beau." Justine laid a hand over her heart and tutted.

"Poor old Beau? He's the one who—"

"And Emmett Lawson as I live and breathe." Justine had a bigger fish on the hook. Greer's luck was Emmett's misfortune.

"Ms. Justine. You're looking . . . healthy."

"My goodness, it's good to see you out and about." Justine cocked her head, her gaze lingering on his legs. "You look better than I expected. Bless your heart."

Greer would have thrown herself into the fray if Emmett had been a stranger to Justine, but he was as familiar with her backhanded sympathy as she was. Why not have a little fun? She shifted to stand shoulder to shoulder with Justine and set her hand on her chest like a mimic. "You don't think he looks a little peaked, Ms. Justine?"

"He's a mite too skinny, perhaps. And goodness me, he needs a haircut."

"I agree. So shaggy and wild." Greer bit the inside of her lip to stifle her laughter. Emmett's expression was a thundercloud, his eyes electric.

Ms. Justine looked over the cart. "Are you working on fattening him up, Greer?"

"That's the plan, ma'am. His mama has been taking too good care of him. He doesn't know how to cook." Greer winked at Emmett. Her tease didn't lighten his expression.

"I see." Ms. Justine's gaze darted between the two of them.

Greer didn't recognize the quicksand until she was already sinking. "I'm helping as an old friend. We're not . . . you know."

"Of course you're not." Justine waggled her fingers and strolled away. "Toodleloo, you two. Have fun."

Greer could only watch her leave. Whispers would sift through the town like smoke, and once the rumor was out, nothing could contain it.

"Your dad is going to haul me in front of the church elders for an exorcism." Greer sent a side-eye toward Emmett.

"Screw him. And screw Justine Danvers." Emmett pushed the cart toward the checkout, but faster now, his gait stiffer, the slight limp more noticeable, as if the confrontation and fallout raised his anxiety more than he wanted to let on.

"Better not say that too loud. Justine Danvers would probably take you up on it."

Emmett's face remained in profile, but she saw a smile tip the corner of his mouth.

They made it through the checkout line and loaded the bags into the trunk of her car without running into anyone else they knew. Small talk filled the distance between the store and his cabin. She pulled to the side of the road by the locked gate, dreading the number of trips they would have to make.

"Hang on." Emmett climbed out, fished something out of his pocket, and fiddled with the lock and chain, finally pushing it open. He gestured her through. The car took a hard bounce off the pavement onto the soft needles. She stopped under the trees and waited for him to slip back in. He'd left the gate wide open.

"Aren't you afraid the Jehovah's Witnesses will sense an opening and come a-knocking?"

"Maybe I'll invite them in and see if they have an insight into why I'm still around and so many of my buddies aren't."

Her foot jerked on the brake, but she gained control over it and coasted along the overgrown ruts that passed for a road. She darted a look in his direction, but he was staring straight ahead. Fractious darkness erupted from him at odd times, only to settle into a bland silence.

By the time they had his kitchen stocked, the sun was falling toward the horizon and a breeze had turned the evening pleasant. Greer dumped the spaghetti noodles into a pot of boiling water, set the timer, and joined Emmett on the porch.

He held out a shot of whiskey. "Unless you'd prefer wine?"

"Do you have wine?"

"No." He made a scoffing sound and tossed his shot back. She did the same with its companion, the slight burn pleasant.

He screwed the top back on the bottle and set it aside. Bonnie had been fed and watered and was playing chase with a fluttering moth at the edge of the porch. Greer half sat on the rail, stretching one leg along the top, and leaned her head against the column. The squeak of Emmett's rocking chair along with the tinkle of the wind chimes settled a contentment she hadn't felt since she was a kid spending her summers reading endless books on the porch swing.

"I can see why you chose to stay out here." She kept her voice soft, as if she might scare away the peace that lurked at the edge of her consciousness.

"I'm staying out here because I couldn't stand Mom fussing over me like I had a terminal illness. The views are a bonus."

"She loves you."

"I have no idea why."

"I don't know, you're not so bad." She let a beat of companionable silence hit before adding, "Once you dig past the jerky outer shell. And I mean dig deep. Like dig-a-hole-to-China deep."

With an agility she didn't anticipate, he shot to his feet and squeezed her leg right above her knee. No one had pulled the "crow eating corn" tickle move on her in two decades.

Laughing wildly, she jerked to get away and would have tumbled over the porch rail into the hydrangeas if he hadn't grabbed hold of her arm to steady her.

"Say it." Laughter threaded his voice.

"No," she gasped out. Tears blurred her vision as his hand continued to gnaw on her leg like a crow.

"Do you give the Lord a biscuit? Come on, say it and I'll stop."

Words were near impossible to string together in her state of tickle torture, and the ridiculous saying had her laughing all the harder. "I-give-the-Lord-a-biscuit!"

Apparently he understood her breathy shout and stopped, but kept her in his grip, his palm sliding enough north on her thigh to add strange dimensions to the pseudo-brotherly moment. Her breaths were labored but she wasn't sure it was all due to their tickle fight. He was breathing hard too, his eyes crinkled and absent their usual shadows.

Instead of being able to catch her breath, it hitched even worse. Her body became aware of his like hunter and prey. What if she grabbed his shirt and pulled him into her? Would he taste of whiskey?

She wasn't destined to find out. The beep of the kitchen timer cut them apart. He stepped back and ran his hands down the front of his pants. Red burnished his cheeks. Whether from the same physical awareness coursing through her or simple exertion, she couldn't discern.

The beep continued like a warning.

"I should get that." She hopped off the rail, thumbed over her shoulder, and backed to the door.

"Need help?"

"No," she said too forcefully. The last thing she needed was being confined with him in the small kitchen. She might continue their foray into adolescent games with a round of Seven Minutes in Heaven. She softened her tone. "Do you want to eat out here?"

"Sure. Let's enjoy the evening."

Greer retreated, gathered her self-control, and returned with two bowls plus a slice of garlic bread each. She sat next to him in a matching rocking chair. They didn't speak or look at each other. The awkwardness of the silence was tempered by the noise of the wind in the trees and the insects awakening for their evening concert.

She shot a side-eye glance in his direction, not turning her head. His pose was pure relaxation, his good leg thrown over the arm of the chair, his other leg rocking him.

The tension holding her in its grip lessened but didn't disappear. Had the lightning strike of sexual awareness been one-sided? Even down a leg, he was still Emmett Lawson, the golden boy of Madison, Tennessee.

She popped up and gathered their empty bowls. "I'll clean up then head out."

"You don't have to—" He bit off his protest and stood, tugging the bowls out of her hands.

What had he been about to say? She didn't have to clean up? Or leave? His face didn't provide any clues, but his stillness was expectant. She wasn't brave—or stupid—enough to ask him what he expected, so she took a step back and tucked her hands into her back pockets.

"Since I cooked, it's only fair you clean, I suppose."

He set the bowls on the side table but didn't draw closer to her. "I appreciate everything today."

"You need a jump for your truck?"

"Don't worry about it. I'll get Dad out here tomorrow."

"That's going to mean leaving the gate open."

"Yeah, I guess it will."

She stepped backward down the steps, hanging on to the handrail, and gave him a teasing smile. "Aren't you worried about the stampede of women who are going to demand to save you with sex?"

"Maybe I'm in the mood to take one of them up on the offer."

She stopped short in the dirt at the bottom of the steps while her stomach wanted to send her spaghetti back up. "What?"

"In case you hadn't noticed, I'm a man, Greer."

Dammit, she'd noticed. Hadn't he noticed her noticing? "Well, I hope you have fun."

That was a lie. She hoped he couldn't get it up.

She couldn't get in her car and moving quick enough.

Darkness closed around her in the trees, and she had to blink around tears to fumble her headlights on. Bugs swarmed in the beams. A lightning bug splatted on her windshield in her line of sight. The windshield wipers smeared its glow.

"I feel you, bug. I feel you."

Chapter 12

Emmett might be down a leg, but he hadn't been neutered. Everything down there was in working order, as he proved on an almost nightly basis. Yet Ryan and Beau had cast bait for Greer right in front of him the day before. And she hadn't seemed the least bit concerned at his threat of messing around with Madison's female population.

Granted, the tentative friendship that had sprung up between them like kudzu was devoid of sexual overtones. Wasn't it? For a moment on the porch after tickling her breathless, he'd sensed . . . something. Something that made him stand up a little straighter. Something that had thickened the air like honey.

But then the moment passed, and she had been back to teasing him like a brother. A concrete foundation had been poured in the construction of their friend zone. Which was for the best. He needed a friend, not a girlfriend or a lover. He touched his stump. Sex was unimaginable.

Was he supposed to keep his prosthetic on? He sure as hell didn't want Greer to see him without it. He didn't want *anyone* to see him without it.

Lying in bed thinking about sex and Greer was a bad combination when he was expecting his dad any minute. With early morning light suffusing his bedroom, he sat up, swung himself to the side of the bed, and pulled on the same pair of khakis he'd worn the day before. If he and his dad were going to get his truck running, he might as well anticipate getting dirty and sweaty.

His prosthetic leaned up against his dresser. He slipped a sleeve over his residual limb and then a special sock with a ratchet sewn in. Standing up, he balanced himself against the wall with one hand while fitting his leg into it. He'd gotten to be expert at lining up the ratchet system that held it in place.

One running shoe was already on his fake foot, so he hobbled to the dresser for a sock for his other foot. He had a stockpile of white athletic socks to match with the one covering his prosthetic. The one time he'd gone barefoot in front of his parents, they hadn't been able to stop staring at his feet—or foot.

The sound of a diesel work truck brought him out on the porch. His dad pulled up beside his old gray Ford F-150. It was a remnant of his high school days. He'd bought a fancy Dodge truck when the army money rolled in, but sold it before he deployed. The logic of making payments on a truck that would sit for a year didn't make sense. He'd planned to buy something fun and risky like a motorcycle when his tour was up, but no more. He was done with risk.

His mom and dad climbed out of the truck. She held a covered dish. His stomach growled before he even smelled it. The spaghetti the night before had jump-started his appetite. A raggedy-sounding meow and slight bump against his leg turned his attention to Bonnie and her empty food bowl.

He poured kibble into the new food dish and Bonnie attacked it the way he wanted to attack whatever homemade goodness his mother had brought him.

His dad pulled out jumper cables from the back of his truck. "You want to pop the hood, Emmett?"

His mom looked . . . worn. Her hair showed gray at the roots and her face was devoid of makeup. Had he done this to her? All his attention had been sucked up by his own needy selfishness, and he had lashed out without recognizing the damage he was inflicting.

"How about we tackle whatever delicious casserole Mom brought before we get all dirty and sweaty?"

His mom and dad exchanged a look. One that encompassed a conversation they would have later about him. A few days ago, he might have had to beat back anger like a whack-a-mole mallet, but this morning, something resembling contentment kept his frustration from spilling over. The bad stuff was still there but manageable.

He threw an arm around his mom's shoulder and gave her a little shake. "Come on in. You and dad can discuss my mental frailties later. I'm starving."

The tentative smile that broke over her face made her look like a hopeful puppy who'd been kicked one too many times when it tried to get close. Another failure and regret to add to the list, right below his inability to save his guys.

"You go sit and let me handle things. Okay?" She waited, her body reflecting a tense defensiveness.

He had blown up at her for less. Sitting and letting someone else handle things had the earmarks of pity. Yet, his mom had fixed him food and taken care of him all his life. Letting her help him would go a long way to returning to their old mother-son dynamic.

"Sure. That sounds great." He brushed a kiss along her cheek.

Her hand flew up to press against the spot before she retreated to bustle around the kitchen. At least he hadn't left her a mess to clean up from the night before. He was tired of letting everyone else clean up his messes. He had to do better. Be a better son. A better man.

He sat on the flower-patterned couch. It had once graced his grandparents' den, and he remembered climbing onto his grandfather's lap to hear his war stories from Vietnam, playing with the same frayed piping he fiddled with now.

His dad crossed the threshold into the cabin as if expecting a booby trap. Instead, the smell of coffee brewing filled the room with welcome, and his dad took a seat in a chair across from him. The silence wasn't wholly comfortable but held a lightness that had been absent for too long.

His mom came out holding two mugs of steaming coffee. "Both black."

"Thanks," Emmett and his dad said in unison.

His mom smiled and looked back and forth at them a few times as if reassuring herself the scene wasn't in her imagination before returning to the kitchen. The church hymn she hummed was one of the few uplifting ones he could remember.

She returned with a tray bearing another mug of coffee and three plates with varying amounts of cheesy sausage and egg casserole. He took the one nearest him, which happened to have a mountain of casserole.

He intercepted another look between his parents but the happy signals his taste buds were sending to his brain overwhelmed any annoyance.

"Someone dump a litter of cats out here?" his dad asked.

"If they did, only one made it. I found her cowering under the porch the other night during the big storm," Emmett said between bites.

His mom cleared her throat and poked at her food. "We heard you went to town yesterday."

If they'd heard he was in town, they also knew who he'd been with. "Bonnie needed a once-over."

"Bonnie?" His mom's brow knitted.

"The kitten. She's named after Bonnie Raitt, the singer? It was Greer's idea."

His dad emitted a huff laden with disapproval, and another meaning-filled glance passed between his parents before his dad glared at him. This one he couldn't let go with equanimity. Emmett dropped his fork, the clatter against the plate ratcheting up the tension. He opened his mouth but his mom preempted him.

"I'm pleased as punch Greer managed to drag you out of the cabin. Did you have a nice time?" It seemed his mom had won whatever power play was occurring between her and his dad.

Emmett let himself relax back against the cushion. "It was good to see Ryan."

It had been good to see him until he'd made a blatant play for Greer right in front of him. That never would have happened in high school.

"I didn't think he was smart enough to make a vet, but he's got a good reputation. Thought about calling him out to the farm to check on Daisy. She's getting close to her first foaling.

Did you eat at the café? I've found their desserts to be the only thing palatable on the menu," his dad said, still edging toward surly.

"I wanted cobbler, but unfortunately, Greer and I were interrupted."

"We heard Beau caused a scene," his mom said.

His dad harrumphed. "Only because that girl—"

"Hush your mouth, Henry."

Emmett had only heard his mom use that tone of voice when he was a kid, and only when he'd deserved a good spanking for talking back. To hear her chastise his dad like a child was strangely satisfying and poked him in the funny bone.

He laughed.

His mom gasped and covered her mouth. His dad put his plate down and sat back in the chair.

"Y'all are killing me." Emmett grinned and shoved another bite in his mouth. "Greer has been a good friend, Dad. Better than I deserve after you complained to Amelia."

"Greer was supposed to leave you alone so you could heal."

"Yeah, well. She wasn't in the service and doesn't follow orders." Emmett scraped the last forkful off his plate. "Apparently, I needed a good kick in the butt more than I needed to sit on my thumbs."

"Is that all she is? A friend?" His mom had perfected the art of interrogation with sugar.

"Only a friend." A pang at the truth of the statement made him rub his chest and retreat to the kitchen for a second helping.

His parents watched him finish off another huge plateful while sipping their coffee and discussing mundane gossip about who was in the hospital and who was on vacation.

His mom gathered his plate a millisecond after it made contact with the table. "I'll clean up. You boys have work to do, don't you?"

His dad rose and rubbed his hands together. "Let's get to it, then. I have chores around the farm to attend to."

A slice of guilt emerged from the clouds of his depression like blinding sunlight. It had been understood from the time his dad retired from the army to take the horse farm over from his father that Emmett would eventually do the same. Now he didn't know if his dad still wanted him at all. His dad's faith seemed shaken. Maybe he'd sell out to some big-shot trainer and take his mom to Florida to retire. It wasn't only a physically demanding profession but required the patience of Job. Emmett was unqualified.

They hooked up the jumper cables, moving as if they had trained together, not needing to speak. His dad cranked the diesel truck and let it run. The noise made conversation difficult, and Emmett was glad.

"Try it now," his dad finally hollered.

Emmett got behind the wheel of his old Ford and turned the key. After one failed try, the engine caught and chugged awake. It wasn't smooth like his Dodge or powerful like his dad's diesel, but sitting in the cab beside him on the worn leather seats was the ghost of his younger self.

Brash, full of confidence, and all in one piece. If he concentrated he could almost grasp some of his ghost's magic. Magic he'd lost somewhere along the way.

His dad disconnected their trucks, and the diesel spooled into silence. Emmett let the Ford run, but climbed out to close the hood and stand in the shade of the cabin, shoulder to shoulder with him.

"Thank you," his dad said, barely loud enough for him to make out.

"I should be the one thanking you and Mom for coming out to help me."

"Then thank you for letting your mother help you. That's all she's wanted since you came home."

Emmett decided to ignore the hint of rebuke in his dad's voice. Their ultimate goal was the same—to make his mom happy. "I'll try to be better."

"I've been at a loss to know what to do. Or say. I'm not sure I've done the right things since you got home."

While it wasn't an outright "I'm sorry," it was the closest brush with an apology his dad had ever had in front of Emmett. "I want you to lay off Greer."

"You sure you and Greer are nothing but friends?" His dad turned, but Emmett kept his gaze on the truck.

"Just friends." The harshest two words in the English language left a bitter taste in his mouth. "I get that in some misguided way you wanted to protect me, but your call to the foundation nearly screwed up Greer's ability to get service hours as part of her plea."

His dad's mouth tightened, and Emmett could almost see his straight-arrow opinion notch for release. Instead, he sniffed, scuffed his boot against a dandelion to uproot it, and said, "I'll make things right with Amelia."

First an almost-apology and now an almost-admission that he'd overstepped. It was a banner day in the sensitization of the Lawson family male. "Thanks, Dad."

"The boys down at the VFW have been after me to drag you down for happy hour."

Emmett knew it wasn't a drink they wanted to share, but

glories of past battles. There was nothing glorious about the heat and filth and death he had experienced.

At his silence, his dad said, "Come on, now, I know you enjoy a good drink."

"I wasn't hungover the other morning." Emmett's defense felt weak considering the number of mornings he had woken up with a blaring headache. He headed to his truck.

His dad followed. "It might help to talk to men who understand. Men like me."

Emmett turned the truck off. "All I've ever heard you talk about is how much you miss the service and how good of a sniper and leader and soldier you were. But to me, all those damn medals lined up on the wall represent death and loss and sacrifices no one should be asked to make."

"If not us, then who, son? Who is going to protect our country?"

Emmett let his head fall back as the mother of all curse words reverberated through the trees. "We weren't protecting our country. We weren't even protecting the people over there. You can't tame chaos. Nothing we did made a difference. My men died for nothing."

"You can't think that way." His dad raised his hand to pat his arm, but Emmett batted it away.

"I can think however I damn well please. The army trained me, but they didn't brainwash me." Resentment and frustration rampaged through him, shredding his previous goodwill.

His dad stepped away and looked to the porch. His mom had come out of the cabin at some point. "Let's head home, Judy."

She took the steps haltingly, the brief respite from her worry shattered. Although his anger had grown as familiar and comfortable as a favorite T-shirt, the foundation for his emotions had been upgraded from sticks to bricks. Enough to overcome the instability.

His parents loaded into the diesel truck and backed up. He couldn't let things end like this. Emmett quick-stepped to knock on the passenger window as his dad shifted into drive. His mom rolled the window down.

What could he offer? A thank-you? An apology? What did they want from him? "You can leave the gate unlocked and open. Come on back anytime. I'd welcome the company."

His mom reached through the open window to hug his neck so tight it hurt, but he didn't complain. He'd chosen wisely. What his mom craved was access to him. Emmett still didn't know what the hell his dad wanted. Probably for Emmett to pull himself together and at least pretend to be normal.

His dad leaned over but avoided catching his eye. "You should come out and check on Eddie. He's missed you."

"Yeah, maybe I will." He'd avoided going to see his old horse Eddie Munster, named because of the exaggerated peak of the dark forelock on his gray coat.

His parents disappeared and left him with a newfound restlessness. He played with Bonnie until she got tired and settled in the sun for a nap. He rocked and stared at the tree line, waiting for something to happen. When nothing more exciting than seeing a deer dash past occurred, he grabbed his truck keys and told himself he needed to keep his battery in working condition.

He found himself driving past many of his old haunts. The high school. The pizza place on the corner that had hosted the football team after home games. The hardware store where he'd gotten his first job stocking shelves. It was all unchanged.

The red and white whirling barbershop pole had him pumping his brakes. Was Mr. Meecham still cutting hair? He fingered his hair where it spilled over his collar then pulled into a parking spot a sedan had vacated.

A bell dinged overhead upon his entrance, and Mr. Meecham walked out of a back room, smoothing a clean white apron tied high around his barrel-like waist. The black end of a comb and the silver loops of scissors stuck out of specially made pockets.

"Well, lookey here. Emmett Lawson."

"Hello, sir. I was hoping you might be able to work me in."

They exchanged handshakes. "Of course. Have a seat. I don't have any appointments until after lunch." Mr. Meecham hit a pedal of the chair with his foot and it lowered to squat on the floor.

Emmett slid onto the buttery, well-oiled red leather, feeling like he'd stepped back in time.

"You want it high and tight or something less military?"

Emmett met Mr. Meecham's gaze in the mirror. "Less military. I'm out now."

"I heard that from your daddy. How's the leg?"

"It's . . . gone." An unexpected, slightly uncomfortable laugh bubbled out.

"Hurt much?"

Emmett found he didn't mind the direct assault of questions. "It's not so bad now, except for the phantom pains."

Mr. Meecham merely nodded and ran a comb through Emmett's unruly mass of hair. Mr. Meecham had served too. Navy, if Emmett's recollections held true. Mr. Meecham had maintained the same military-style buzz as long as Emmett had known him. He also cut hair with military-style efficiency and precision. He was finished with Emmett in ten minutes.

Emmett looked at himself in the mirror. His shorter hair threw his cheekbones in sharp relief. As if on cue, his stomach growled. He required cobbler, stat. More important, he *wanted* some cobbler.

He followed Mr. Meecham to the checkout counter and pulled out his wallet.

Mr. Meecham waved him off. "On the house. For your service and sacrifice."

Anyone else might have put Emmett's dander up with such an offer, but Mr. Meecham eyes held a pain he'd never noticed as a kid. Or maybe Emmett had to have experienced loss in order to recognize it in others.

"Lost my best friend in an accident on board the ship. Lost another one to suicide after we got home," Mr. Meecham said.

"I'm sorry for your loss." Emmett wished it didn't sound like such an overused platitude.

Mr. Meecham gave a dismissive grunt. "You should come down to the VFW some evening. It's not all old men anymore." His smile was kindly and crinkled the corners of his eyes.

"Dad invited me, but—" Emmett shook his head.

"Your dad has some sad stories." Mr. Meecham's smile flipped into a grim frown.

"He does?" The surprise must have shown on his face.

Mr. Meecham narrowed his eyes. "Have the two of you not talked?"

It was a loaded question. They didn't talk so much as argue. Arguments punctuated by silence. Emmett ran a hand through his freshly trimmed hair, then lifted it in farewell. "Thanks for the cut, Mr. Meecham. Maybe I'll see you down at the VFW one night."

He had no intention of stepping foot in the place, of course. After a double helping of peach cobbler at the café, he was back in his truck. If he headed back to the cabin now, he would pour a row of shots out of sheer boredom, but for the first time in too long, obliterating his ability to remember didn't appeal.

Instead, he found himself pulling onto Lawson Lane, the long, paved driveway leading past the stables and to the main house. Parking in the shade of the horse barn, he slid out of the truck and took a breath. The loamy air settled a deep-seated comfort on him.

He stuck his hands into his pockets. The chuffs and stomps of the horses drew him inside the barn. He stopped in the entrance and blinked, letting his eyes adjust. It was cooler inside and he took a deep breath. Hay, leather, and manure swirled to tease his senses with memories.

Good ones of him waking at dawn with his grandfather to shovel manure or feed the horses, when his family would visit over the holidays. His grandfather had bought Eddie Munster for him when he was ten. He'd been a young horse, and Emmett had spent every waking, and some sleeping, hours in the barn with Eddie. Back then, being on the back of the horse was pure magic. Leaving the farm at the end of the holidays to return to the base his dad was stationed on had been gut-wrenching.

Then, when his grandfather had passed and they'd settled at the farm, Emmett had taken care of Eddie and the other horses before school. Sure, he'd hated life on cold winter days when he couldn't feel his fingers gripping the handle of the shovel, but even then, he'd felt like he was doing something important.

The barn hadn't changed. It was neat and orderly, but Emmett expected nothing less with Alfie Woodard, the long-time farm manager and horse trainer, in charge. As much as Emmett loved Alfie, he was glad the barn was absent its human keepers.

Grabbing an apple from a sack Alfie kept stashed in his desk,

Emmett padded softly down the row of stalls. As if Eddie could sense him, he stuck his head over the top of the stall door and neighed. The familiar dark forelock was curled to the side of his pricking ear, stark against his light gray face.

A wave of warmth enveloped Emmett as he offered the apple to Eddie. "Sorry I haven't been out to see you like I should."

Eddie neighed and crunched the treat. Emmett wrapped his arms around the horse's neck, embarrassing tears pricking his eyes. He hadn't cried before or after his amputation. He hadn't cried the first time he'd tried to walk on the prosthetic. He hadn't cried the day he received his discharge papers. But with his face buried in the mane of his best childhood friend, tears leaked out.

Emmett thought about his dead sergeant. A man who'd trusted Emmett's orders and followed them without question. Orders that had gotten him killed. Disentangling his fingers from Eddie's mane, Emmett stepped away, but the horse nudged against his shoulder and snuffled against his neck.

Emmett closed his eyes. What did he deserve? What was his penance? Was it his leg or did he need to sacrifice more? His thinking was warped. He knew it, yet couldn't stop himself from spiraling into the darkness.

He turned his back on Eddie and the barn and walked away. It was only when he was back in his truck jouncing from the grass to the blacktop that he glanced in his rearview mirror. His dad was silhouetted against the house, his hand raised as if he'd been trying to get Emmett's attention.

Emmett focused on the road ahead of him.

Chapter 13

Greer smoothed her white oxford shirt into her black pants, took a deep breath, and stepped into Becky's Bar and Grill. Late-afternoon sunlight cut through the windowless room, drawing the eyes of two men sitting at the bar before the door closed. Only the cheap clock above the door gave any indication as to the time of day.

Although smoking wasn't allowed by law anymore, the scent had permeated the walls and rugs and maybe even the wood. No amount of cleaner would ever eradicate the smoke. The undercurrents of cigarettes supported the lingering smell of stale beer. She'd spent the better part of ten years in bars not so different from Becky's and discovered both anxiety and a strange comfort in her surroundings.

She had texted Emmett her hours but kept herself from begging him to stop by—barely. A friendly smile and some moral support would help her face old friends who had expected more from her than to be slopping beer and Long Island Iced Teas in Madison.

Why would he subject himself to stares and gossip? Getting him into the store had been a huge victory. His voluntary presence at a central hangout in Madison would be a miracle.

Becky was behind the bar ticking off items on a tablet. The man across from her swiveled around and patted the stool next to him. Greer smiled tightly, lifted the hinged bar top, and joined Becky on the working side of the bar. A white apron hung on a peg, and she tied it on.

While her shift didn't officially start for another half hour, Greer wanted to get a feel for the space and make up for the bad impression she'd left as a customer. "What can I do to prep?"

Becky looked over her reading glasses and smiled. "Glad you're here, honey. I hate to throw you in the deep end, but Edgar's babysitter is sick. He has to wait until his wife gets off her shift. Think you can handle the bar on your own for the first half of the night?"

"Of course I can." Her heart kicked a hornets' nest of nerves in her stomach. She glanced down beneath the bar, her brain inventorying her basic needs. "We'll need more beer glasses."

"There's a crate in the back." Becky turned back to the wall of liquor bottles. "You'll need another bottle of Jack and more Bacardi for sure. I'll bring that out. Can you check the kegs?"

"Will do."

Greer started moving and didn't stop. People trickled in at a steady rate and stayed. The noise swelled, but all she could see was the wall of customers standing two deep in front of the bar top. Several old friends lit up when they saw her, but the conversations were thankfully brief due to the crowd and noise.

There was no sign of Emmett. Disappointment bothered her like lemon on a paper cut.

"Hey, Greer!" Ryan Humphries stood at the far end, a grin on his face. "Fancy seeing you here. How's the kitten?"

"She's good. Emmett is fattening her up." She wiped her hands on the bar towel she'd thrown over one shoulder and side-stepped closer. "What can I get you?"

"Have you got an IPA on tap?" he asked.

She nodded, poured a glass, and returned with a coaster. "Do you want to start a tab?"

He slid over a twenty and winked. "Keep the change."

"That's crazy, Ryan. At least let me save it for another drink."

He put his hand over hers and squeezed. It was slightly sweaty. "No, keep it. I can't have another in case there's an emergency."

She extricated her hand and tucked the money into the pocket of her apron. "You get called out a lot at night?"

"Springtime is the worst. Calving season. Time waits for no man."

She thumbed over her shoulder. "Beer waits for no man either. Better get these glasses filled before there's a riot."

Ryan stayed planted on his corner stool and nursed his beer. Even though she tried to ignore him, every time she glanced in his direction, he was watching her with a goofy, good-natured grin on his face. Hyperaware of his gaze, her scalp prickled with sweat, and she bobbled her next couple of glasses before finding her equilibrium.

Whenever she moved within earshot, Ryan would call her over and attempt to engage her in conversation. She was too frazzled and overwhelmed to do more than respond with a bare-minimum politeness.

It was a relief when a handsome black man in his mid-twenties scooted behind the bar with her. She had vague memories of him cutting her off the night she'd lost her damn mind with Carrie Underwood. As she filled two beer glasses from the tap, she gave him a grimace-smile. "Edgar. I don't know if you remember me—"

"Hard to forget the woman who got in a fight with the juke-box." His smile was wide, but faded as he scanned the crowd. "Man, it's hopping tonight."

Greer finished pouring the beers, wiped a hand over her apron, and offered it for a shake. "I hope you won't hold my behavior that night against me. I'm usually pretty chill. Greer Hadley."

"Edgar Canterbury. No worries. Let's get this mass fed and watered." He moved past her to take orders from the far half of the bar. When she glanced that way again, Ryan was gone. Had he received an emergency call or had her brusque attitude shut down his obvious interest?

She didn't have time to worry about it. Even with the two of them, they could barely keep up. "Is it always like this? I don't remember it being so crazy the night I was here drinking," Greer asked as they crossed paths at the register.

"Friday and Saturdays are always crowded but this might be a record. Becky hired a musician this weekend."

Greer hadn't realized there would be live music. A tiny voice inside her head railed that it could have been her if she wasn't such a coward. She ignored it and concentrated on her job, making two Jack and Cokes and a Tom Collins.

The strum of a guitar jerked her hand and she spilled simple syrup over the bar top. She bit her bottom lip and wiped up her mess. With sticky fingers she poured two more beers from the keg, the head of foam on the second signaling the keg was on its last beer legs.

The musician was tuning his guitar and Greer noted his A string was sharp. She waited for the guitarist to fix the offending string, but the next chord hit her as slightly off. Slight enough that no one else was likely to notice, but every strum grated along her internal ear.

A man rapped an empty beer glass in front of her. "Another one, please."

"It'll be a minute, sir." She turned to Edgar. "We need to tap another keg."

He gave her a salute and disappeared into the back as a folksy version of "Brown Eyed Girl" quieted the crowd. Most of the people at the bar turned to watch. The man's voice was older and rough around the edges but pleasant. Also familiar. She stood on her tiptoes and caught a glimpse over someone's shoulder.

Aaron Nash. A middle-aged, journeyman musician who had been a regular staple in Nashville's dive bars long before she'd hit the circuit. He was well past his prime. Record executives were after young, attractive singers they could wring dry before moving on, and Aaron had only ever been an average songwriter.

Although considering he was performing and she was waiting for a keg to get tapped, who was she to judge success? Edgar rolled the new keg over and deftly changed the hoses.

"He's pretty good, huh?" Edgar nodded to the beat.

The offending string twanged and made her shoulders hunch. "Yeah, he is."

Aaron launched into a set of classic rock and good-old-boy

country. Songs everyone knew the words to and soon a chorus of a few voices joined in a sing-along. The mood in the bar lifted even higher.

Aaron might not be the most innovative musician, but he could read a crowd. No doubt his tip jar would be overflowing by the end of the night. The wall of people at the bar thinned out. It was then she noticed him.

Emmett stood in the shadow of a vertical support beam close to the wall, wearing his cargo pants, a plaid button-down, and a frown. His arms were crossed, and he gave off a general fuck-off vibe that seemed to be working.

He wasn't looking at the crowd or at Aaron, but at her. She had a feeling he had been watching her for a while. Instead of being freaked out like she had been with Ryan, a seed of grate-fulness sprouted in her heart. He'd come.

She tapped Edgar on the shoulder. "Can you cover for a couple of minutes?"

"Go on. Things will be slow until the singer takes his first break."

Greer slipped out from behind the bar. A scrum of partiers moved into her path like a herd and she stopped to let them pass. A hand landed on her arm from behind. Annoyed, she shook free and glanced over her shoulder. It was Deputy Wayne Peeler, except he wasn't in his tan uniform but jeans and a T-shirt.

"Surprised to see you working at the scene of the crime." His toothy, predator-like smile set her on edge.

"All recovered?" She darted a glance toward his crotch be-fore shuffling a step away. Her path to Emmett was still blocked by the milling group.

"Good as new. Want to give it a look-see out back?"

"Uh. No." The crowd in front of her thinned, and she took another step away. "See ya."

"Got yourself a pity project, huh?"

She stuttered to a stop and half turned. "Excuse me?"

"Him." Wayne chucked his chin toward where Emmett had straightened, his hands balled at his sides.

Greer stepped in front of Wayne, her back to Emmett in case he could read lips. "He's not a pity project."

"What is he, then?"

"He's none of your business."

Wayne gave a snort of disbelief. Rumors of her grocery store sojourn with Emmett had trotted through Madison like the Pony Express. Even her mother had asked her deliberately vague yet leading questions about Emmett.

She performed an about-face and weaved her way around people and tables to Emmett. Nothing about his slightly aggressive stance changed. But something *was* different. He'd gotten a haircut. It made him look more mature, yet reminded her of the Emmett from high school at the same time. The thick waves were only partially tamed and fell over his forehead. Her fingers itched to push through his hair and explore, like she'd imagined doing so many times stuck behind him in class. She trapped her hands in her back pockets.

"I wasn't sure whether you'd actually show." She had to raise her voice to be heard but no one seemed to be paying them any attention.

"What'd Wayne want?"

"Wanted to give me a hard time about the other night." She couldn't verbalize the sexually tinged threat that emanated off Wayne. It was something she'd dealt with enough as a single woman working late nights in Nashville but hadn't expected to

face in Madison, her safety net. But she'd impugned his mascu-
linity the night of her arrest, and he was the type of man who
had to reassert it somehow.

With Emmett's gaze still intensely focused over her shoulder,
he leaned closer so she could hear him over the music and crowd
noise and said in a lowered voice, "I never did like the Weasel."

"Yeah, me neither, but now that he's got his panties in a wad,
it's best to leave him alone to untangle them."

Although Emmett didn't smile, he transferred his gaze to
her and the ready-to-pounce tautness of his body eased. "You're
surprised to see me?"

"Well . . . yeah. How many times have you left the cabin
since you hunkered down there?"

"Three times, if you count right now."

"I'm honored." Her sarcasm was tempered with honest-to-
goodness honor. She couldn't fathom how difficult it must have
been for him to step out of his fortress of solitude and into the
chaos of Becky's. It was like facing a phobia of spiders by wallowing in a vat of them.

"Don't get used to it. After this I'm going to need a month of
alone time to recover." While amusement lightened the words,
she sensed the real desire in him to retreat as soon as possible.
"Have you been catching up with old friends?"

"A few, but mostly everyone just wants their drink. Ryan was
here for a while, though." She bit the inside of her mouth. "I
know it sounds crazy, but I think he was working up the courage to ask me out."

"Doesn't sound crazy at all." His statement made her heart
swell and pump a few beats faster until he added, "In school, he
went after anything with legs, boobs, and a decent face. The ink

is barely dry on his divorce, though. He's probably looking to rebound if you're into that."

It took a hot second to unpack his implications. Legs, boobs, and a decent face—was that how Emmett saw her? Real empowering. What niggled at her even more was the fact he didn't seem at all bothered Ryan might ask her out.

Which was fine. They were just friends, after all, and Emmett was giving her friendly, useful advice. Advice that made her want to punch him in the face. "Thanks, I'll keep that in mind when I accept his invitation."

"Why in the world would you say yes?"

"Maybe I'm looking for a rebound. You said yourself he's a nice guy. Do you know any other reason I shouldn't go out with him?" She tensed.

His jaw tightened and his blue eyes narrowed. "No reason at all. Go for it. Enjoy your rebound with Ryan. How's the bartending going?"

Enjoy her rebound? What an asinine thing to say. Hurtful too, considering . . . No, she couldn't consider it. Instead, she forced a smile but it was brittle from the blistering tension between them. "Crazy busy but oddly enjoyable. It feels good to put in an honest day's—or night's—work. Edgar hasn't held my jukebox-fighting antics against me."

Emmett raised his hand, and she waited for his move, but he only tucked a piece of escaped hair behind her ear with a gentleness that belied the almost ferocious look on his face. The shiver his touch invoked was nothing like the distaste from Ryan's brief but sweaty hand-holding. Her breath caught, waiting for his next move, but there was none. He resumed his fuck-off stance.

"When did Becky start bringing in live entertainment?" He leaned into her even though they were already close enough to hear each other. His scent muffled the stale smoke and beer of the bar, and reminded her of the cabin and night air.

She swallowed past a sudden lump and fiddled with the strings of her apron. "Since tonight. Aaron's been gigging for a long time, though."

"You know him?"

"The Nashville music scene is smaller than you might think. If you're out there playing shows, you eventually meet all the other wretched souls trying to break through."

"You've really given up?"

Her feelings about leaving Nashville and abandoning her dream were complicated. "I wonder sometimes if I'd worked a little bit harder, hustled for one more show, written one more song, if it would have made a difference."

"It's not too late."

"That dream is dead." She never wanted to relive the humiliation of the Bluebird. "I need to figure out what's next."

"You should ask Becky about playing one night." Emmett's lecturing, know-it-all tone on top of his blessing for her to date another man rubbed salt on the still-oozing wound.

The thought of stepping in front of a bar full of people had her breaking out in a panicked sweat. She wiped her forehead with the bar towel stuck in her back pocket. "You are so full of it. Another lecture about giving up and how I should get back in the game. What about you?"

"What about me?"

"You're going to turn into a hermit who collects cats. People will whisper about your strange ways and you'll become a cautionary tale for children. Poor, crazy, old Emmett Lawson. Been waiting to die for fifty years. And when you do, your army of feral cats will eat your face off."

"At least I didn't half-ass the last decade of my life. I gave everything for what I believed in. Even my fucking leg." He hunched even closer until they were face-to-face and whisper-yelling.

"That's not fair. I put my heart and soul into my music until it sucked me dry. You think my dream was to be thirty and bartending for a living?"

"You think I want to be a cripple?" A bitterness to match her own laced his voice. "You think I want to relive all those men's deaths every time I close my eyes? Grow the fuck up, Greer."

He turned and stalked out. She was torn between anger and shame. Yes, her troubles paled in comparison to his, yet he'd made it sound like she was a quitter. She wasn't. The trouble was her panic onstage had finally overtaken any pleasure she'd once gotten from performing.

The thought of losing their friendship punched a hole in her gut. He would probably be perfectly happy at the cabin with an army of cats, but she couldn't imagine not being able to spar with him. She'd been mean because he'd hurt her feelings like she was a teenager. Maybe she *did* need to grow up. An adult apology was in order. Could she catch him in the parking lot?

She took a step toward the door when Aaron's smoky voice registered. "I'm going to take a quick break, but I'll be back."

A wave of people crashed over toward the bar. She couldn't leave Edgar on his own. It would be a sprint to get everyone served before Aaron took up his guitar for his second set. Aaron sidled up to the edge of the bar.

She traded two longnecks for cash and cocked her head. "What can I get you, Aaron?"

A shot of surprise crossed his face. "Greer Hadley? Damn, girl, what are you doing in this backwater slogging beers?"

"I grew up in this backwater."

"Gimme a Coors Light. Trying to keep my girlish figure." His laugh was like sandpaper.

She uncapped a bottle and plopped it down. "Your A string is a smidgeon sharp. It's driving me bonkers."

"You kids with your perfect pitch . . ." He shook his head and took a drag off the bottle. "These folks are drunk enough not to care."

"True." When Aaron tried to pull out money, Greer waved him off. "On the house. You want another to get you through the set?"

She didn't wait for his affirmation but handed over another bottle of beer. He saluted her with it, smiling but with a quizzical look on his face. "Are you taking a break from Nashville for the summer or did you leave for good?"

"For good, I think."

He gave a slow nod. "I think about leaving sometimes—I have a standing offer at my brother-in-law's insurance agency—but performing is like a drug. I get a high, even in a place like this."

He returned to his stool, and everyone followed like he was the Pied Piper. It was an amazing feeling to be able to command a crowd like that. The rush of performing was a drug to her too, but her addiction had turned dangerous to her psyche.

Customers flitted to the bar while Aaron played his second, and last, set. A final rush of partiers got drinks when last call was announced. Wayne still hung around the periphery but didn't approach her again.

As the last song of the night, Aaron played "The Fireman,"

classic George Strait. The crowd's off-key and off-tempo singing almost drowned out his voice. Becky joined Greer and Edgar behind the bar to change out the register drawer.

"Looks like my experiment paid off," Becky said. "Live music plus drinks has loosened pockets."

Edgar was counting out the bills from the tip jar. "You got that right. This is the most tip money I've ever seen."

"You two split that up however you want." Becky propped the drawer on her hip. "You did good tonight, Greer. You want to work tomorrow night too?" At Greer's nod, Becky made a note in the ledger lying on top of the drawer. "Let me know how many hours you want each week, and I'll work you into the schedule."

"Thanks for taking a chance on me."

Becky flashed a smile before disappearing. Greer turned back to Edgar, who had divided the tips into two unequal piles. He pushed the larger stack to her.

"No. We should split it down the middle." She pushed the bills back.

"But I was late. You worked more hours. It's fair." He nodded.

"You did all the heavy lifting of a barback on top of bartending." She took the stacks and deftly recounted, splitting them equally and shoving half at Edgar. "I insist."

He shook his head but smiled. "Thanks. I appreciate it. Things have been tight lately with the baby. Who knew something so small could be so expensive?"

Aaron walked over with his guitar case. "I'm out of here. Good to see you again, Greer."

They exchanged a handshake. His fingers rasped over the back of her hand, his calluses the work of years. She watched him walk out the door to the next gig and felt a shot of both relief and jealousy.

By the time Becky emerged from the back, Greer and Edgar had cleaned and organized the bar area for the next day. "You kids are done. I've got you both down for tomorrow night too. Another musician is coming so expect a busy but lucrative night."

Greer waved good-bye and pushed out the front door into the sultry night. She looked to the sky and felt her world expand from the windowless bar to the stars. A deep breath cleared her lungs with earthy scents from a nearby farm.

She didn't know what she wanted, but it wasn't to toil away for someone else slogging drinks the rest of her days. She felt . . . empty. At one time, music would have filled the void. Now she foundered for purpose and clarity.

Clumps of people had moved the party to the parking lot, laughing and talking. While everyone seemed friendly enough, she knew better than to take chances. She dug through her purse for her travel-size can of pepper spray.

"I feel like it's my duty to protect the male citizens of Madison and see you to your car." Wayne materialized from the shadows of the wall. She yelped and clutched her purse closer.

She waved the can of pepper spray in his face. "You were about two seconds from being miserable. You should never sneak up on a woman in a dark parking lot. What if I was packing heat?"

He gave a dismissive huff. "This is Madison, not Nashville."

Madison had a dark underbelly, just like any town, but instead of arguing the point, Greer walked around the side of the building toward the back of the bar. She hadn't considered how isolated and dark her parking space would be at midnight. Passing by a hollering group of questionably legal boys, she was even slightly grateful Wayne had hung around.

She unlocked her car using the fob, and Wayne stepped

ahead, but instead of opening her door for her he blocked her path. All she wanted was to climb behind the wheel and be alone. "What are you doing?" she asked.

"You owe me, sweetheart."

"Yeah, I don't think so." She forced her voice to remain cool even as her insides jostled. The group of young men had moved on, the sound of engines firing and gravel crunching leaving her and Wayne too alone for her comfort.

"You humiliated me." He banged a hand on the roof of her car.

She gripped the pepper spray tighter, her finger on the trigger, and took a step back. "What do you want, Wayne?"

"I want you to go out with me. I'll even take you to the country club."

It was the last thing she expected to come out of his mouth. Her answer was cold and short. "No."

His lips thinned and red burnished his cheeks. "Is it because Beau and I are friends?"

"No. It's because you don't even like me."

His gaze trekked down her body and back up, leaving her craving a bath. It was all about dominance and pride with Wayne. "Give me one good reason why you won't go out with me."

He shifted and blotted out the interior car lights. His face was a dark blob, and as if she were answering a Rorschach test, she said the first thing that popped into her head: "Emmett."

Wayne reared back and muttered, "Just like fucking high school. I should have known."

"What are you talking about?" She still had hold of the pepper spray and wouldn't hesitate to use it.

"He could have any girl he wanted back then. Guess not much has changed. Even down one leg." He took a step toward her. She tensed, but he sidestepped around her.

"He's waiting for me. I'll see you later." She winced at her knee-jerk politeness. She had zero desire to see him ever again.

She had the car on the road in less than five seconds. Distracted, she tapped her thumbs on the steering wheel. It wasn't until she was at the stop sign where one direction would take her home and one would take her to Emmett's cabin that she noticed the headlights behind her.

Was it Wayne? Was he checking her story? She squinted in the rearview mirror. A black truck. A good percentage of Madison residents drove a black truck. It could be anyone. She took a left, down the road less traveled. The truck turned to follow.

She mumbled a string of curse words and held on to the steering wheel even tighter. If Emmett's gate was locked, she was screwed. The truck trailed far enough behind to keep her guessing. She turned down the narrow blacktop that led to Emmett's gated grassy lane.

The truck seemed to hesitate. Or had her perception of time slowed? The truck continued down the main road and Greer collapsed back in her seat. Her headlights cut through the wide open gate, and a swarm of bugs greeted her as she drove beneath the pine trees.

She continued on, craving the safety and danger lurking at the end of the rutted path. No lights were visible. What in God's green tarnation was her endgame—she hit the brakes—wake him up, apologize, and drive off? It was a plan, if not necessarily a good one.

She coasted closer. A rational person would call or text him tomorrow to apologize. She stopped again. Her fear of Wayne was a bad aftertaste that needed a chaser. If anyone could understand, it would be Emmett, right?

She crept forward again. Unless he was sound asleep. She

was an idiot to be here this late. As she swung her car into a U-turn, her headlights caught on Emmett, standing at the top of the porch steps, his shoulder propped against the wood pillar, his hands stuffed into his pockets. Had he watched her dithering the entire time?

She turned her car off, blind in the sudden darkness. Nothing moved and for a moment, she wondered if she'd imagined Emmett standing there because he'd set up camp in her head.

She slipped out of the car and stumbled toward him. The moon was a mere sliver in the sky and offered no physical or psychological illumination. Even the bugs seemed to wait for her move. Finally, the call of a whip-poor-will broke the silence.

"I'm sorry for bothering you so late." When he didn't acknowledge her, she squinted. "Are you there, Emmett?"

"I'm here." His voice rumbled like thunder in the clear night. "Why'd you come?"

"A couple of reasons." She shivered even though the night air was warm, and plowed ahead. "Just so you know, I don't want an army of feral cats to eat your face."

"How comforting." This time the rumble in his voice edged closer to laughter than anger.

"Do you find this amusing?"

"No." A chuckle burst out of him. "Actually, a little. It looked like you were doing your best to talk yourself into turning around."

"I was worried I might wake you or, based on your track record, you might shoot me."

"What's the other reason?"

"Huh?"

"You said you came for a couple of reasons? The feral cats being one. What else?"

"It's dumb."

"Try me."

"Wayne walked me to my car tonight."

The porch creaked as his shadow shifted. "I take it he wasn't doing it out of the goodness of his heart."

She gave a little laugh, but it petered into nothing. "He wanted me to go out with him as an ego salve for that other night, I think."

"Did he threaten you?"

"No, but . . ." Feeling more and more like she'd overreacted, she took a step backward toward her car. "I should go."

"Wait." His voice brooked no argument, and she froze. "Come on in before the mosquitos get ahold of you. There's something I need to say too."

Her eyes had adjusted enough to see the porch steps. He opened his front door and she followed him inside. The darkness shaded deeper and left her blind. He didn't turn a light on.

Even though it was darker and more isolated than the back parking lot of the bar with Wayne, she dropped her purse at her feet, pepper spray included. No fear rose up to clutch her around the neck in a stranglehold.

"I'm sorry if I came off as a condescending ass in the bar. I have no right to tell you what to do when my life is as unsettled as yours," he said.

He sounded sincere enough even though his face was unreadable in the dark. The long, low shadow of the couch was behind him. She closed the distance between them, but everything remained unclear—his face, her intent, his feelings.

"You don't really know why I left Nashville."

"No, I don't," he said softly. "Maybe someday you'll trust me enough to tell me the story."

"Maybe I will." She owed him more. "You'll figure things out, Emmett."

"Maybe I will." The smile in his voice sounded like the one that crinkled up his blue eyes and made them spark with mischief.

She rubbed her shaky hands down her jeans. He was a mess, and so was she. Their lives were caught in stasis between past and future. Eventually momentum would carry them away from each other.

But this pocket of time seemed to exist just for the two of them. Time to heal wounds both physical and emotional. The tether binding them grew shorter and shorter, and she shuffled toward him, her breath coming as if she were running.

"Greer?" The longing he imbued in her name reeled her the rest of the way in.

In the dark she misjudged the distance and hit his chest with enough force to send him back a step, his butt landing on the back of the couch. She didn't let the embarrassment washing through her take hold. The darkness lent her bravery.

His position put them face-to-face. She wrapped her arms around his neck and notched herself between his knees. His shoulders moved and she tensed. Would he push her away? Ask her what in the heck she was doing?

His hands came around her waist and slipped to her hips, but he didn't pull her forward. His hesitation made her hesitate in turn. Was he not attracted to her?

Or . . . was his confidence as shattered as hers? Had he let any woman close enough to touch him since his injury? Did he think losing part of his leg somehow made him less attractive? Less of a man?

She tightened her hold and leaned into him, brushing her

nose along his until her lips met his in a soft, brief kiss. "Is this okay?" she whispered with their lips still in contact.

"It's certainly a surprise." He nipped her bottom lip playfully.

"Good or bad?"

"Very good. Dare I even say, great?" He clutched her hips tighter and pulled her flush against him.

Her exhale was equal parts relief and pleasure. He wanted her. She speared her hand through his hair and twisted the strands in her fingers, her sigh reminiscent of the high school girl she'd been. "Your hair looks good."

"Spur-of-the-moment decision."

"I didn't come here to kiss you. I mostly came to apologize." He pulled away and she followed, craving more of his . . . everything. "Is this an extension of your apology?"

She sensed his mood shift and refused to allow him to retreat, fisting his hair and holding him in place. "You're worried this is a pity kiss."

"Isn't it a little?"

She'd hung out with enough musicians to recognize an ego hound from fifty feet, but Emmett wasn't the type to need his ego stroked. He needed to be picked up from the despair he'd wallowed in the last few months.

"You're hot as sin, Captain Lawson. I've been thinking about this for a while, only I wasn't sure you were into me."

He walked his hand up her spine, slow and sensuous, to tangle his fingers in her hair and cup her nape. He pulled her mouth to his, then deepened the kiss, his tongue making contact with hers for a split second before retreating. "Not into you? How could I not be into a woman whose favorite pastime is to put me in my place?"

"Your dad's right; I'm kind of a mess."

"Ditto." The word was muffled against her mouth. "Also, can we not talk about my dad?"

Untold minutes passed in an exploration of lips and bodies that kindled the ember of her attraction into a four-alarm fire. His hands were magic. Vibrations of pleasure sang through her like a perfectly composed song.

"Oh my God, I lied to my mama." She nuzzled his neck and breathed in his scent. Honeysuckle and warm grass. God, she probably stank like whiskey and smoke. He didn't seem to mind.

"About what?" he asked as he laid a path of kisses from her temple to her mouth.

"I told her you were like an annoying brother." She slipped her hand under his shirt to his warm, solid back. "But you're so not. Well, at least not the brother part."

"I would hope not. We might be in Tennessee, but that shit is still illegal."

She laughed and for the first time in a long time, she felt light. Light-headed and lighthearted. Could they eradicate the darkness they battled together?

With a tentativeness at odds with his usual brashness, he skated a hand up to tease the side of her breast, his thumb caressing the underside.

She popped to her toes and let her weight fall fully into him. He wobbled on the edge of the couch, then they were falling. A metallic thud rang out followed by a crash. Something had shattered.

Only their rapid breathing filled the pause. She was on top of him but cattywampus on the couch, one leg over the back, the other dug into the cushion at his hip.

"You okay?" he asked.

"Yep. How about you?"

He scooted them into a prone position, side by side and facing each other with her back against the cushions. Dangerous and tempting. She notched her leg between his and initiated another kiss. They made out like teenagers, feeling each other up from the outside of their clothes, for what felt like hours.

Turned on beyond anything she'd experienced, she was more than ready to hit a grand slam, yet he didn't seem inclined to move beyond first base even when she ground her hips against him. His control waxed as hers waned.

She slid her hand over his hip and down his leg until her fingertips hit the carbon fiber of his prosthetic. He froze and pulled her hand away, holding it too tightly. Unsure, she froze as well, and waited for his reaction.

He pushed her away and sat up, his elbows on his knees and his head resting in his hands. She scrambled up and pressed her hands together on her lap. Now that her body was free from his spell, she was silent as her head whirred to life. What now? Was their friendship irrevocably changed?

"You'd better go." The words shot arrows into her heart.

"Okay." She took a deep shuddery breath but refused to beg or pressure him. It was like they'd shone mirrors on each other, neither of them willing to share their true selves. She rose and shuffled toward the door, shards of whatever they'd broken crunching under her shoes.

With hope taking a last gasp, she hesitated with her hand on the knob, but he didn't stop her. He remained still and silent in the same hunched, defensive posture on the couch. Unable to locate the words to traverse the distance between them, she walked out the door.

The soft meow of Bonnie drew tears. She crouched on the

porch stairs and gave the kitten the affection her master was unable to accept. She left, her car creeping through the grass, sure Emmett would appear in her rearview mirror like in one of her favorite rom-coms to stop her. He didn't, and she pulled onto the blacktop, lonelier than she'd felt in forever.

Chapter 14

Tuesday afternoon, Greer stifled a yawn as she stepped into the Music Tree Foundation toting a guitar case and beginner guitar lesson books. Saturday had been another late night spent working behind the bar at Becky's.

Guilt sent her to church on Sunday morning after a few hours of sleep, and she'd desperately needed toothpicks to hold her eyes open during the sermon. Sandwiched between her parents on the pew, she'd felt about nine years old. Except her mind had kept drifting to Emmett and the very adult encounter they'd shared Friday night.

He hadn't called her, but then again, she hadn't reached out to him either. As the rejected party, she had her pride to shore up like a house of cards. Still, she wondered. And worried about him despite telling herself he wanted neither from her.

Emmett's mother and father hadn't coerced him into rejoining their flock of sinners, and she could only imagine his caustic commentary if they had.

The rest of Sunday was spent cooking with her mom. By Monday, the late nights of her weekend and early Sunday had caught up with her, and she'd slunk out of bed at ten in the morning.

Could she even hold down an eight-to-five job?

With her future as foggy as ever, she focused on her session with Ally. Ally needed her; Emmett did not. He had to figure out how to pry his head out of his own butt. She couldn't do it for him.

Ally had all kinds of potential. Potential Greer didn't want to see frittered away. If she nagged Ally, she would come off sounding like a teacher or parent and drive Ally's frittering level to eleven. Greer had to play it cool.

Ally showed up fifteen minutes late and out of breath. "Sorry. Had some stuff to take care of."

When a slingshot *What kind of stuff?* nearly shot out of her mouth, Greer put on a smile she didn't feel and kept her voice casual. "No worries. I brought you something."

Ally narrowed her eyes. "What?"

Why did she fall back into a position of suspicion with any offer of help? Greer pushed the guitar with her foot, under the table and still in its case, until it met resistance in the form of Ally's combat boots.

Ally ducked her head and gasped. A look like a kid coming down the stairs Christmas morning passed over her face before she shut it down with a mask of teenage nonchalance. "That's for me to use today?"

"Yes, but also for you to take home with you and practice on. It was my very first guitar. I'm pretty sure the spirit of my teenage angst is lurking somewhere in the body. I have the feeling you two would really hit it off." Greer pulled the canvas bag of instruction books onto the table between them. The worn book she pulled out had pages falling out. It was filled with classic rock songs. "You'll have to experiment with what learning style suits you best, but this worked for me."

Ally flipped one open to "Imagine" by The Beatles. Greer had played it so often, her fingers changed chords on an invisible fret in her hand. When Ally only smoothed her hand over the page, Greer added, "If this music is too old-fashioned, some of these other books have more modern music."

"No," Ally said sharply before her tone softened and her gaze lifted to meet Greer's. "This works. I'll take good care of your guitar, I promise."

Greer believed her. Ally's surface sass had peeled away and revealed a core of honor. Whatever trouble Ally had landed herself in wasn't because she was a bad kid but because she'd been desperate. Was *still* desperate if Greer's instincts weren't off-kilter.

"Before I show you some chords, let's take a look at the lyrics you've been working on." Greer reached out and made a grabby hand.

Ally gave a groan but rustled around in her backpack. "They still suck."

"They are allowed to suck. That's what we'll fix during many rounds of edits."

The notebook paper Ally passed over was rife with eraser marks and crumpled as if she'd gotten frustrated and given up at least once.

"'Dark Side of the Mountain,'" Greer read aloud, accompanied by another groan from Ally. "Great title."

Greer put the girl out of her misery and read the rest silently. The lyrics were timeless and heartfelt and could have been set to an alternative rock cadence or bluegrass. It was like she'd bled on the page. That's what good songwriting was all about, tapping straight into the emotional vein, harrowing yet cathartic.

"This is good. Real good." Greer peered over the paper at Ally, who squirmed and picked at her fingernails. Greer put her hand over Ally's to stop the carnage. "Sharing your work is hard as hell, and I can't honestly say it gets easier, but I promise it won't go beyond the two of us in this room—unless you want it to—so be wild and unafraid."

"What do you mean, unless I want it to?"

"I started writing songs when I was about your age and eventually performed them."

"I'm not good enough."

"Yes, you are, Ally. Your first try is better than some musicians who have been around for decades. Songwriting is a talent separate from playing or singing. It can be developed, but a person has to have the kernel of genius to nurture."

"And you think I have a kernel or whatever?"

"You've got something special." Greer put the paper down, tilted her head, and studied Ally. "What do you think? Did you enjoy the process?"

Ally crossed her arms over her chest and didn't meet her eyes. "It was harder than I thought it'd be. If I had talent, wouldn't it come easy?"

"Talent is like getting a leg up, but it won't get you over the wall. Success only comes if you work and practice day after day, year after year."

Ally's gaze dropped to hers with the force of a hammer. "Then why did you give up?"

The little brat had tangled Greer in her own motivational web. Now it was Greer's turn to study the white-painted cement walls. "The pressure and disappointment got to me. One night I had a panic attack onstage and can't bear the thought of getting back up there."

"You're scared." Incredulity sailed Ally's voice high.

"I'm not scared." The knee-jerk denial came out with blistering intensity.

"Prove it." Ally reached into the case and held the guitar out, her eyebrows raised.

Greer scooted back in her chair as if the guitar were weaponized. Ally *bocked* like a chicken. Was she going to wuss out in front of a teenager? As if her arm were shot through with cement, she took the guitar, the strings biting into her palm.

"Hand me a pick, you little punk."

Ally offered one between her index and middle fingers along with a smirk.

Greer settled the guitar across her lap. The curves of its body fell into place like a puzzle piece finding its mate. She ran her hand up the neck, the strings taut and smooth and familiar. It had been her first love, her first guitar. A slight, discordant twang reverberated.

Her heart galloped like a fear-crazed racehorse. A clammy sweat broke over her neck and back, and her hands shook. Panic. The same reaction she'd experienced onstage at the Bluebird.

"Hey, are you okay?" Ally's voice came from a long tunnel.

Greer met the girl's huge eyes. She looked freaked out. Greer's own words circled her mind. It was just the two of them and nothing she did would go beyond the four walls. If Ally could be vulnerable in front of Greer, could she not attempt the same?

With a shaking finger, she plucked the low E string. Without having to think, her ear registered the tone as flat. She adjusted

the tuning knob and plucked it again. The sweet tone counter-
acted her bitter panic. She repeated the task for all five strings.

Muscle memory was a beautiful thing. Her fingers created
a G chord, and she strummed. Then C and back to G. She repeated the three chords, this time humming the familiar melody of "Amazing Grace." On the third line, she closed her eyes
and sang, *"I once was lost, but now I'm found."*

She sang through the chorus once and|let the last note ring
out. Silence overtook the room, and Greer opened her eyes. Ally's
eyes were wide and unblinking and her mouth was parted. She
looked hypnotized.

A new melody weaved into Greer's head, as if playing "Amazing Grace" had thrown open a locked door. It happened that way
sometimes. As if some higher authority gifted her music. Why it
was happening now after a dry spell of months, she wasn't sure.

Greer strummed the chords straight. The addition of a minor chord gave the tune a haunting feel. She glanced down at
Ally's lyrics and started a rhythm, giving the old-timey melody a modern feel. Then she added Ally's lyrics, modifying her
rhythm to fit the syllables.

It was rough and needed massaging, but it was a song.

She strummed the last chord, then grabbed a blank sheet of
music and jotted down the chords and rhythms before she lost
them.

"How'd you do that?" Ally scanned over her paper of song
lyrics as if she'd missed something.

Greer laughed, feeling as if the darkness inside of her had
finally lightened to gray with the promise of a new day. "I don't
really know. It just came to me. How'd you like it?"

"For a second, I didn't even realize you were singing my
words. It was great."

"Because your lyrics are great."

Ally picked at her fingernails and the compliment squatted between them, unaccepted. At Ally's age, Greer had been full of optimism and bravado. Life had been a cushioned ride with seat belts. It wasn't until later that life had removed the gloves and knocked her around. Ally had already experienced enough hard knocks for a lifetime.

Richard would be arriving any minute to take their room. Greer stacked Ally's music on the books. "How's school? Any more trouble?"

Ally gave a less-than-enthusiastic one-shouldered shrug. "It's fine."

"Yeah, sounds like everything is fabulous." Greer didn't bother to mask her sarcasm and was rewarded when Ally quit staring at the table.

"It's nothing you can help with so let it go."

"I can't fix the fact your dad is gone, but I can listen if you want to talk instead of keeping everything bottled up inside."

Ally made a scoffing sound and performed an epic eye roll. "You sound like a therapist."

"Are you seeing a therapist?"

"I have better things to do."

"Like shoplifting and getting put in this program?" As soon as the words popped out, Greer bit her lip. She'd pushed too hard. "Ally, I'm sorry. That was harsh."

Ally shoved papers and books into her backpack and stalked out of the room.

Had Greer burned all the progress they'd made to the ground? She stood and gathered her things. Ally had taken her stack of lyrics and the guitar manuals, but in her snit, she'd left Greer's old guitar. Sensing an opening, Greer packed the guitar in its case and took off at a run, but Ally had performed her typical vanishing act.

Returning to Amelia's office, she knocked. "I need a favor."

Amelia swiveled in her chair to face Greer. "What?"

"I want to drop my old guitar off at Ally's place as a surprise. Could you jot down her address?" Greer attempted to inject innocence into her smile, but her lips trembled from the weight of fakeness.

Amelia narrowed her eyes. "It's not my practice to give out personal information."

"I realize that, but she can't carry her backpack plus a case all the way to her house. This will be easier."

Amelia rifled through folders and wrote something on a sticky note. "Here."

"Thanks." Greer took the note and tried to place the street name in her mental map of Nashville, but couldn't.

"Do you want me to sign your sheet while you're here?"

"What? Oh, sure." Greer fished it out of her satchel. She'd forgotten all about it.

"Three more weeks and you'll have your hours." Amelia handed it back.

"What? No, that can't be right." She ran her finger over the hours and did a mental tally. Amelia was right.

"I'd love to have you stay on as an actual volunteer. Your forthrightness seems to work with certain personalities."

"You don't have to sound so shocked about it." Greer shot her stepcousin a smile before backing out of her office, impatient to find Ally. "I'll think about it."

In her car, she entered the address in her phone. A digital tack pinpointed an area of Nashville that wrestled with crime but was on the cusp of gentrification.

Winding her way through the streets, she kept her eyes peeled for Ally but didn't spot her. She most likely took the city bus. Greer's GPS led her to one of four duplexes squeezed together on a corner. Sparse grass poked through dirt and gravel to form a front yard. A rusting kid's bike leaned against the brick front of one porch while a container of flowers added life and color to the duplex next door to Ally's, whose house number was peeled halfway off.

Greer climbed out and pulled the guitar case with her, nerves making the handle slip in her palm. She knocked and waited, noting the tear in the screen and the long scratch in the paint of the door.

She knocked again. This time the door opened. The woman standing in the crack bore enough resemblance to Ally to tag her as her mother, but she was fairer-skinned with straight dirty-blond hair in need of a wash hanging to her shoulders.

"What do you want?" The lack of welcome in her manner set Greer back a step.

"My name is Greer Hadley. I'm working with Ally at the Music Tree Foundation. Has she mentioned me?"

"No." Ally's mother sent her gaze down Greer's body and back up as if checking for threats. A sigh framed her next words. "What's she done now?"

"Nothing." Greer tempered her shock at the cynical question with a smile and added, "Nothing bad, I mean. She's actually demonstrated enormous talent."

"What?"

"That's why I'm here." She held up the guitar case. "I wanted to drop a guitar off for her to practice on. If you don't mind, that is."

The woman's shoulders relaxed. "She's doing well?"

"Very well." Greer nodded and waited.

"All right then, you'd better come on in." She swung the door open wider, and Greer stepped into a small entry that opened straight into a cozy den. "I'm Karen, by the way."

It was no different than the apartments Greer had rented her years in Nashville. Nondescript with no personality. At first, Greer had done her best to make them a home, but she'd learned the futility of that after her third move into progressively smaller places. Eventually, they became only a place to sleep.

Karen had tried to liven up the beige walls and carpet. A color-blocked rug in reds and blues gave life to the worn, stained carpet and a houseplant that had seen better days sagged next to a small flat-screen TV on top of a wooden bureau that was of good quality but had suffered scars.

A picture hanging slightly askew on the wall drew Greer closer. Karen joined her and straightened it. A wedding photo featuring a handsome dark-skinned Latino man in an army dress uniform and a younger, less worn version of the woman at Greer's shoulder radiating happiness and hope.

Karen had been a kid when she married. She probably wasn't more than half a dozen years older than Greer, yet those years represented a gulf of experience and grief Greer didn't know how to bridge.

"My husband was killed in action," Karen said softly.

"Ally told me."

"Did she?" Karen's voice reflected her unsettled expression, as if speaking of his death aloud gave pieces of their memories away. She reached out and touched his face. Numerous smudge marks on the glass indicated the picture was a talisman of sorts.

"All I can offer are my sympathies, which never seem like enough. I guess that's why people feel the need to bring food to the bereaved."

Karen's laugh was full of the same resentment and irony as Ally projected. Was it inherited or a learned behavior? "We had to throw out garbage bags of food afterward. The other wives in his company—the ones whose husbands survived—meant well, but I could smell the relief on them like cheap perfume. Not that I blame them. I'd been in their shoes—cooking casseroles and counting my blessings. I pray to God none of them end up in mine."

"Things have been hard?" Even though Greer posed it as a question, the answer was in the way Karen's shoulders rolled forward and the lack of care she took with herself.

"Javier and I were young when we married. He had already joined up, and I stayed at home. We wanted more kids but I guess it's a blessing we only had Ally."

Greer stepped farther into the apartment. The shelf of a pass-through window to the kitchen was stocked like a small bar. An economy-size bottle of Jack was bookended by a bottle of Bacardi and the familiar amber of tequila. Smaller, airplane-size bottles were lined up like foot soldiers in front.

"Are you working?" Although Greer was not here to judge another woman's rock bottom, Karen's raggedy old concert T-shirt and faded yoga pants didn't qualify as business-casual attire, and a faint hint of whiskey tickled Greer's nose.

"I was working down at the Country Kitchen restaurant, but"—she cleared her throat—"things didn't work out. You know how it is. So we're stuck in this crappy place for now."

"Doesn't the army provide some sort of benefits for you?" It felt crass to be discussing money as a benefit of her husband's death. An inadequate, ignoble trade-off.

"Javier arranged a trust for Ally for the majority of his benefits. He wanted her to go to college so bad. Neither one of us had the opportunity."

"Does she know about the trust?" Greer asked.

"Yes, and she's insisting she's not going to college so we might as well break the trust and spend the money." A hint of Ally's stubbornness tightened Karen's mouth even as her chin wobbled slightly. "I should be able to take care of us until I can get her off to college."

Karen was a mother doing her best in unimaginable circumstances. "You're doing the best you can."

"Am I? I wonder sometimes." Karen gestured toward a cozy den. "Come on in. Want something to drink?"

"Water's fine. Or iced tea if you've got it," Greer said, mainly to have something to do with her hands. They wanted to form chords and strum as if the session with Ally had woken them from an enchanted sleep.

While Karen was in the kitchen filling glasses with ice, Greer picked up a picture of Ally sitting in her father's lap. She was ten or eleven but dwarfed by her father, who wasn't looking at the camera but adoringly at Ally, grinning for whoever was taking the picture, presumably Karen. The innocent happiness made Greer's chest ache with might-have-beens.

"Javier loved her so much. They got along better than Ally and I ever did. The one thing we can agree on was how awesome her daddy was."

"She's a tough kid." Greer meant it in every possible way. Strong, but also hard to handle.

"She's secretive and distant and I have no idea what's going on in her head."

"Isn't that all teenagers?"

Karen huffed a laugh and looked toward the window even though the curtains were drawn. "She's changed schools enough, I assumed it would be an easy transition for her, but she's gotten into trouble since almost the first day."

How much to tell her mother without betraying the tenuous trust Greer had built with Ally? She was saved from making a decision by the creak of the front door opening and the thud of Ally's backpack hitting the floor.

"I'm home." Ally's voice was monotone and didn't invite questions.

Karen rose. "Your friend Greer stopped by with a surprise for you. A guitar. I didn't know you wanted to learn to play. You should have told me and I could have—"

"There's nothing left to pawn, Mom." Ally turned to Greer with a face of stone. "You shouldn't have come here." Unfortunately, she didn't say it in the Southern way of *you shouldn't have*, but . . .

"Well, I did." Greer settled herself back on the couch and took a sip of tea. "A perfect amount of sugar in the tea, Karen."

"Javier grew up in Georgia and was particular about his sweet tea." Karen aimed a melancholy smile at the glass.

Greer recognized that Ally's lyrics were inspired by her mother's endless well of grief. A new melody meandered through Greer's subconscious, flitting like a lightning bug showing itself in flashes too ephemeral to catch.

"What about extended family? Do you have any close?"

"A few cousins I haven't talked to in years. I came from what might qualify as a white trash upbringing. Not that I realized it at the time. Everyone else was just as poor," Karen said.

"How did you and Javier meet?"

Ally slunk farther into the den but didn't sit. Greer did her best not to acknowledge her existence, sensing her interest in a story she must have heard before but perhaps not for a long while.

"I dropped out and followed my high school boyfriend to Atlanta. When the relationship ended, I got a job waitressing at a bar the boys from Fort Benning frequented. I was young, and it was fun." Her smile turned inward. "One night, I met Javier."

"He was fun too?" Ally asked.

"He was more than fun. He lit up my world. I was a goner and so was he. We got married three weeks later."

"Three weeks? Mom! You were barely eighteen. You won't even let me date." Ally stepped forward and crossed her arms over her chest as if she were the parent and Karen the child. "I can't believe you've never told me this before."

Karen's laugh lightened the shadows and revealed a beauty sadness had veiled. "You weren't old enough to handle the truth. Anyway, you're smarter than I am. Smart enough to put your college money to good use."

"Why are you telling me now?"

"Because you can handle the truth. You can handle anything life throws at you."

Ally made a dismissive noise but it came from a tear-clogged throat. "What else haven't you told me?"

"Nothing. Nothing at all." Karen's eyes said differently, but some memories between a man and a woman weren't meant to be shared. "Aren't you going to thank Greer for stopping by with the guitar, Ally?"

Greer took the change in subject as a dismissal, put her glass on the side table, and stood. Karen followed suit.

"Thanks," Ally mumbled.

"I had an idea to bounce off you. Walk me to the car?" After saying her good-byes to Karen, Greer waited until Ally reluctantly followed her outside.

Ally kept her gaze aimed toward the ground and scuffed her shoes through the weeds growing along the cracks of the sidewalk. "What's your idea?"

"I don't actually have one." When Ally still didn't look up, Greer said, "I wanted to apologize for overstepping and coming here without asking you."

"Oh. It's okay."

Unable to leave it at that, Greer tried again. "Your mom seems nice."

Ally shrugged. "Are we done? I have homework."

When Ally turned, Greer caught her wrist. "Can I do anything for you guys? You mentioned a pawnshop and—"

"Yeah, you can mind your own damn business." Ally shook loose of Greer and stalked back inside, letting the door slam behind her.

"That went well," Greer muttered as she climbed behind the wheel, wondering if she'd seen the last of Ally.

Chapter 15

Emmett lobbed off another low limb of the crepe myrtle and tossed it into the pile of trimmings. The hydrangea bushes no longer threatened to swallow the cabin and the tree looked neat again. Next up was clearing leaves out of the gutters. The last hard rain had revealed clogs.

Wiping his forehead with the hem of his T-shirt, he made his way to the shed in the back of the cabin. He'd found yard tools hanging along the wall at the front along with a row of grass and pest killers that lent a chemical smell to the hot box-like space. Venturing farther into the dimness, he squinted toward the corners but saw nothing resembling a ladder. He would have to borrow one from the farm.

Although it was inevitable, he wasn't sure he was ready to head back to the Lawson homeplace. He'd text his mom and have her toss a ladder into the truck. Along with a casserole. His appetite had grown to monstrous proportions and a frozen pizza wasn't going to satisfy him.

The sound of a vehicle echoed through the pine trees. A buzz of anticipation burned through him like he'd injected whiskey straight into his jugular. *Greer*. But it wasn't Greer's vanilla sedan. An unknown truck, and a big one, pulled up toward the cabin. His anticipation faded into curiosity and caution.

He made his way around the side of the cabin, lurking at the corner to scope out the possible enemy. While the truck was unfamiliar, the muscular black man who slid out was not. His shaved head reflected the sun.

Terrance moseyed up the front steps and out of sight. The pound of a fist on the door scared a nesting bird from the eaves. The blue jay squawked in protest as it landed on the branch over Emmett's head. If only Emmett could train the mean little cuss to attack on cue. The image of Terrance cowering for a bird would be worth millions on base.

"To what do I owe this pleasure?" Emmett swaggered from around the house to casually lean against the bottom rail of the stairs. "You here to recruit me?"

Terrance took the steps two at a time and pulled Emmett into a bear hug, lifting him off the ground. "Something like that, you hermity bastard."

Terrance pulled back, looked Emmett up and down, and thumped him on the shoulder hard enough to send vibrations down his arm. "You're looking a sight better than you were last time I saw you."

Considering the last time had been at Walter Reed after his amputation, Emmett could only imagine. "I'll always be better-looking than you, Terrance, down a leg or not."

It wasn't strictly true. Terrance was a bear of a man who attracted women like a beekeeper attracted bees, utilizing a smoke show to get their honey before leaving them with broken hearts. Or at least bruised ones. Emmett had never been able to switch off the gentlemanly conscience bred into him like his eye color. He'd been the Boy Scout. Not prudish, but unwilling to take part in the bar hops and one-night stands prevalent in a single soldier's life.

"How's your stump?" Terrance asked bluntly.

Emmett grinned. Most people felt the need to dance around the question—which was ironic, given the topic.

"What's so funny?" Terrance was always afraid to be left out of the joke. Or worse, to be the butt of one.

"Glad to see you is all. Come on in. I'll get us some drinks." Emmett led the way up the stairs, his self-consciousness at being watched maneuvering his prosthetic acute but manageable.

The air-conditioning inside had a hard time keeping up with the ninety-plus-degree temperature on top of 100 percent humidity. Emmett flipped the overhead fan on and headed straight into the kitchen to pull out a container of sweet tea he'd brewed that morning.

"Dang, you're like domesticated or something." Terrance took a Mason jar of iced tea and killed it as if he'd been wandering the desert for days. He held it out for a refill. "That's almost as good as my mama brews."

Emmett topped his jar off and gestured toward the den. They sat and Terrance propped his feet up on the coffee table and groaned as his head fell back in a pose of relaxation. A comfortable silence mustered around them.

"I'm getting deployed again," Terrance finally said.

Emmett's stomach flopped. "When?"

"End of the summer."

"Where to?"

Terrance hesitated. "Guess I'm not allowed to say, but it's not a cush assignment."

"Any assignment can go FUBAR in a blink. Even the cush ones." Fucked up beyond all repair pretty much summed up his life. Or it had. Slowly, painstakingly, he was mending.

Terrance lifted his head, his eyes shining with understanding, but also with the relief it hadn't been him. Terrance's orders the day of the ambush had taken him and his men on a different route. The area had been in U.S. hands for so long, everyone—including Emmett—had grown complacent. Chance. Fate. What ruled their lives?

The whys tried to engulf Emmett. Why him? Why *not* him? The merry-go-round usually whirled him until he was sick, but this time he had the strength to step off. No answers were to be found there.

"Yeah. I'm feeling it more this time," Terrance said solemnly. Introspection wasn't a natural state for him.

"Feeling what?"

"Jesus, don't laugh, okay?" At Emmett's nod, Terrance said, "My fucking mortality."

Terrance had come to the wrong person if he expected Emmett to dole out reassuring platitudes. "You might die. Statistically speaking, the more deployments you take, the longer you stay in, the more likely your number will come up."

Terrance rubbed a hand over his scalp. "Thanks for sugarcoating it for me."

"I hope you didn't come here expecting some rah-rah patriotic bullshit."

"No, I didn't." Terrance hunkered farther into the cushions. "I came to ask for a favor. And to extend an offer."

"Is this a good news, bad news situation?"

"Depends on your outlook, I guess." Terrance pulled a throw pillow into his lap and fiddled with the fringe along the edge. His unrest was unusual. He'd grown up in rural Alabama and from the time his dad had given him his first gun at seven, he'd spent every minute he could in the woods hunting. He could maintain a still alertness longer than anyone Emmett had ever met. It was both enviable and eerie.

"Spit it out. You're making me nervous." Emmett tried not to squirm himself.

"I'm an only child and my dad died a few years ago." Terrance knew Emmett knew all this. Emmett had attended the funeral. "My mom has a couple of cousins, but they aren't close. She's not good with money and I need . . . I need . . ."

"Someone to look after your mom in case something happens?"

"Yes," he said on a huge breath. "I know it's a lot to ask."

It was a lot to ask. Especially of a man who had spent the last weeks and months attempting to disconnect himself with the world. Terrance had been by his side since officer training. The experiences they'd shared had forged their friendship in fire. How could he say no?

"No," he said on a whisper.

Terrance let his face fall onto the pillow. As if he'd received a physical blow, Emmett felt the pain of their friendship fracturing.

"You're not going to die, Terrance," Emmett said, even though he no longer believed the good guys always won.

"You of all people can't say that. Look, I get it. We're not family. I shouldn't have asked considering . . ."

"Considering what?" Emmett's tone hardened.

Terrance sat up and met Emmett's gaze. "Considering you've

all but given up on living. I would never have pegged you as a quitter."

"Quitter? Taking my discharge because my leg got blown off is not quitting."

"You quit on those boys."

Numbness spread from Emmett's chest outward. His sweat-soaked shirt turned clammy against his skin. He clutched his knees to hide his shaking hands. If he closed his eyes, he would be on a blood-soaked dirt road, his ears ringing from the blast, choking on dust. His sergeant would be there, reaching for him with terror in his eyes.

"I did my best. I made a tourniquet and dragged myself—"

"Jesus, I'm not talking about the ambush. Everyone knows you did everything you could and then some. I'm talking about right here, right now. How many of those guys would rather be in your place right now, alive? What are you doing out here, man, except wasting your life?"

"Fuck off." His plans for his future had been upended in a millisecond. He'd expected to move up the ranks, retire from the army just like his dad and his grandfather before him, and take over the horse farm. He'd failed his family name, he'd failed his men, he'd failed himself.

"When's the last time you lived a little? Had a drink, had fun, kissed a girl without feeling guilty?" Terrance asked with the patience of a therapist.

Guilt tracked him like his shadow, always there but only revealed in certain circumstances. Like after the unexpected kiss with Greer. At the touch of her lips, his failures and his leg had faded from his thoughts. His physical response had been quick and volatile and had left all other emotions dwarfed.

His last months had been spent enduring the impersonal

touch of doctors and therapists. He'd forgotten how soft a woman's body was and how amazing a woman's needy hands felt against his skin.

That it was Greer—hot-tempered, sass-mouthed Greer—had only raised the stakes. She wasn't some random woman he was using to get back in the saddle or for a sexual fix. She'd been hurt, the reality of it still raw in her eyes, and he didn't want to add to her pain. But he would. As soon as her hand trailed down his leg and wakened the shorted-out nerve endings close to his amputation, he'd come to his senses.

He would disappoint Greer, just like he was disappointing Terrance, just like he'd disappointed his dad.

Terrance killed the last of his watered-down tea, set the glass on the coffee table, and rose. "I'll get out of here, so you can continue to sit on your ass."

"I wasn't sitting on my ass when you got here." Defensiveness leapt into his voice, but it was bogus. He'd spent the majority of the time since his discharge planted in a rocking chair with only Jack for company. That was slowly changing, though.

Emmett trailed him to the door and stood at the top of the porch steps. The air between them snapped with contentiousness. Unable to bear the thought of adding one more regret to his stash, Emmett hopped down the stairs on his good leg and knocked on the truck's driver's window.

Terrance rolled it down, smirked, and quirked an eyebrow. "What is it, asshole?"

His response settled Emmett. They would be okay. "I don't want to give you a big head, because Lord knows, you can barely get that eight ball through the neck of a T-shirt as it is, but . . ." He paused to assemble his thoughts. "You might have a point. About the wallowing thing. Believe it or not, I'm working on figuring things out."

"Glad to hear it. I'll shoot you a text before we fly out."

The waters between them had calmed. Terrance had his window halfway up, when Emmett put his hand over the top. "Hang on. You said you had a favor and an offer. What was the offer?"

Terrance ran a hand over his chin. "Hell, I nearly forgot. The Colonel wants me to find out if you'd be interested in a job."

It was the last thing Emmett expected. "Doing what? Cleaning his personal shitter with a toothbrush?"

Terrance barked a laugh. "As a contractor helping manage special projects."

"Why me?"

"Colonel Harrison seems to remember a captain who was diplomatic and well-liked but could come down like a hammer. I *think* he meant you." Terrance's teasing sarcasm felt like a big brother's; like family.

"I'm not sure I'm ready."

"Get ready because he wants an answer by the end of the month. It pays well, and you'd be a welcome sight on base."

Nothing could compare to the atmosphere on a military base. The one time Emmett had been back for a checkup at the VA medical center, he'd both missed it and couldn't get away fast enough. Could he work on base as a civilian and not feel left behind watching friends like Terrance climb the ranks?

Emmett stepped back and waved Terrance down the lane, standing in the sun until the rumble of his truck faded into birdcalls and solitude.

A *meow* swung his attention to the here and now. Bonnie sat at his ankle and stared off to where Terrance had disappeared.

"Done hiding?" He scratched her behind the ears, inciting a loud purr. The kitten had at least doubled in size and filled out with regular feeding. "Probably a good thing you didn't show yourself. Terrance would bust my ass if he knew I'd adopted a kitten."

He retreated to the cabin, fed Bonnie, and paced. The offer from Colonel Harrison was another ingredient in his stew of confusion. He hadn't considered his future since he'd come back to Madison because he hadn't felt like he deserved one. Was Terrance right? Was he letting his men down by living half a life and denying himself love and friendship and a purpose?

He had to get out of his own head. More often the silence and solitude he'd sought weren't comforting but oppressive. He changed shirts and fired up his truck. The rumble of the engine in his chest and the feel of the leather under his hands was like clutching a security blanket.

He headed toward the farm with the excuse of borrowing a ladder. Not only would honest manual labor distract him from a looming decision he didn't want to make, his exhaustion would leave less room for nightmares.

He bounced off the driveway and cut across open grass for the barn. Alfie was in the paddock with a young stallion, putting him through his first paces.

In his mid-fifties, Alfie had been part of the farm as long as Emmett could remember. To say his face was weathered was a compliment to driftwood. The scars from skin cancer removals pocked his forehead and nose, but he was still lean as a stalk of okra with ropy muscles and a spry, bowlegged gait.

Emmett grabbed an apple and a brush from the stable and found Eddie Munster munching grass in the shade of a water oak to the side of the barn, his tail twitching lazily. When he spotted Emmett, he tossed his head and chuffed a greeting. Emmett took his time giving the horse the treat and a thorough brushing, keeping half his attention on Alfie and the young, high-strung but beautiful stallion.

Yes, he'd missed his horse, and he also missed the excitement of watching the yearlings grow in their confidence as they learned their craft. Emmett wasn't ready to abandon his life of limbo, but with the Colonel's offer on the table, he had decisions to make. Decisions that would alter the trajectory of his life.

Alfie sent the stallion toward the water trough and approached Emmett and Eddie Munster with a shy smile. "Well, I'll be. That you, Emmett?"

Emmett patted Eddie's rump before making his way around to shake Alfie's hand. "I stopped by last week but you must have been up at the house. How are you?"

"No worries God can't handle. The missus and I have been praying for you."

The platitude usually got Emmett's hackles up, but Alfie didn't say it in a bless-your-heart, backhanded way. He spoke from a place of true faith. Faith that eluded Emmett.

"I appreciate it. How're the horses?"

"We've got two ready to foal. Another three to be shipped to their new owners. Business is good." Even though Alfie spoke all good news, troubles trenched his forehead and his lips pursed as if there was more to be said.

"What's going on? What are you not telling me?"

"Not my place." He hustled past Emmett toward the stable.

Emmett could barely keep up. "You can't leave me hanging like that."

Alfie stopped at the roomy birthing stall on the end of the stable and pulled out a carrot. A placard painted with the name

Daisy hung askew off a hook to the side. Heavy with foal, the tan mare that had been to visit Emmett months earlier lumbered to poke her head over and snuffle at the treat.

"No, *you* shouldn't leave it like that. Talk to your daddy."

"I'm just here to borrow a ladder."

"I keep them where I always have. Help yourself." Alfie patted the mare on the neck as she crunched the carrot.

Emmett felt dismissed by a favorite teacher after failing an exam. If the farm was in trouble he wouldn't put it past his dad to use it as leverage to get him back into the fold. If not the farm, then what was wrong?

After spending a few minutes with the mare, Emmett pulled a paint-stained A-frame ladder out of the storage room and slid it into his truck bed. He'd gotten what he came for, and it would take hours to get the gutters cleared. The air was thick and portended an afternoon thunderstorm. He needed to get to work.

He sat behind the steering wheel, his hand on the key but not turning it. The sweat creeping down the side of his face was the only thing that moved. The string of curses he let ring out made him feel marginally better. He climbed out, slammed the door, and trekked toward the big house.

A glance over his shoulder revealed Alfie standing in the door of the barn watching him. He waved a white cleaning rag in acknowledgment. That felt about right. A white flag of surrender.

An awkwardness descended when he faced the front door. He'd walked straight in countless times, dumped his backpack or rucksack on the floor next to the stairs, and headed straight to his dad's office or the kitchen, depending on how hungry he was.

That boy was a stranger. Should he knock like one?

He forced his hand to squeeze the latch. The door opened
and blessed cool air took him in its grip and swept him inside.
The smell of baking drew him toward the kitchen. He'd snuck
out enough in high school to have memorized the creaky boards.
Except a board that used to be safe creaked under his foot. Time
had crept in and changed the map in his mind.

His mom called out, "Is that you, Henry? The banana bread
is still warm if you want a slice with butter."

Emmett stopped trying to muffle his steps and walked into
the kitchen, but his mother hadn't heard him. She pushed a
piece of her graying bob behind an ear while she wrapped up
a loaf in a colorful dish towel. He knew without a doubt it was
for him.

"I'd love a piece if you have it to spare."

She started with a gasp, then laughed. The pure joy on
her face pained him, because it emphasized the anguish he'd
brought her. He joined her at the counter. She had a streak of
flour on her cheek and tears shining in her eyes.

"I'd hug you but I'm all sweaty," he said.

"I don't mind a little sweat. I'm married to a horse trainer,
after all." She leaned toward him and he wrapped her in a hug.
She felt more delicate in his arms than he remembered. Closing
his eyes, he could cast back to when her hugs had been all-
encompassing, making him feel safe through every move they
made as a family.

During those first few days at a new school when no one invited him to play at recess or sit next to them at lunch, he'd had
her hug to welcome him home and assure him he would make
new friends and find his place. She'd always been right.

She pulled away to cut him a slice of banana bread. A fallen
tear had streaked the flour on her cheek. Shooing him to the

table, she lay the plated slice in front of him, the butter already melted, the smell intoxicating. He ignored the fork and used his fingers, eating the bread in three bites.

Before he even swallowed, his mom put another, thicker slice on the plate along with a glass of milk. "Thanks," he mumbled.

"Don't talk with your mouth full, Emmett."

He might as well have been fourteen again, sitting at the kitchen table being smothered in banana bread love. Why had he been in such a hurry to grow up and leave home? Why hadn't he appreciated the bubble of protectiveness instead of railing against it?

When she placed a third slice on his plate, he pushed out the empty chair next to him with his foot. "Why don't you sit down and have some with me?"

She hesitated but returned with a half slice and a cup of coffee, her genteel manners making him feel like an animal. He picked up his fork and cut off a wedge when what he really wanted was to bite into the loaf. At the rate he was eating, he would need to start working out again.

"I saw Alfie out at the barn. The man doesn't ever change," he said merely to jump-start the conversation.

"Age creeps up on us all, Emmett. It's the way of life." Something in her tone made his stomach bottom out. Her sudden smile lightened the moment. "What brings you by the house?"

"I needed to borrow a ladder to clean the gutters at the cabin."

She patted her mouth with a napkin, her body rocking forward enough to signal her need to admonish him to be careful because of his leg. He tensed. Instead, she nodded. "I can't remember the last time it's been done. The farm keeps your father so busy."

She rose and collected their plates. He shifted in his chair to watch her put them in the sink, her back to him. Something about the droop of her shoulders set off warnings.

He rose and came up beside her, resting his hip against the counter. "What are you not telling me?"

"Nothing." She dried her hands on a dish towel and disappeared into the pantry.

He followed and blocked the door like a crossing guard. "I might agree except Alfie insinuated—"

"It's nothing you need to worry about." His mom collected a fresh bag of flour and a can of peach pie filling.

"Is the farm in trouble?"

His mom took a step forward, but he didn't budge. She made an exasperated sound and popped her hip. "The farm is fine. Your dad's not getting any younger, you know."

She jabbed the can of pie filling into his stomach. He stepped back and took the filling instinctively, letting her sidle around him.

"Is Dad having health issues?"

His mom pulled a *Southern Living* cookbook off the packed bookcase in the corner and flipped through it, her gaze downcast. "His cholesterol was a bit high at his last physical, but otherwise he's as healthy as an ox."

If it wasn't the farm and it wasn't his dad, then . . . "What's wrong, Mom?"

"It's probably nothing more than stress and exhaustion. The doctor is running more tests." She licked her index finger and kept flipping.

"What prompted the tests to begin with?"

"I was feeling worn down. Turns out I was anemic."

"Okay . . ." He drew the word out as his mind turned the information over. "Can't they give you iron supplements for that?"

"Yes, but the doctor wants to rule out any underlying causes. I've got an appointment to get scoped next week."

The lump in Emmett's throat grew into a boulder. "Are they talking cancer?"

"That's always a possibility at my age, of course." Her serenity with the unknown was enviable. "Or it might be stomach ulcers or a host of other things. God's will be done."

Emmett grit his teeth. He trusted medical science far more than the intangible hope preached every Sunday morning. "You'll follow up on everything the doctor wants you to do, right?"

"Of course I will." She turned another page. "Aha, there it is. Skillet cobbler. Betsy Shannon's husband was released from the hospital this morning. Massive heart attack, but they say he's going to be okay. Lots of family in, so I'm going to take them dessert."

He didn't remember Betsy or her husband. "That's real sweet of you, Mom."

"Can you stay for dinner?"

"Not tonight." He wasn't sure how to sit across the dinner table with his mom's news as the centerpiece and the realization that his parents hadn't told him because . . . why? Had they only wanted to protect him or had they worried he was too unstable to handle bad news? "The gutters need cleaning before the afternoon storm rolls in."

"Tomorrow, then? I'll make pot roast."

He couldn't deny the hope in her eyes. "I can't turn pot roast down."

"I need to thank Greer." She gave a little laugh.

"For what?"

"For making me promise not to bring you any more food. Hunger is a powerful motivator."

Emmett drew in a deep breath, everything becoming clear. Instead of resentment or anger, amusement surfaced. Greer had awakened his appetite in more ways than one. "I'll let her know next time I see her."

"Are you going to see her soon?" The glance his mom sent him under her lashes was rampant with curiosity.

After the way he'd ended their encounter Saturday night, he wasn't sure Greer wanted to ever see him again. He owed her something—an apology for starters—he just wasn't sure how much he had to give. "I hope so."

Leaning in, he kissed his mom's cheek and took a deep breath, the smell of baking mingling with her signature perfume. He wasn't sure what it was, but she'd worn it for as long as he remembered.

He shoved his hands into his pockets and headed to the front door, his gaze on his feet and his mind miles away. He pulled the door open as his dad pushed, throwing them both off-balance. Emmett grabbed his dad's shoulder, and his dad grabbed Emmett's waist in a weird dance position.

"Sorry," Emmett said before his worry and frustration at being kept out of the loop got the better of him and he whispered, "Why didn't you tell me about Mom?"

His dad gestured him outside and closed the door behind him. "Let's walk."

Although his brook-no-argument tone grated and reminded Emmett why he'd been so eager to grow up and leave the nest, he complied. They were silent until they got halfway to where he'd parked his truck in the shadow of the barn.

"How serious is it?" Emmett asked softly.

"We don't know yet. It could be minor or cancer or something in between. Won't know until she's scoped."

"What happened?"

"She passed out in church one Sunday morning while singing 'Nearer, my God, to Thee.'"

"I've faked having to go to the bathroom to get out of singing that plodding behemoth."

His dad barked a laugh. "Not my favorite either."

"When did this happen?"

"Two weeks ago."

Emmett stopped short and muttered a few choice curses. "Why didn't you tell me?"

"You have enough going on without piling on more troubles."

"I'm not fragile."

"Neither is your mother. She'll be fine." His dad spoke with the conviction of a true believer.

"And if it turns out to be something bad like cancer?"

His dad's face sagged for a moment, betraying his age and worry, before reassembling into a mask of strength. Maybe his mom needed him to be artificially strong, but Emmett would appreciate the unvarnished truth.

"Then we'll fight it."

They entered the dark barn. Through instinct or self-preservation, Alfie had disappeared like a sprite.

"Do you need help?" The question was out before he could stop it.

"With your mother or the horses?"

"Either. Both."

His dad rested his arms across the stall of Daisy the pregnant mare and didn't even look in Emmett's direction. "Got someone in mind?"

The offer from Colonel Harrison played on repeat in Emmett's mind. He wasn't sure if he even wanted the job on base, but if he accepted, Fort Knox and Madison were close enough for him to manage. "Don't be obtuse. Me, of course."

His dad turned his head to look out the barn door. There was nothing to see but white fences and June bugs skipping along the swaying grass.

"Do you want me to come with you to Mom's appointment?" Emmett asked.

"There's no need for theatrics." Only his dad would equate offering support as making too big a deal of the situation. "How long has it been since you've ridden?"

"Since that last time I was home before . . ." Would his life forever be classified in terms of before and after? Emmett clanked his prosthetic against the steel gate. "Not sure I can ride anymore."

"A good rider uses his hips and knees to control a horse. Why don't you at least give it a shot?"

He couldn't see a way out, but even more, he didn't want to look for one. It was time to test his limitations. "How about before dinner tomorrow night? Mom's promised me a pot roast."

"I'll have Eddie Munster saddled and ready." He clapped Emmett on the shoulder and headed out, hands in pockets, head down. The same way Emmett walked when deep in thought.

Emmett waited until his dad disappeared inside the house before climbing into his truck and heading back to the cabin. Emmett set up the ladder and began decluttering the gutters. The promised storm sent him seeking cover on the porch, but it blew through quickly, and he got back to work. Once he got used to climbing up and down and finding his new point of balance on the ladder steps, the work became mindless.

Maybe a new point of balance was what he needed in general. The inability to recapture the moment before his world exploded was difficult to accept. Yet no amount of Jack or hours of rocking or guilt would turn back time to save his leg or his men. His life would never be the same, but the corollary wasn't that his life had to be worse.

As the sun sent orange fingers of light across the sky like a fist closing into darkness, the sound of a car shifted him on the ladder. Of course it was Greer. She seemed to appear to him at crossroads, representing choices to be made. Opportunities to be accepted or rejected.

She slid out of her car and shielded her eyes to look up at him, but didn't say anything. With her hair twisted off her neck and dressed in a form-fitting T-shirt, a striped skirt that fluttered above her knees, and flip-flops, she could have starred in a magazine ad for a beach resort, luring vacationers like a siren.

She deserved a good grovel. When a woman like Greer offered a fraction of herself, a man would have to be an imbecile to turn her down. Just call him Emmett the Imbecile.

With his focus on putting things right between them, he descended the ladder, only realizing when he approached her, he'd lost any self-consciousness about his leg or the hitch in his step.

In the South, food was the glue that united a community. Families came together over Thanksgiving meals and churches gathered for potlucks. Food was offered as a form of sympathy or when forgiveness was sought.

"I'm sorry for being an idiot. Can I make it up to you? I have steaks and potatoes. This time I'll cook," he said.

They held gazes and much passed between them in only a

few blinks, leaving a foundation of forgiveness, which was more than he felt he deserved.

"I like my steak medium well if you're taking orders." She brushed past him to the porch steps, pausing to give Bonnie a rub behind the ears. "She looks good." Over her shoulder, she added, "So do you, by the way."

A zing went through him. If he wasn't mistaken, her gaze was flirtatious as it traveled his body. Maybe he hadn't completely blown his chance after all.

"Now that I've started, I can't seem to stop eating. Pretty sure I killed half a loaf of banana bread with my mom earlier, and I'm still hungry."

Instead of settling in on one of the rockers, she followed him into the kitchen to help. Once the potatoes were in the oven, a salad put together, and the steaks marinating, he asked, "You mind if I clean up? Steaks won't take long in the cast-iron skillet."

"Go for it. I'll make myself at home."

He retreated for a quick shower. With his hair dripping cool water down his neck, he rifled through his drawer for a pair of cargo pants. They were all dirty. His only option was dirty pants or clean shorts. He murmured a curse and pulled on the shorts before reattaching his prosthetic.

As an engineering marvel, his prosthetic was a thing of beauty. Its dark gray lines reminded him of modern architecture. He'd had the option of a flesh-toned leg, but he wasn't going to pretend the device was a substitute for the real thing.

With a clean T-shirt halfway on, he paused. Music drifted through the closed door. Not a radio, though. No, it was his guitar in the hands of a gifted musician. All Emmett's self-consciousness was swept away by the song—classic Dixie Chicks—as he walked out of the bedroom.

Greer looked up from playing and smiled, but didn't stop singing. *"Cowboy, take me away . . ."* Her gaze took him in from head to toe but didn't linger on his legs. He stared right back at her. The oven's beep silenced the music.

"That'd be the potatoes." She leaned the guitar against the coffee table.

As he made his way to the kitchen to heat the skillet, he said, "I thought you were done with playing."

"My mental block broke loose during a session with one of my foundation clients, Ally." She propped her shoulder against the jamb leading into the kitchen and sketched out her interactions with the teenage girl in stark facts, but he could see behind them. For better or worse, Greer was emotionally involved.

"How do you feel playing again?" He glanced over as he forked the steaks into the super-heated skillet. The poof of smoke and aroma had his mouth watering.

She tilted her head back and closed her eyes to answer. "Like a well that had been drained refilled. It was the strangest feeling. Ally wrote the lyrics to a haunting, painful song. A melody popped into my head fully formed, and I was playing before I second-guessed myself."

"Selfishly, I'd like to hear you play more often. Why don't you ask Becky if you can play one night?"

"No one wants to hear me. They want a professional." She scuffed her flip-flop against the wood floor and didn't meet his eyes.

"You are a professional."

"Not anymore I'm not. I'm a bartender who needs to figure out what's next."

He shrugged and let it go. If she wasn't ready to examine

her baggage, he wouldn't bust down the door. "You could teach music."

She shot him an incredulous look. "You think schools would trust me to mold young, impressionable minds?"

Laughing, he transferred the skillet to the oven and set the timer. Taking on a more serious tone, he said, "It sounds like you've managed to break through to Ally. She blew off everyone who tried to help, and now she's written an amazing song with your guidance."

"She did the hard work." Her obvious pride reflected how attached she'd become to Ally.

The oven beeped again and he pulled on an oven mitt to retrieve their sizzling steaks. "Inside or outside?"

"Outside."

They fixed their plates and headed to the porch. Balancing his plate on the rail, he cleared the small side table of empty beer bottles and the half-empty bottle of Jack he hadn't touched for days. She was close enough for him to make out the striations of green and brown in her irises.

"It would mean I'd have to go back to school." She picked up their conversation as if the thought had been rolling around her head since he'd tossed it in her direction.

"I'll bet the community college could get you started."

"I don't have any money."

"You could take classes during the day, bartend at night." *Or play.* He took a bite of steak to occupy his tongue.

"What if I'm not smart enough?" She poked at her potato.

"You're plenty smart." He took a bite of his steaming loaded baked potato and nearly moaned. How had he survived on frozen food and chips for so long?

"I have enjoyed working with Ally and the other two veterans Amelia assigned me."

"I've been replaced?" He widened his eyes in fake astonishment. "What are they like?"

"Neither of them have shot at me, so an improvement?" Her smile took any sting out of her tease.

"But not as interesting as me, huh?"

While she sketched out the two men's histories, he polished off his potato, skin and all. His plate was clean while she still had most of her potato and half her steak left. He eyed the meat like a wolf.

She laughed, and without him asking, pushed the steak onto his plate. "You weren't lying about your appetite."

He mumbled a thanks around a bite of her steak.

She finished her potato and rocked in the chair, her gaze on the horizon. "How're your parents getting on?"

"Fine." His polite response was knee-jerk, but troubles tumbled like a rockslide he couldn't keep contained. "Actually, no, they're not. Mom is getting some tests run next week and Dad's worried."

She stopped rocking. "What's going on? I hadn't heard anything."

"Apparently she passed out in church a few weeks ago. Turns out she's anemic, which can have many causes, one of which is cancer."

"Oh my. I'm sorry, Emmett. How is she handling the situation?"

"She invoked God's will like any good Christian, but that's bullshit. God doesn't save you because you're worthy or sinless or whatever. It's chance and genes."

"But she finds comfort in the thought and a good attitude can go a long way."

"What if she doesn't follow up with a specialist or—"

She squeezed his hand—hard. "It's your mom. You're scared."

"What if—" He swallowed, looked at his feet, and shook his head, unable to put his worst fears into words.

She tilted her head. "Surely you can't think any of this is your fault?"

"No. Maybe? What if the stress worrying about me brought on ulcers or triggered some negative reaction in her body? I've seen big men, strong men, crumble under stress."

"You're questioning everything, which is a normal reaction to unsettling news, but it doesn't help anyone. Think about what you can do to help her."

"For one, not be such a self-centered jack-hole."

Her laugh was husky and banished a portion of the heaviness weighing on his chest. They rocked in synchronicity. Her hand was still on his and he rearranged both to lie palm to palm, fingers linked. He felt like he was thirteen again and at the movies with a girl for the first time. His arm tingled and not only because it was falling asleep.

"Your dad will need to be with your mom at appointments." A leading edge was in her voice.

"Two mares are ready to foal . . . I don't know if managing the farm is the life I want."

"It doesn't have to be forever. Have you thought about what's next for you?"

He chuffed a laugh. "I'd planned to do a whole lot of nothing, but it looks like that isn't an option. Actually, an old army buddy came by and extended a job offer from my former colonel."

She stopped rocking. "What? Where?"

"A contractor managing special projects at Fort Knox. It would pay well. It's familiar. It's not far. I'd be able to come back to Madison as often as I wanted."

"Sounds like too good an opportunity to pass up." Although her words hinted at her blessing, a sadness within them spoke to the doubts he harbored about leaving Madison with so much unfinished business. "When does the job start?"

"I don't know, but he'll need an answer soon. I'm not sure what the right thing to do is."

Her hand twitched in his. "You have to do what's right for you."

He sensed she was giving him an out. An out of whatever was brewing between them. Deepening their relationship would only make things more difficult in the months to come, yet he couldn't seem to help himself.

"I hope I didn't hurt your feelings the other night." His voice came out low and rough.

"Trust me, I've survived worse humiliations." Her tone was rife with the desire to move on to a different subject.

He couldn't, though. Not until she understood what had really happened. "It wasn't you. I mean, it was but not because I didn't feel things. And stuff." His brain had shut down and stopped supplying coherent thoughts. He was a plane going down in a crash.

"It's okay, Emmett. We can be friends. Or whatever."

Her cheeks were apple red, and she had straightened and scooted toward the edge of her seat like a bird ready to fly away, but he held fast to her hand, desperate to pull out of his tailspin.

"I haven't been with a woman in a while. Especially one like you. I was deployed for almost a year and then since I lost my leg . . ." He took a deep breath.

"Like me? What does that mean?" She was looking at him now, her eyes like blades ready to eviscerate him.

"A woman that I . . . *like*. Care about. You know." He waved his free hand as if he could conjure prettier words out of the air. Nothing came. He might as well write her a note with check boxes.

"Oh. I see."

He wished he could see what she saw. Blind, he bumbled ahead anyway. "I'm worried you'll be freaked out or turned off by my leg. Or what's left of it."

There. He'd said it.

She blinked a few times at him, her mouth in a little O of understanding before a not-so-innocent smile crept over her face. "You know it's another appendage altogether that I'm interested in, right?"

His breathing accelerated like a Mustang at a drag race. "Yeah?"

She pursed her lips as if considering the point—or more likely holding back the shadow of a smile making her eyes sparkle and giving him life. She stood and tugged him inside until they were caught in an eddy of cool air.

Her kiss knocked him back on his heels. Literally and figuratively. He backpedaled until he hit the wall. The empty picture frame around the hole he'd punched into the drywall fell to the floor, the sound of wood splintering unmistakable.

"Why is every time we try this something gets broken?" He gave a little laugh, turned them, and pushed her against the wall.

What was next to be broken? His heart? Was it even possible to break something that was still wounded in ways he didn't recognize? He shoved the thought away.

He herded her to the bedroom, their hands busy on each other's bodies, pulling and tugging at the fabric impeding their ultimate goal. They fell sideways on the bed, his feet hanging off. She hooked a leg over his thigh and pulled his leg between hers, resting her calf along his cold, non-feeling prosthetic. Except nerve endings sent phantom tingles down his nonexistent leg as if he really could feel her touch.

This time he didn't stop her hand when it traveled down his leg, but he couldn't stop the tension from roiling his stomach and tensing his muscles.

"Does this work better with it on or off?" she asked with her lips in contact with his throat.

"I don't know. I haven't had sex since before. Would you be more comfortable if I kept it on?"

Part of him—a sizable part—wanted her to say yes. Wanted to maintain the illusion everything about him was whole and undamaged. But a kernel deep in his heart wanted the opposite. He wanted to bear himself so no secrets remained.

"Take it off," she whispered.

It was his dream and his nightmare. He hadn't allowed anyone to watch him take the prosthetic off since the last day of his physical therapy. He sat up on the side of the bed and paused with his fingers on the button that would release the heavy-duty ratchet holding his leg in place.

He looked over his shoulder. She had rolled onto her back and scooched up his pillows, her hands linked behind her head.

"You sure about this?" he asked.

"Yep. While you're at it, take off your pants too, big guy."

Unbelievably, a smile surfaced from somewhere deep inside, unlocked by her teasing words. Was she really so confident or was she trying to set him at ease? Did it matter? She was in his bed and ordering his pants off.

Once decided, he made quick work of his leg and his pants. His shirt followed it all to the floor for good measure, leaving him in nothing but his boxer briefs.

Her gaze traveled down his body to his residual limb then back to his chest. With a decidedly naughty grin, she stretched her arms out and made grabby hands. "Come here."

Chapter 16

In the darkness, her breathing slowed and her body turned boneless. Emmett was curled behind her, his arm heavy across her waist, their edges tucking against each other as if carved from the same piece of wood. Strangely, the aftermath felt more intimate than the sex. More . . . important. Like the resettling of the land after an earthquake. Rivers reshaped and new landmarks formed.

Except, sex wasn't an apocalyptic event. Sex was merely a salve so they could lift themselves up and move on a little less injured. Or had the sex acted as a distraction from the confusion and uncertainty of life?

Whatever. The sex had been good. No, it had been *great*. Not that she had expected Emmett to be anything less, but she hadn't been confident his leg wouldn't hamper him or make things weird like it had the night on his couch. Far from the awkwardness she'd feared, coming together with him had been natural.

Now what? The actual sex might not have been awkward but her mental wrangling about the meaning sure was. Not to mention the bombshell he'd dropped about a potential job at Fort Knox. She wasn't upset. The job sounded perfect for him, and it would get him out of the cabin and back into the world. She wouldn't be the one to hold him back no matter how sad the thought of him gone made her feel.

He kissed a sensitive spot below her ear, inciting shivers. "You good?"

"I'm fine." Her pat answer was one she'd give to an acquaintance asking after her health and she stumbled to add, "I'm good. Great. I thought we synced up well." What was she babbling about? They weren't phones. Trying to save the moment, she asked, "Are you good?"

"Better than." The breath he took transmitted to her through his chest. "You weren't freaked out or whatever?"

She was freaked out but not for the reasons he worried about. His lack of a limb was the least of it. She turned onto her back. Although the shadows were deep, the open curtains striped his face with filtered light.

She laid her hand along his cheek. "You are sexy no matter what. The proof was in my orgasm, so for Pete's sake, quit harping on your leg or lack thereof."

His cheek moved under her hand in a smile. "You certainly have a way with words."

"I was always better with the melody than the lyrics." She fiddled with the edge of the sheet as she considered the wisdom of cracking open her own insecurities. "What are we doing?"

"Cuddling?"

A quick laugh popped out before she could slam a lid on it. "I mean, *us*. Don't misunderstand. I'm not expecting some heartfelt declaration, especially with the future up in the air, but we were friends before, and I don't want this to screw that up."

"We're still friends." His pause was weighed with his own varied thoughts. "But there's no reason we can't be more than friends until things shake out, right?"

"Your parents hate me."

"They do not."

"Okay, not your mom, but if we were in high school, your dad would ground you from seeing me."

"No, he wouldn't."

"You didn't see his face when I went by your house. He wanted to sweep me out of his house like dirt."

"Come with me tomorrow night for dinner with them." He launched the grenade with a casualness that shocked her.

She sat up, her sexual lassitude gone. "That's a terrible idea."

"Actually, it's brilliant. You'll defuse the tension."

"I'm more of an instigator than a defuser. Anyway, you and your parents need to have some serious discussions."

"I don't think my mom wants her medical issues to over-shadow everything. With you there, we can be normal. Or at least pretend to be normal."

She eased back down but still clutched the sheet under her chin as if limiting physical exposure could protect her emotion-ally. "It would be too much like we're . . . *together* together."

He peeled away from her and laid on his back, no longer touching her. "No problem. I get it."

She propped herself up on her elbow. The distance between them settled an anxious pit in her stomach. "What exactly do you get?"

"After what happened with Beau, I can't say that I blame

you. You want sex without complications. Fine by me." It didn't sound fine by him.

"I never said I was just here for the sex, dumb-butt." Maybe calling the man whom you liked more than a little and had rocked your world a "dumb-butt" wasn't romantic or sensitive, but his assumptions were making her mad. "I failed at my dream career. I'm completing court-ordered volunteer hours. My current job is a step above menial labor. I'm thirty and have no clue what I want to do with my life. Why would you want to be with a mess like me?"

"I thought we'd already established I'm as big a mess as you are if not bigger."

"Not reassuring, Emmett. Two messes make one ginormous mess."

"How about we come at it from a different angle?" He played with a lock of her hair that had fallen across his chest. "You care about other people. You work hard. You can laugh despite setbacks and challenges. You don't put up with my BS. And I'm one hundred percent confident that you'll figure out your life and make yourself proud."

His confidence in her might be misplaced, but it was like being given a boost over a wall that had seemed insurmountable. She'd caught the worried glances her parents exchanged on a daily basis. They loved her and would support her, but they feared for her future.

Her laugh was choked by rising tears. "Is this how you got your men to walk into danger? Because I have to admit, you're motivating."

She sensed the change in atmosphere around him like a barometric drop signaling a storm front. He spoke in a low voice. "I never sent a grunt into danger with a pep talk."

She swallowed, cursing herself. Her teasing had scratched open a wound she couldn't heal with a trite platitude or even mind-blowing sex. It ran deep and was a trauma he'd have to tend to and heal himself—like she had to blaze a new future for herself—but that didn't mean she couldn't pass him some bandages.

"I'm sorry. That wasn't something to joke about." She stroked the back of her hand down his face. "You received the Silver Star for your bravery."

"I didn't deserve it," he said softly.

"What are you talking about?"

"The bomb went off and I just lay there." His voice was barely audible now.

"You were gravely injured. In shock."

"If I'd been faster with a tourniquet, my sergeant might have made it. Even a few seconds might have saved his life."

She searched for words of wisdom but none appeared. All she could cobble together were useless words of comfort, which she murmured in his ear while stroking his hair and hugging him close.

Finally she said, "Fate controls all of our lives with a few seconds. A few seconds faster or slower and maybe you could have avoided a car wreck. A few seconds is all it takes to miss your train or bus and get you fired for being late to work. A few seconds can save a life or take one. You did everything you were capable of doing in those few seconds."

His long sigh seemed to whisper his disagreement. Nothing she said or did would convince him he was blameless. It would have to be a conclusion he reached after wrestling with the whys and wherefores over the course of months or years or decades. All she could do was hold him tighter.

Eventually, their conversation veered to more mundane top-ics. High school memories, funny stories from her time in Nash-ville and his time in the service, books and movies.

Her phone flashed a text from the nightstand.

It was ten and her mom was wondering where she was and when she'd be home. "Speaking of high school, my mom is ask-ing when I'll be home. I'd better go."

"I have a news flash. You're thirty and allowed to stay out after dark." He tugged her back down to him.

She laid half on his chest and kissed him, the newness of the feeling thrilling. "I'm living under their roof and basically dependent on them. I don't want to thumb my nose at their sen-sibilities. They would freak out if they knew what we've been doing. I'm pretty sure they think I'm still a virgin."

Regret and longing entwined. She wanted to spend the night in his bed and wake at dawn to make love to the sound of the world coming alive. The urge revealed parts of her heart she thought slashed and burned, and quickened her hands as they pulled on her clothes. It was too much, too fast.

"Come to dinner with me tomorrow night," he said.

"Emmett." A warning lowered her voice. "I shouldn't. Any-way, I have to work at Becky's tomorrow night. More live music. I can't pass up the extra tips."

"Maybe I'll stop by." His tone probed for a sign of welcome.

She pulled her T-shirt over her head. Was the ground as shaky on his side as it was on hers? "I'd love to see you."

"Should I have my mom call your mom and ask if we can have a sleepover?" He wore nothing but a grin. A laugh burst out of her.

"We'll see." She leaned to plant a quick kiss on his mouth, but he wrapped a hand around her nape and deepened it. By the time he released her, she was breathless and rethinking her responsibilities.

Another text from her mom popped up, breaking the mood. She shuffled toward the front door, only hitting her shin once.

"Sweet dreams, Greer Hadley." Emmett's voice carried from the bedroom before she stepped out the door.

Sweet or erotic or fearful, her dreams were sure to star Emmett Lawson.

She sent her mom a text and headed home, taking back roads and letting her mind wander. What did she want to do with the rest of her life? She'd thought every avenue to music had been blocked but she'd only abandoned the main thoroughfare. Teaching was an alternative that would never have occurred to her without her detour through the Music Tree Foundation.

The times she'd spent there had been challenging and rewarding and frustrating. And surprisingly, she was good at what she did there.

She parked and tiptoed through the kitchen door.

"I was getting worried." The voice came from the shadows of the kitchen table.

Greer let out a yelp even as her brain registered the rollers her mother slept in every night and the scent of cold cream. She was conservative and old-school and had never understood Greer's propensity for adventure and oftentimes trouble.

"Sorry, Mom." Greer gave her mom a kiss on the cheek and sat next to her, picking up a cookie on the plate between them. "I was hanging out."

"With anyone I know?"

"Emmett Lawson." The silence was unsettling, and like a teenager lobbing excuses and lies, she babbled. "He adopted a kitten. Did you know he used to play guitar?"

"Do you think it's wise to get involved with someone right now?"

Of course it wasn't, but when did she ever cave to what was "wise?" Maybe her problem was she didn't rely on logic but her unreliable feelings.

"Believe me, I didn't plan on anything happening."

"Greer." Her mother covered one of her hands and squeezed. "Your life is off track at the moment. I have no doubt you'll find your footing, but until you do, no good can come from a relationship."

"It's not a relationship. We're hanging out." Her heart thumped as if lodging a protest. They'd slept together. Greer was old-fashioned enough to classify that as a relationship.

"I don't want to see you get hurt again, honey."

"Me neither. I'm figuring things out." She took another cookie to give herself time and courage. "I might go back to school."

Her mom's lips parted on a sharp intake of breath. "For nursing?"

"No. For teaching music. I've enjoyed volunteering at the foundation. I'm good at it."

"I thought your intention was to leave music behind." A questioning lilt threaded her words.

"It was, but I . . . can't. It would be like donating an organ. And not my gallbladder. Something vital, like my heart." Greer braced herself for another lecture in practicality.

Her mom smiled, but it was tinged with worry. "Your dad and I had given up hope of having children when I got pregnant with you. It was a miracle. You were born a dreamer, and for two no-nonsense people like me and your father, raising you was like entering a brave new world."

"What are you trying to say? I should get my head out of the clouds?"

"No. I'm saying music feeds you as surely as these cookies do. I'm glad you aren't going to give music up. Any student would be lucky to have you as a teacher."

Greer looked to the ceiling and blinked the tears back. "You think I can do it?"

"I know you can."

"I'm going to go by the community college and make an appointment with a counselor to see where I need to start." The vague plans Emmett had etched in her subconscious coalesced into stark black-and-white. "I'll bartend to pay tuition and get my own place—"

"No need to waste money on rent. We love having you home."

Greer raised her eyebrows but didn't argue. They might love it, but they worried and fussed over her like she was sixteen again. Still, having some direction for her life would relieve the stress she'd put them under the last few months.

"Okay. I'd love to stay here." More needed to be hashed out. Being an adult living with her parents meant not allowing herself to slip back into childish roles. "But I'm a grown-up, Mom. A curfew isn't going to work for me." Greer prayed her mom cottoned to what she was insinuating without going into details.

"I realize you're grown." Her mom tapped the table, the only reflection of her discomfort. "How about you text with an ETA so we don't pace the floors waiting for you?"

"And if my ETA is the next morning?"

The rhythm her mom tapped sped up. "Then, we won't expect you for dinner."

Greer let out her breath and relaxed into the chair. For the first time in a long time, when she thought about the future, desperation and anxiety took a backseat to anticipation. She went to bed and did indeed dream of Emmett.

Flipping through the brochure she'd picked up at Madison Community College, Greer walked by Amelia's office the next afternoon.

"Greer! You have a second?" Amelia called out.

Greer checked her watch and ducked into the door. Her session with Ally was scheduled to start. If Ally even showed up. "What do you need?"

"The end is near." Amelia linked her hands and gave Greer a look over the tops of her glasses. "I need to know what your plans are going forward so I can reassign your clients if needed."

At the beginning, amassing the hours had seemed monumental. Now that the finish line was within sight, it felt like a blink of time. "I can hardly believe it."

"What do you want to do?"

Greer waved the brochure. "I'm enrolling at the community college."

"Studying what?"

"Music education."

A self-satisfied smile spread across Amelia's face. "Fantastic. You probably won't have time to continue to volunteer, but you're always welcome."

Even though her life was about to get exponentially more complicated, she wouldn't abandon Ally or the others. Somehow, she would make it work. She opened her mouth to tell Amelia just that when a monotone voice spun her around. "Are you ready?" Ally stood hunched under the weight of her back-pack.

"I'm ready." Greer followed Ally down the hall to their room and closed them in. She'd talk to Amelia afterward. "Have you been practicing?"

Ally didn't answer, but she ran her thumb along the tips of her fingers.

"You'll build up calluses the more you play and your fingers will stop hurting."

Ally performed the ubiquitous teenage blow-off, a shrug accompanied by a lack of eye contact.

"Are you still mad I dropped the guitar at your house?"

Ally finally looked at her and the roiling emotions on her face set Greer back in her chair. Ally pointed at the college brochure. "What's that?"

"I'm going to college. Better late than never, right?" Greer smiled but when Ally remained stone-faced, she cleared her throat and continued, "Music education."

"What about your service hours?"

"Actually, I'll have satisfied them in a couple of weeks."

"So that's it? You're not coming back, and I'll get assigned to freaking Dicky again." Ally made a gagging sound.

"I didn't say I wasn't coming back."

"Amelia said you wouldn't have time."

"The summer semester starts soon, and I'm not sure what my class schedule will be yet, but I'd like to keep meeting even if we have to work out a different time. Saturdays, maybe? Or I could come to your house."

"Mom won't want you there."

"She doesn't like me? I thought I made a decent impression."

"It's not you in particular. She doesn't like people around when she gets . . . sad. And she's sad a lot."

Was "sad" teenage code for "drunk"? "Your mom told me her last job didn't work out. Is she looking for another one?"

"I think so."

"What about the cousins and aunts your mom talked about? Ever see them?"

"Nope." Ally made the word pop.

"What about your dad's family?"

"They're in Mexico. Dad came over with his brother, but he went home a long time ago."

Greer could only imagine the difficulty of navigating the grief and trauma of losing a husband without support. Yet Karen still had Ally, and Ally needed her.

As alone and lonely as Greer had been in Nashville, her rock bottom had been bedrock made by people who cared about her—her uncle Bill, her parents, Amelia, and even now Emmett. Given the time and safety to regain her footing, she'd discovered a new strength and purpose.

Could she provide the same for Ally and her mom?

"How about we get to work?" Greer asked in an artificially light voice. "Let's see if we can massage my melody and your lyrics into a kick-ass song."

Chapter 17

Emmett woke at dawn in peaceful increments instead of jerking out of one of his usual nightmares sweating and heaving breaths. He was alone but not lonely. The small dark corner of his world was expanding. He turned his face into the pillow and breathed in a faint flowery scent.

He still couldn't believe Greer Hadley had been in his bed. Naked. Doing things with him he hadn't been sure he'd ever do again. But here he was lying in an empty bed with an idiotic grin on his face smelling pillows. Where were the singing cartoon birds and bunnies?

Slowly, though, his expanded world revealed its troubles and conflicts. His mom and dad. The horse farm. The job offer from Colonel Harrison. The knot in his stomach unspooled to reveal dread, excitement, and nerves. It was as if his life had been sitting static in a pinball machine, waiting for someone to launch him back into motion.

His recent days had dragged by as if minutes were hours.

Today, he wasn't sure he had enough time to accomplish his plans. He hauled himself out of bed and used furniture to hop his way into the bathroom to shower.

Once he was dressed, prosthetic included, he fed Bonnie then ate a bowl of cereal while the kitten chased a moth. He was in the truck and on the main road by the time the sun crested the horizon in a blaze of orange.

He pointed his truck toward Nashville on a quest that would likely prove fruitless. The first pawnshop he hit was seedy, with no sign or memory of Greer's guitar. By the third shop, he decided all pawnshops had a melancholy air no matter how bright or clean or welcoming. It emanated from the items for sale. Items parted from their owners because of hard times and necessity.

On reaching the seventh shop, he'd given up hope of ever locating her guitar. He stepped to the counter, where wedding rings were displayed under the glass. How much sadness and anger and heartbreak resided in the simple bands of silver and gold?

He focused on the clock over the doorway to the office instead. It was early afternoon, he was starving, and his dad would expect him before dinner for the ride he'd promised.

When no one came out to help him, he wandered over to the wall hung floor to ceiling with guitars. All different styles from acoustic to electric and an array of colors. He felt like Indiana Jones faced with the task of choosing the Holy Grail from the assortment of chalices. Which guitar would Greer have played?

Definitely acoustic and a traditional natural-wood finish. He gravitated to a dozen or so in the middle. One had a strap tooled with mustangs. Not that one. Another had a simple black leather strap. Another no. The guitar closest to the ceiling had a brown leather strap tooled with flowers. An electric sense of

elation zagged through him, as if the woman herself had saun-
tered into the room. He took the guitar down and turned it to
examine the body.

Nothing. He had hit another dead end.

"That's a Martin. Not cheap." The manager had snuck up
behind him and was wiping his hands on a paper towel, the
faint smoky scent of barbecue clinging to him. "Plus, it has Dolly's John Hancock on the base."

"Excuse me?"

The manager flipped the guitar up and tapped a black signature on the bottom of the base. It was only a few inches long
and faded. Emmett touched it with his thumb, then positioned
the guitar across his body and strummed a chord. The richness
of the sound registered in spite of the instrument being badly
out of tune.

"I'll take it."

"Don't you want to know how much it is?"

"I don't care. Ring it up." He had just identified himself as
an easy mark. Not only that, but he had no idea what the going
price for a used Martin was these days. It didn't matter. He
pulled out his credit card. The guitar was priceless.

The manager reeled off a number that seemed reasonable
and even threw in a black case from the back room. Emmett
stashed the guitar in the cab of his truck, even belting it in for
the ride home. With no time to drop it at the cabin, he drove
straight to the farm and parked near the barn.

His dad and Alfie were standing in front of Daisy's birthing
stall, their heads close. The whirring fans muffled his steps and
made it impossible to hear their conversation. Only the horses
acknowledged him with a flick of their ears.

"How is she?"

Both men startled. "You scared a year off my life, Emmett," Alfie said with a tease after he recovered. "She's in labor."

Emmett stood behind his dad. Either Emmett had grown or his dad had shrunk. The odd realization hammered home the passage of time.

He turned his attention from the existential to the real. Tossing her head, the mare paced and circled the stall, occasionally pawing the hay. Her belly was distended and her discomfort obvious.

"Are you going to call Ryan in?" Emmett asked. The mare was a first-time mother and at a higher risk for complications.

"Alfie and I were discussing that. If things continue to progress, we'll let nature take its course. Lord knows, I've delivered more foals than Ryan. I'm going to have to postpone our ride though. Your mother is going to tan my hide, but I'll most likely miss dinner too."

"I'll hang with you." The offer popped out before he could examine the ramifications of spending hours with his dad.

"I'd like that, son." His dad turned away before Emmett could register the emotion on his face, so he took his dad at his word.

"How about I break the news to Mom? If she gets mad, I'll play the one-leg card."

His dad's burst of laughter was like a relief valve. "Put on some puppy-dog eyes and score us some food too."

Emmett picked at a sliver of wood on the top of the stall. "Any word about Mom?"

"We won't know anything definitive until the appointment, but she's feeling better." The slug of emotion in his dad's voice said more than a shed tear.

Emmett meandered from the barn to the house. Regular

food and exercise had strengthened him and his gait was no-
ticeably smoother. He'd turned a corner and left his shadow
behind. Once inside, he followed his nose. The aromas coming
from the kitchen reminded him of Thanksgiving—meats and
vegetables and desserts.

His mom stirred the pudding for the layers of bananas and
wafers at her side. There was nothing like warm homemade banana pudding.

He cleared his throat to gain her attention. "Smells amazing
in here."

She smiled and pushed her hair off her forehead with one
hand while continuing to stir with the other. "I'm at a delicate
stage with the pudding or I'd give you a hug. I thought you and
your dad were going for a ride?"

"Rain check on the ride. Daisy is laboring. Alfie and Dad
don't want to leave her in case of complications."

"They've been worrying over her all week like two mother
hens. Your dad has it in his head that her progeny will fetch top
dollar. Dinner's ready if you want to catch a bite to eat before
things get exciting."

"I volunteered to keep him company. Will you mind terribly
if we eat in the barn?"

Her sigh was one of exasperation but also resignation. Their
dinners had often been interrupted by horse-related emergen-
cies. "Is Alfie staying too?"

"I assume so."

"Let me fix you three plates."

"You're the best." It wasn't a platitude but the truth. He put
an arm around her shoulders and hauled her into a half hug.

"You're going to make me scorch the pudding." His mom
batted him away, tested the consistency, then poured it over the

bananas and wafers. Emmett snuck a spoonful while she fixed the plates.

Back in the barn, the three of them ate standing up in a semicircle around the stall door. Alfie volunteered to return the plates to the house, and Emmett and his dad moved into the birthing stall with the mare, keeping a safe distance.

"How is she progressing?" Emmett asked.

"She's been restless all day."

Something in his dad's voice had Emmett asking, "Worried?"

"Not yet, but she waxed two days ago. I was expecting her to foal last night." In preparation for foaling, a mare often leaked colostrum. The colostrum dried and formed what looked like dripped candle wax.

"Mom said this foal could be special."

"Its sire is one of the best Tennessee walkers in the country."

Emmett let out a low whistle. "How much did that stud cost?"

"Five thousand."

The figure was staggering considering there was no guarantee the farm would recoup the money. Genetics were a roll of the dice. The foal could be stillborn or have a defect that would hamper its potential. And even if the foal was top quality, it would be months before its value became clear during training.

"What can I do?" Emmett asked.

"Nothing to do but wait."

They took up the vigil on a bale of hay, shoulder to shoulder. The space was intimate, with the sun dropping below the trees on the horizon.

"I wasn't sure what you needed me to do or say when you

came home. I'm sorry I handled things badly." The words stumbled out of his dad's mouth.

The apology was like a kick from a mule to Emmett's chest, setting his heart to skipping along too fast and erratic. "I didn't know what I needed either. All I know is that I'm not a hero like you or Granddad."

"Why do you keep saying that? You received a Silver Star."

"I didn't feel heroic or brave. If you want the truth, I was scared shitless."

His dad shifted on the bale of hay to meet his eyes. "Son. We were all scared shitless. It's a constant state of being when you're in action. As a solider, your training allows you to function with the fear."

Emmett leaned his head against the stall and took a deep breath of the stagnant, humid air. There was truth in his dad's statement. A good soldier trained until performing their duty was second nature. "You were scared?"

"Every day."

"I remember your old army buddy coming around and telling stories about how you saved his life by jumping that guy with a knife."

His dad's arms were crossed, and his chin was tucked down. "I wasn't driven by a noble urge to sacrifice myself to save him. I was desperate and panicked and was only thinking about surviving myself. You were barely two years old, and I'd been gone more than I was home."

"But you always said being deployed was the best time of your life."

"It some ways, it was. In others, it was the worst time of my life. I had nightmares for months after I came home. Killing a man at close range and watching the life drain out of his eyes, knowing he may have had a wife or son or daughter at home, wrecked me."

A memory popped into Emmett's head. It was the night after his dad's army buddy had visited to reminisce. With teenage hunger driving him out of bed for a midnight snack, he'd spied his dad sitting at the kitchen table with an almost empty whiskey bottle. An anxious, unsettled feeling had Emmett creeping back to his room unseen.

"Did you talk to Granddad about it?" Emmett asked.

"Back then, you didn't talk about it, but I could tell he'd seen even worse in Vietnam. When you've seen death, when you've killed someone, it haunts you. Changes you. Just like I could see the changes in you."

His dad's truths settled around them. Finally, Emmett asked, "Do you still have nightmares?"

"Time has dulled the memories. Made them bearable. But I don't want you to feel like I don't understand, because I do."

A harsh groan came from Daisy's chest, followed by several chuffs as if she were practicing Lamaze breathing. Emmett was quiet, waiting for something momentous to happen, but she continued to circle the stall and paw at the straw.

His dad's voice was soft. "You know, I had no intention of coming back here and taking over the farm."

Emmett couldn't contain his astonishment. "What? I thought taking over had always been your plan."

"My plan was to make the army my career and retire a general. I wanted to travel the world with you and your mother."

"We lived all over the country."

"We did, but as the years went by, I began to see this piece of land—this farm—not as an anchor but a salvation." His dad rubbed a hand over his whiskered chin. "I'm not saying it has to be your salvation too, but you need to find something to hang on to or your demons will eat you alive."

Emmett leaned his head back and closed his eyes. His demons took a bite every chance they got. "It was supposed to be a routine patrol, you know? My company had done dozens. All without incident. We were prepared. We were always prepared, but maybe we had gotten complacent? I don't know."

He paused for a moment as the scene manifested like a movie. "It was hot, but the sky was a cloudless blue. It reminded me of a Tennessee summer day. In fact, I had slowed my pace to stare up at the blue. My first sergeant got farther ahead of me than usual. He turned around to chap my hide about being slow."

If he concentrated, he could hear the *clomp* of their boots in the dirt and feel the hot sun beating down. He could even see his sergeant's good-natured, shit-eating grin.

"It was like flipping a switch from order to chaos. An explosion knocked me to the ground. If I'd been on my sergeant's heels like I should have been, I would have died too."

"You realize the space you'd put between you and the explosion saved the lives of the men behind you too," his dad said softly.

"Maybe, but maybe if I'd been concentrating on my surroundings and not the fucking sky, I would have noticed something. I would have been able to . . ." He leaned over his knees and held his head in his hands. What could he have done differently except die?

"You aren't a superhero. You couldn't have predicted when or where an ambush might take place."

"I knew my leg was messed up bad. Worse than feeling pain, I couldn't feel it at all."

"You were in shock," his dad said softly.

"I got on my knees and returned fire. I don't know how many insurgents were out there or how many I hit. We were pretty exposed, but there was a ditch. I don't know how long it took me to notice my sergeant was down. Too long. I grabbed his flak jacket and dragged us both into the ditch. He was still alive, but the blood . . . an artery had been hit. I tried to put pressure on it, then a tourniquet, but . . ." Blood had puddled in the dirt underneath them. "He knew it was over."

Emmett scrubbed his face with both hands as if that could erase watching a man's eyes go blank as he tried to speak words lost to death.

"What happened then?"

"I crawled over to the next wounded man. His face was burned. I had to check his pocket to know it was Jenkins." A pause as Emmett swallowed down his rising bile. "He made it, though."

"The report said you saved his life, Emmett."

They'd told him the tourniquet he'd applied had saved Jenkins's life and his leg. But had he even wanted to be saved? A nurse had wheeled Emmett into the burn unit at Walter Reed while he'd been recovering from his amputation and Jenkins hadn't wanted to talk to him. The burns had left him unrecognizable.

"Two other men credit you with saving their lives that day. Being a hero doesn't mean you aren't scared. It means you do something to help even though you *are* scared."

Memories circled like carrion ready to take their pound of flesh. "I'll never feel like a hero," Emmett finally said.

"You don't have to, but people need heroes. They need to

believe in good and evil, right and wrong. The gray areas in between don't inspire others to want to be better. Do better."

"I don't want to be anyone's inspiration."

His dad let out a sigh. "I almost begged you not to go into the military."

Emmett raised his head. "What? Why?"

"Because you had a vision of service that was a mirage. Same way I did, and probably your granddad too. But, son, freedom needs warriors. Warriors to battle through the gray in between. I didn't say anything, because I knew you had the strength of character to understand the truth of that someday."

A question that had hammered at Emmett popped out. "What was the point?"

"What do you mean?"

"What was the point of my men's sacrifices? The defense of a pocket of land with no strategic worth?"

"I can't answer that, but all the threads weave together and connect in ways big and small. When just one of those threads are cut, it can all unravel. You don't know what sort of horrors you prevented with your patrols."

Although the words had the veneer of wisdom, Emmett would need to turn them over and examine them from every angle.

The mare tossed her head, gave a distressed whinny, and laid down on her side. A gush of fluid streamed over the hay.

"Her waters broke. We need more light." His dad's voice gained urgency.

Emmett grabbed the electric lantern Alfie had left hanging on the top of the stall. "What now?"

"Pray things go smoothly."

He knelt next to his dad in the straw. Daisy flicked her bound tail and gave another chesty groan. Alfie joined them and stood against the wall, a silent observer.

Ten minutes passed as they watched the birth sac ease out inch by inch with each agonized push.

His dad muttered a curse. "The foal is stuck with one leg in and one out."

"What do we do?" Emmett asked.

"We help her out." His dad looked over at him with a small smile. "Go wash up."

"Me? No. You or Alfie should do it." Although he'd watched a few births from afar over the years, he'd never gotten down and dirty.

"Come on, boy." Alfie gestured to the stall door. "I'll get you fixed up."

Emmett followed Alfie to the industrial sink in the corner, where he produced a medicinal-smelling harsh soap and scrub brush. Emmett cleaned his hands and nails and rinsed with almost scalding water.

Holding his hands up like he'd seen television doctors do, he reentered the stall and dropped to his knees. The impact sent nerves burning in his stump, but his discomfort was forgotten as he followed his dad's directions.

"Can you feel the leg?"

The leg was wet and slippery. It took three tries before Emmett got a grip on the spindly limb. "I've got it."

"Slow and gentle is key. A foal's legs are delicate at this point and you could break it if you aren't careful."

Sweat dripped off Emmett's forehead as he concentrated on easing the leg out. "Got it!"

As soon as the foal was aligned properly, Daisy bore down

again and the foal slipped halfway out, along with a flood of birth fluid that wet the knees of Emmett's pants. He scooted backward but stayed close.

His dad turned to Alfie. "Get us a towel, would you, Alfie?"

A brown towel was produced and his dad rubbed the birth sac away from the foal's mouth and head. The rest of the foal was birthed onto the straw with little more effort required from Daisy.

"What a beauty," his dad whispered. Checking its hindquarters, he grinned at Emmett. "A colt."

After rubbing the colt down, his dad backed away and Emmett followed. Daisy gathered herself to stand, the afterbirth yet to pass, to lick her newborn and nudge the colt to his belly. His gangly front legs splayed out in front of him.

Less than fifteen minutes later, the colt rose on shaky legs and went in search of milk. Tears stung Emmett's eyes. The scene was both common and a miracle. A common, everyday miracle. An oxymoron that made perfect sense in the moment. A swell of emotion filled his chest.

Being with Greer had dug a well inside of Emmett, but it was seeing the foal born that filled it with hope. Even after its hard entry into the world, the foal found the strength to rise on wobbly legs, and the exhausted mare welcomed him with licks and her milk. A new life had begun with Emmett's help.

Once the afterbirth was delivered, the three men replaced the messy straw with fresh and let mare and colt bond in peace.

"Everything will be all right now," Emmett's dad said.

Although Emmett knew his dad was referring to Daisy and her colt, the statement took on a bigger meaning in Emmett's psyche. Things would be all right. Not without obstacles or hardships or grief, but all right.

"You want a drink?" His dad clapped him on the shoulder.

Emmett's shirt and pants clung to him in a mixture of sweat and afterbirth. "What I really want is a shower."

"Come on up to the house. You still have some clothes stashed in your old bedroom."

Emmett and his dad strolled to the house, serenaded by the insects and with the stars putting on a show overhead.

He stopped his dad before they reached the porch. It was difficult to find the words. "I think I want to stick around."

"You tired? Your mom keeps a clean set of sheets on the bed."

He shook his head, frustrated at his own lack of clarity. "No. I mean stay in Madison and work on the farm. With you. If you still want me, that is."

His dad dropped his head back and looked to the sky, his voice thick with emotion. "Of course I still want you, but only if you're sure it's what you want."

"I wasn't sure until now."

"Don't let the high of seeing a foaling influence you. The days are usually more mundane. Full of hard work and even harder decisions."

Emmett had lived and worked on the farm in high school, so he had some idea, but as a teenager he'd been sheltered from the hard stuff. "Terrance came down this week with a job offer on base as a contractor overseeing special projects."

His dad whistled low. "It's more than you'll make here. Less work too. Why wouldn't you take it?"

"The army is my past. I'm ready to serve in other ways. You and Mom need me."

His dad ran a hand down his face. "We will manage fine. Don't give up a good opportunity for us."

"It's not just for you. It's for me too. I'm ready to settle down and plant roots."

"Does this have anything to do with Greer Hadley?" His dad's voice veered slightly suspicious.

"No." Emmett reexamined his feelings. "Maybe. I don't know what's going on with us, but she's been good for me. Doesn't take my crap and knows when to give me a good swift kick. Why don't you like her?"

"It's not that I don't like her. She's nice enough, and her parents are good people."

"Then what is it?"

"She's a dreamer. Unreliable. She's liable to take off and not look back. I don't want you to get your feelings hurt is all."

An initial guffaw at his dad's protectiveness faded as the realization swept over him: It was too late. Greer had already worked her way into his life and heart. He didn't know what—if anything—he meant to her. It could be he was her project or her rebound or just a way to pass some time, but his feelings were involved in a big way.

It didn't matter. Even if things ended in a relationship trauma unit, he would survive and be a better man because he'd known her. "You don't need to worry about me."

"I'll always worry about you. It's my most important job." His dad squeezed his arm and strolled up the porch steps.

Stunned, Emmett was slow to follow. He understood now. Finally. Although Emmett didn't agree with his dad's methods, he couldn't fault his heart. His dad had never been his adversary but his ally.

His mom fussed over them, relieved about the successful birth and ecstatic at the changed vibe between Emmett and his dad. Anything he could do to relieve her stress was a positive.

He checked his watch. Greer would be busy behind the bar, but he didn't mind. He'd hold down a barstool and watch her work until her shift ended. "I'm going to get cleaned up and head out, but I'll be back in the morning to start work."

"Start work?" Wrinkles deepened between his mom's eyes.

"Emmett is going to start helping out around here." It wasn't often his dad smiled, so the grin that spread over his face made an impression.

His mom gave a little gasp, her eyes shining. "That's wonderful. Just wonderful."

When she moved to hug Emmett, he held her off. "Unless you want to take a shower too, I'd hold off on the hugs."

He retreated to his old room and the connected bathroom. He stripped out of his clothes and pulled his prosthetic off, wiping it down. The hot shower loosened his stiff muscles and the stress over the difficult birth.

Cleaning up after hard, dirty work made him feel useful and accomplished. Sitting on his butt out at the cabin the last few months hadn't been healthy, physically or psychologically. If Greer hadn't marched out and dragged him back from the brink of his depression, would he still be sitting out there drinking himself to death? He wasn't confident he would have found the bravery to run the gauntlet of his fears without her shove.

He scrubbed himself clean, climbed out, and hopped by his dirty clothes to rifle through his dresser. It was filled with old high school T-shirts. He pulled on a blue one with his senior year printed on the pocket and the high school football team's tiger mascot on the back. It was tight but would have to do.

Pants were another matter altogether. His only choice was

a pair of cargo shorts that left his prosthetic exposed. As he found a pair of old tennis shoes, he put a nail on the coffin of the self-consciousness he'd wrestled with since losing his leg. His insecurities might not be buried yet, but they had one foot in the grave—so to speak.

He smiled. Greer would have thought that was funny. His leg was sore from the day's work, his limp more pronounced on his descent to the kitchen.

His mom greeted him with a hug and a plate of banana pudding. He devoured it and held his plate out like Oliver Twist for more.

"Tomorrow morning, we'll take that ride I promised you," his dad said. "I've got some ideas for the south pasture I'd like your opinion on."

"Sounds good." He checked his watch. "I'm going to head out."

His parents stood on their front porch and waved him off, illuminated in his rearview mirror until he hit the main road. He glanced at the guitar in his passenger seat. The road led him straight to Greer.

Chapter 18

"There is he?" Becky paced behind the bar and cast a glance up at the clock for the hundredth time.

Greer doled out another beer and took the cash, stuffing the extra into the tip jar for her and Edgar to split at the end of the night. The bar was hopping, but its failure to deliver live music after everyone had paid a cover charge was fueling an undercurrent of disappointment and aggression.

"At this point, you may have to give people their cover money back. I don't think this guy is going to show." Greer didn't know the musician Becky had hired for the night's gig.

"Is there anyone we can get over here on such short notice?" Becky asked.

Greer filled a glass with beer and passed it down the bar, making a note on the customer's tab. While she had connections, anyone she called now would never make it in time. "Not for tonight. I can make some calls and probably find someone for tomorrow night, though."

"What a nightmare," Becky muttered and continued her pacing.

A set of broad shoulders caught Greer's attention. Her heart danced the cancan, and her huge smile made her feel goofy. Still, she didn't take her eyes off him as she sidled down the bar in his direction, filling two orders along the way.

"Hey, big guy. What's your poison? It's on me."

"Surprise me with something on tap. Just one, though."

"Drinking is kind of the point of coming to Becky's. It's not known for its ambience." Teasing Emmett was her new favorite pastime.

"I'm here because you're here." Although a smile tipped his lips, his blue-eyed gaze pierced with a sharp truth that both thrilled and terrified her. "Have you talked to your mom about a sleepover yet?"

His T-shirt was tight across his shoulders and chest . . . and well, everywhere. His hair was damp and rumpled in a sexy-messy kind of way. It was a ridiculously good look for him.

"I might have mentioned my need for more freedom since I'm technically a grown-up."

"I'd say thirty qualifies."

"Most of the time I feel like I don't know anything about life, but then, I saw eighteen-year-old baby-faced kids today on campus at the community college and realized I've lived a lifetime."

He perked up. "What were you doing on campus?"

"Registering for the summer semester."

"Way to go." His smile was a combination of I-told-you-so and pride.

Filling drink orders pulled her away from him, but every time she glanced in his direction—which was every five seconds or so—he was watching her in a way that made her overfill a glass of beer and bobble a bottle of gin. It shouldn't matter what he thought, but somewhere along the way, it had started to matter. *He* mattered.

When she weaved her way back to his end of the bar, he asked, "The flyers advertised live music. What's the holdup?"

"The dude never showed. Becky is beside herself. She charged a cover for the first time tonight."

Becky joined her at the bar. "This is a nightmare. I can't think of any other option than to . . ." Her head tilted and her eyes narrowed on Greer. "You could play."

"No." A cold wave of panic flooded Greer, tingling her fingers.

Becky gasped and took hold of her hands. "Why didn't I think of this before? You have the experience. You could do it. Will you?"

"I can't. I don't have my guitar."

"I happen to have a guitar in the truck." Emmett thumbed over his shoulder.

If Becky didn't have hold of her hands, Greer would have catapulted across the bar top to slap a hand over Emmett's mouth. "Isn't that convenient," she said caustically.

"It certainly seems fated." Emmett shrugged.

Becky's voice was begging. "I'll cover the bar and pay you for the set and a bonus too."

"I can't. You don't understand."

"Please, Greer." The lines around Becky's mouth and eyes were cut deep with worry. She was independent, decisive, and not used to having to ask for favors. She'd also taken a chance on Greer when she'd been at her lowest.

Her instinct to say no and stay safe warred with her desire not to disappoint anyone else in her life. The room was filled with regular people, not record executives. Her performance meant nothing. Except it felt like she was facing a jury ready to hand down a death sentence.

Emmett leaned over the bar and took her hand. His was strong and warm and alive while hers felt like a dead fish hanging from her arm. How was she supposed to play a guitar when she couldn't feel her fingers?

"You can do this. Trust me." A tiny portion of his confidence transferred to her.

Enough to have her whispering, "Okay. I'll try."

"Yes!" Becky did a fist pump and wasted no time in dragging Greer from behind the bar by her upper arm and parting the crowd with a hollered, "Coming through, people!"

She pushed Greer toward the simple wooden stool sitting behind a microphone stand and scooted behind the lights and soundboard in the corner. The lights came on in a blaze, blinding Greer. What was once a familiar spot felt foreign.

No way could she do it. But before she could take a step back into the shadows, Emmett was there with a guitar.

"I want to leave." She clutched his arm.

Emmett's broad shoulders blocked the glaring lights. He was a mountain she wanted to shelter beside. "If you want to leave, I'll get you out. But you can do this, Greer."

"I've run away or messed up everything in my life."

"Not true and you know it. Look at me."

She squinted, looking for a lifeline in his eyes.

His lips tipped into a smile she couldn't return because her mouth was so dry. "My legs. Check out my legs."

She dropped her gaze. He wore shorts, his prosthetic visible. Through the dread and tension, she found an answering smile. "You've got a nice set of gams there, Emmett."

"Thank you." He leaned closer and touched his forehead to hers. The restless, impatient audience disappeared. "You dragged me back to the land of the living. Let me be here for you."

He straightened and when she would have followed him to stay close, the hard body of the guitar came between them.

She took hold of the neck instinctively. Her finger glanced over a small notch near the third fret. Her attention snapped from him to her guitar. *Her* Martin. She ran her other hand over the flower-tooled strap before looping it over her head. She slipped the body up and tapped Dolly's signature.

"Where? How?" Words deserted her. She hugged the guitar. It was like being reunited with a loved one after a tragedy.

"A million pawnshops later . . ." He made a sweeping gesture.

"You did that? For me?"

He tucked a lock of hair that had come free of her ponytail behind her ear. "I would do a lot more than brave a few seedy pawnshops for you."

She wanted to grab his T-shirt and drag him to her for a kiss. Confess what was written on her heart. But a *whoop-whoop* from the crowd and a few yells to "get the show on the road" broke the illusion that only the two of them existed.

All she could do was nod at him and slip onto the stool, her guitar settling into her lap naturally. She strummed and adjusted the tuning before shifting her attention to the microphone and the audience.

She flipped the switch and leaned close. "Everybody doing all right out there?"

Her voice reverberated and a cheer went up from the crowd. Her gaze found Emmett, standing to the side where the light faded, his shoulder propped against the wall, his arms folded over his chest like he was guarding her. And wasn't he? Not physically, perhaps, but protecting her heart and soul while still encouraging her to fly?

Closing her eyes, she launched into "Crazy On You," a classic Heart song, up-tempo and rocking. When she heard the lyrics ricocheting back at her from the crowd, she opened her eyes. People were dancing and tapping their feet. No one was judging her and finding her lacking. Their enjoyment in turn relaxed her.

Her ability to read crowds hadn't faded over the months she'd been out of the spotlight. This crowd wanted familiar songs they could sing along to. The songs flowed as if released from a dam, flooding her insecurities and reminding her how fun performing could be when the crowd was into it.

An hour and a half later with her voice sore and her shirt clinging to her back with sweat, she announced a break. "Make sure you tip your bartenders well."

The crowd moved like a flock from the dance floor toward the bar while she made like a homing pigeon for Emmett.

He handed her an ice water and she killed it. He turned to the small table behind him and handed her another one. Her thirst appeased but not satisfied, she sipped.

"You were fantastic. How'd it feel to perform again?" he asked.

"Scary at first, but I loosened up. Not sure how much more my voice can handle, though. I'm out of practice."

"Damn, I'm proud of you."

Tears rushed to her eyes and before she questioned herself, she nestled into his chest and wrapped her arms around his waist. Rubbing her tears into the soft cotton of his T-shirt, she mumbled, "Sorry I'm a sweaty, gross mess."

"I don't mind." He laid a kiss on her temple. "You should have seen me earlier. I was a walking biohazard."

"What happened?"

"Helped Dad with a difficult foaling at the farm."

She pulled back, studying him. "Was that good?"

"It was terrifying and exciting and cathartic. So, yeah, I'd say it was good." He'd gained a new peace and it looked good on him.

"You talked to your dad."

Surprise had his eyebrows popping up. "How'd you guess?"

"You seem lighter. Less restless. Dare I even say happier?"

"Seems like today has been a big day for both of us." His smile spoke of conversations they would have later.

Fear sped through her like the first tremor of a massive earthquake. He'd made a decision about the job offer from Fort Knox. Had he taken it?

Becky bustled over, a grin on her face. "My God, you were incredible. Everyone is raving. Are you good for another set?"

She cleared her throat. She would need a gallon of honey tea in the morning. "A short one."

Becky clapped with the excitement of a five-year-old being promised ice cream. She handed a slip of paper over. "Requests if you know them."

They were all bar standards. Lighthearted and easy. Greer looked up and nodded, but Becky had disappeared back behind the bar.

"I guess I'd better earn my keep." She held up the paper and turned away. Stopping halfway to the stage, she turned back. "Will you still be here when I'm finished?"

"Do you want me to be?" No tease lightened his voice or expression, and the question didn't seem a simple one.

She didn't hesitate even a millisecond. "Yes."

"Then, I will be."

She nodded, her throat so tight she wasn't sure how she was supposed to sing. Men like Emmett were throwbacks to another age. Even his months of isolation and wallowing at the cabin couldn't hide his true nature: trustworthy and honorable. Whether he wanted to accept it or not, he *was* a hero. Better than saving her, he'd given her the courage to save herself.

She slid onto her stool and set the list of good-time bar songs aside. She would sing those songs and make the crowd happy, but first, she needed to sing a song for herself. And for Emmett.

She squinted against the colored lights shining up from the floor and searched the crowd. She didn't see him, but he was out there. She knew because he'd told her he would be. He was a man who stuck.

She mindlessly strummed a chord and then another before the song registered in her ear. It was her song. The one she'd played at her high school talent show so many years ago. Her come-out. Written when she was too young to understand heartbreak, the lyrics took on new meaning a decade and more later. She didn't fight the compulsion to flay herself open and bleed out on the bar floor. That's what good songwriters did.

The last plaintive note faded. The silence was only heartbeats long, but in that time, her chest swelled. Applause thundered like a wave through the room, whoops and hollers cresting above it like whitecaps.

Moments like this reminded her why she wrote and performed from the heart. And this moment was enough. She didn't need the adoration of millions. She needed only to touch the hearts of those within her reach.

"That was called 'Lost Souls.' And I wrote it a long time

ago." More whoops had her smiling. "Now, how about we kick it up a notch."

She launched into the list of requests, still riding a high. The set wrapped with the classic "Friends in Low Places" by Garth Brooks. Everyone had their arms thrown around someone's shoulders and were belting it out in a cacophony of mismatched pitches and rhythms.

Greer smiled when the two men who had nearly come to blows earlier exchanged a high five. She'd taken a frustrated crowd and turned them into good-natured, love-thy-neighbor putty. As the last note faded, the stage lights turned off and the overhead lights came on, the starkness sobering. It was like taking off beer goggles the regretful morning after.

The crowd quieted and shuffled out the door and into the parking lot. Greer packed up her guitar, running a hand down the strings. She'd thought the day she'd sold the Martin had been her lowest. If only she'd known how much farther she had to fall, but how sweet the climb would be.

She snapped the case's lid closed and picked it up, the familiar weight a comfort beyond measure. Talking to Becky at the bar, Emmett leaned against a stool, his legs crossed at the ankle, his prosthetic on top. It was part of him but didn't define him. Not by a long shot.

As if his senses were still honed from the battlefield, he turned and watched her approach. The fluorescent overhead lights threw his face into a mixture of shadows and relief, sharpening the blade of his nose and cheekbones. His lashes cast dark crescents and hid the expression in his eyes.

"Ready to head out?" he asked.

"I need to help clean up." Her voice was hoarse.

Becky threw a rag over her shoulder. "No, you don't. Head on out."

"I'll leave your half of the tips with Becky," Edgar said with a smile. "Great job, by the way."

"Thanks, but I didn't earn the tips. You and Becky did all the work. Buy something for that baby of yours."

Edgar shook his head and set his chin. "No way."

"Yes way. I insist. I'm getting paid to play, right, Becky?"

"Of course. You want a regular gig?"

Her breath caught before a grin broke out. "I would love one. I can still bartend, though, right? I'll need the extra money for school."

"Sure thing, sweets." Becky pulled out a pack of cigarettes and tapped them on her palm with the ease of a lifelong smoker no amount of public-service messages would dissuade. "Now if you'll excuse me, I need my fix."

Emmett got up, stuck his hands in his pockets, and nudged his head toward the door. They fell into step shoulder to shoulder. The air retained the heat of the day even at midnight, but it was clear and the stars blinked in the sky like they were communicating in Morse code.

"Can I carry that for you?" He glanced down at her guitar.

She tightened her hand on the handle. "Honestly, I don't want to let go of it. I might even sleep with it tonight."

"That's a shame. Here I was hoping you would sleep with me tonight." The honeyed tease in his voice made her heart pump faster, and it felt as if the same honey had invaded her veins, sugaring her limbs.

"I might be persuaded to leave it next to the nightstand."

"I'll put it right next to my leg."

She couldn't help but laugh. "I can't tell you what it means to have her back. Thank you."

He took her free hand in his and pressed a kiss on her fingers. "You would have eventually gone to buy it back."

But she wouldn't have. Without him, she would have missed the guitar the rest of her life. His gift had mended her soul, and in return, she had given Emmett something even if he chose not to recognize or take it—her heart.

It was crazy. She'd thought Beau had broken her heart, but he hadn't. It had been performing that had done the damage. Once she'd rediscovered the joy in music with Ally, her heart had emerged from exile, whole and beating and ready.

Beau was a stranger. She'd loved the idea of him and what he represented. Emmett was a friend and a lover and she loved every obstinate, funny, sweet part of him. They were starting new chapters in their lives. Was it best to turn to a blank page?

Maybe, but not tonight. Tonight she would love him without words.

"My place?" he asked.

"Definitely. My mom is on board with not checking up on me at all hours, but even she would freak out if you were in my bedroom come sunrise."

He threw his head back and laughed. No sarcasm or irony weighed the sound. Unable to help herself, she stepped in front of him, wrapped her free hand around his nape, and pulled him down for a kiss.

When their lips separated an inch, he whispered, "What was that for?"

"That was for being an amazing person, Emmett Lawson."

"Why, Greer Hadley, you're going to make me blush." His

put-on Southern belle accent had her giving a breathy laugh before pulling him in for another kiss.

They separated like two magnets being forced apart, and she followed Emmett's truck to the gate he now left unlocked. As soon as they met at the foot of the porch steps, their bodies reached for each other. This time humor replaced their awkward fumbling, but the urgency was still there, driving them hard.

It wasn't until she was cuddled into him, her head on his shoulder, that sadness had room to grow. She would miss this. Miss him.

"You made a decision about the Fort Knox job, haven't you?" she asked.

"How'd you know?" He yawned, his breath stirring the hair at her temple.

"You're not fighting the current anymore." She clutched him closer but knew when the time came, she would let him go. Not without heartbreak, but without regrets. She wouldn't be his anchor.

He grunted. "I'm going to turn it down."

His announcement pulled the pin of a grenade in her chest. She rose on her elbow. His eyes were heavy-lidded with exhaustion, but he looked content and, dare she say, *happy*?

"What are you going to do instead?" she asked through a tight throat.

"Work the farm. Dad is going to retire someday, and Mom deserves a vacation whenever she wants." Worry crinkled his eyes.

She smoothed her hand over his forehead and into his hair. "You're staying out of family obligation?"

"Partly. But mostly I'm staying because I forgot how joyful the work can be. There will be hard days and lots to learn, but helping that colt into the world and watching him rise even after everything he'd been through was amazing. I'll never forget it."

"You're staying in Madison." She stated the obvious because it felt like a dream.

"Yep."

"What does that mean for us?"

"What do you want it to mean?"

Dammit, why did he have to lob the hot potato back to her? "Did you recognize the song I sang?"

His smile unfolded slowly, lazily. "It sounded like the one you sang at the talent show, but different somehow."

"I hadn't lived with heartbreak and love back then. Now I have. That song was for you, Emmett."

"I felt every word in my bones."

The grenade detonated and she buried her face in his neck so he wouldn't see the messy aftermath. "Oh God, why do you have to be so nice?"

He rolled her onto her back, looming over her, his residual limb between her knees, the weight of his thigh holding her in place. "You must be punch drunk with exhaustion. I'm not nice, sweetheart."

"True enough. You can be arrogant and rude and domineering and kind of an asshole on occasion."

His barking laugh contained plenty of sarcastic self-deprecation this time. "You make me sound like such a catch."

"I can be flaky and stubborn and let my anger get the best of me too often," she added.

"What you're saying is neither one of us is perfect."

"I should have said that you're perfect for me." Seeing his

eyes widen and his mouth part, she realized she'd said too much and launched into a babbling backtrack. "I mean, not *perfect* perfect. Just sort of great. Let's go to sleep."

Hopefully, she'd die peacefully in her sleep and not have to deal with the embarrassment of facing him in the light of the morning.

"Hold up. You can't expect me to sleep after you tell me I'm perfect for you." His voice was rife with laughter.

She huffed. "I said no such thing. In fact, my point was that you aren't perfect in the least, you're just—"

His breath warmed her mouth a heartbeat before his lips took hers in a kiss so sweet it made her ache like her entire body was a tooth and he was a vat of sugar. She grabbed him and held him close despite her mortification.

With his lips still pressed against hers, he whispered, "I think you're perfect too, wild woman."

She felt the words as much as heard them. Felt them in her bones the same way he'd felt her song.

This time the sex was slow and sweet, her body handling the intricacies of a love she wasn't quite brave enough to declare. She fell into a deep sleep, not plagued with worry for the first time in months.

Sun poured onto the bed, and Greer stretched under the covers, bolting upright when she realized she was alone and Emmett's prosthetic was gone from where it had guarded her guitar as promised. She listened but heard nothing coming from the other room.

Grabbing up her clothes, she hightailed it into the bathroom and grimaced at her bedhead and the circles under her eyes.

Late nights used to not sap her energy like this. A blush kindled and spread like her body was dry tinder. Her exhaustion might have more to do with the life-affirming sex that had kept them up until the wee hours.

Dressing in her clothes from the night before, she made a note to at least stash some clean panties in one of his drawers. No sign of Emmett in the cabin and his truck was gone. She was alone.

She banished the ghosts of insecurities taking shape and wandered into the kitchen in search of coffee before she slunk home to her parents. Even though she and her mother had come to an understanding, it was still going to be weird to look her in the eye and know that *she* knew where Greer had been and could take a good guess at what she'd been doing. Or *who* she'd been doing.

The coffee in the pot was still hot and a note with her name on it sat propped on a mug.

Sorry to leave you, but I promised to help my dad.

Hang out as long as you want.

Lunch later?

E

She dropped the paper, poured a cup of coffee, and padded barefoot to the porch. Lounging in a patch of sun, Bonnie lifted her head and gave her a sleepy blink. Her food and water dishes were full.

The cabin was peaceful, starkly different from her last grungy apartment in Nashville. The sounds of nature drifted on the breeze, musical in their own way. She leaned against the porch post and let the sun dance behind her closed eyes. As a kid, she'd lie out in the yard and pretend the sun sparks were cameras going off after she'd killed it onstage.

She smiled, picturing her younger self and the innocence of her dreams. No pang of sadness or regret marred the memory. Her priorities had shifted from fanciful to concrete. Now that she'd gotten a taste of helping people, she was addicted.

Her path forward had become clear and wide open. She would work her schedule so she could still volunteer at the Music Tree Foundation a few hours a week, and she could continue to write music and play at Becky's while she earned her degree.

The only worry marring her contentment was Ally. Maybe by the time they met again, Greer would have had a revelation. But for now, she had her own personal revelation to meet for lunch.

Chapter 19

By the time Tuesday rolled around, Greer was a mass of excitement and nerves. Thankfully, the Music Tree Foundation had become a comfortable place. She exchanged greetings and chitchat about the streak of unusually hot days with another volunteer before making her way to Amelia's office.

Amelia looked up when she walked in, a question in the wrinkled set of her brow. "Have you made a decision about continuing?"

"Yeah. I want to keep volunteering if you're willing to schedule around my classes, but I'm committed to making it work. Surprised?"

"A little. You've never struck me as the sort to settle down or commit to anything."

Greer's pursuit of music had been inherently selfish and for a long time, the music had been enough for her. It was only now that she'd formed connections that she understood what had been missing.

She shrugged. "Things change. People grow up. It took me a little longer than some."

"Would this have anything to do with Emmett Lawson? A little birdie told me you and he looked pretty cozy at Becky's this weekend." A tease made Amelia's eyes sparkle, and Greer realized with a start that Amelia had turned into an honest-to-goodness friend.

"I suppose I should thank you for your personal cowardice in sending me out to help him." Greer ended her eye roll by giving Amelia a smile.

"Ha! I knew it." Her mouth tightened but her voice retained a lightheartedness. "The man is wild. He nearly shot at you, for goodness sake, which makes him the perfect kind of crazy for you."

"He's definitely my kind of crazy." Greer bit the inside of her mouth. "I wasn't too enthusiastic when Uncle Bill assigned me hours here."

"Yeah, I noticed," Amelia said dryly.

"Volunteering here has been . . . life-changing." It sounded melodramatic and trite, but it was the truth. "So, you know, thanks." She mumbled the last, the burn in her face signaling her extreme embarrassment.

Amelia's voice grew softer. "People don't understand that the volunteer gets as much out of it as the client. There's a happiness to be found helping others. I'm lucky to have found my calling early."

Emotion ripened in the room. Greer blinked back tears. It was too much. She had to pull herself together before she met with Ally. "God, no wonder Uncle Bill likes you more."

A laugh burst out of Amelia. "My killer potato salad won him over."

"He is a potato salad connoisseur." Greer glanced at the

clock and stuck her head out the door to check the hallway. Ally should have come in by now.

"What's wrong?" Amelia asked.

"Ally's late." Greer checked their usual room in case Ally had somehow slipped by. It was empty. Dread crept up her spine like a tour group stampeding across her grave.

Greer paced while she waited. Teenagers possessed an unreliable internal clock. Ally had likely gotten distracted and didn't realize the time. Thirty minutes passed. The cement block walls pressed in on her, and she retreated to wait outside. Heat wavered off the black tarmac of the streets. The few people out scurried from car to building and back again without lingering in the scalding sun.

Greer paced in the shade of a tree. What if Ally had been kidnapped or was lying in a ditch somewhere? Despite the heat, a chill raised goose bumps on her arms. She was overreacting. How many people actually ended up in a ditch? Probably not enough to register statistically on a list of things that could happen to wayward teenagers.

Greer had been a wayward teenager once. Thinking she was following in the footsteps of great musicians, she'd smoked cigarettes and pot and made poor decisions. She'd been dumb, but Ally was smart.

Except she had shoplifted and gotten caught. She hadn't done it selfishly or to rebel, but to do something nice for her mother. Moving to the parking lot, Greer tossed her purse into the passenger seat, slid into the oven of her car, and headed toward Ally's house.

After a wrong turn sent her down a street that had her locking the doors, she found Ally's duplex and parked at the curb. A knock on the door yielded no response. She sidled behind an overgrown bush, its twigs tangling in her hair, cupped her hands, and looked through the window. The interior was dim, with no signs of life.

What now? Why hadn't she ever thought to get Ally's number?

Pulling out her phone, she texted Amelia and asked if the files contained a number for Ally or Karen. While she waited, she backed down the walk, keeping her eyes on the front door as if Ally might pop out.

"Hello there, young lady." A black woman had emerged from the duplex next door with a watering can. Her front stoop was overrun with hanging boxes full of colorful flowers along the rails. "Can I help you with something?"

Greer crossed the sparse grass of the yard. The woman's white hair and barely lined face put her anywhere from sixty to a hundred years old, but based on the stoop of her shoulders, Greer guessed she was at least eighty.

"Your flowers are lovely." Greer hoped her smile read as reassuring and trustworthy. "I'm looking for Ally Martinez. Your young neighbor. She missed an appointment with me after school."

The woman pursed her lips and emitted mild disapproval. "She's a nice enough girl. Helped get my groceries up the steps a few times. But that mother . . ."

"She recently lost her husband. He died serving in the military."

Pity tempered the woman's expression. "I didn't know. Neither of them mentioned it."

"It's still raw." Greer didn't add that it was the pity Ally tried to avoid. Her experience with Emmett had taught her that. "No one seems to be at home, but I was under the impression Karen was between jobs. Anything unusual go on over there today?"

"Shenanigans were going on not an hour past. Mother and child in a screaming match. I was ready to call the authorities, but they both disappeared and all fell quiet."

"Any idea where they disappeared to?"

"None, dear. I'm sorry."

"That's okay. You've been a help. At least I know she made it home from school." Greer gave the lady a wave and retreated to her car.

Her options were limited. Driving the streets would be the equivalent of a Where's Waldo game. Even if Amelia came through with a number, Ally might not reply.

She had dinner plans with Emmett. Leave or stay? A web of indecision stymied her, and she drummed her thumbs on the steering wheel, waiting for something to happen to break the stalemate in her head.

Her phone dinged. She fumbled to unlock her screen. It was Amelia and the text was simply a name and phone number. God bless the woman and their burgeoning friendship.

Greer pressed the number but got Ally's voicemail. She left a brief message, knowing Ally might not even check. Greer typed out a long text explaining her every worry, but backspaced before she was foolish enough to hit *send.*

Missed you at the foundation. Everything okay?

The reply came fast and was disappointing. *Y*

Her thumbs hovered before typing out, *Went by your place. Need help?*

Greer roasted for ten minutes waiting for a reply that never came. She let out a groan and banged her head against the seat. There was nothing else she could do unless Ally reached out to her. She headed back to Madison with a sense of uneasiness.

Emmett was waiting for her on the porch with an ice-cold beer. She took it and killed half in one go.

"Rough day?" His smile had lost most of its bitterness with life.

She walked into his chest and notched her head against his shoulder. His scent was fresh in the stagnant air. She needed a shower after sweating on her trek around Nashville, but she needed his steady advice even more. "Ally was a no-show. According to their neighbor, Ally and her mom got into a huge fight then disappeared. Not sure if they are together, though. It feels like something is wrong."

"Did you text or call her?"

"Both. She texted that she was okay."

"You don't believe her?"

"No, but I have no clue where she is."

"Unless you want to stake out her place, you'll have to wait until she's ready to talk about it."

"But I want to help." She let her head fall back to look in his eyes. What she saw made her heart double Dutch. Tenderness and regret and love.

"I know. She's got to want help, though."

"You didn't want help."

"True. But you knew where I lived and wouldn't leave me alone even after I threatened to shoot you."

"So you're saying I *should* stake out her place."

"No. Maybe?" He ran a hand through his hair and gave a little laugh. "Hell, I don't know. Your methods did work for me."

She stepped out of his arms. "I'm going to hop in the shower."

"Casserole still has twenty minutes so take your time."

She took her beer and retreated to his bathroom to let the

water wash some of her tension away. Her request to store underwear at the cabin had turned into him cleaning out an entire
drawer in his dresser for her use. Unpacking an assortment of
clothes and toiletries had felt like a giant leap for mankind. Or
at least her-kind.

The *ding* of her phone echoed against the tile. Not bothering
with a towel, she dripped onto the floor and read the text from
Ally.

Can you come get us pls?

Of course. Where?

Somewhere on Cuthburt.

Cuthburt Road was no place for Ally or her mom. *ETA is
45 min. Are you somewhere safe?*

Greer clutched her phone tight at the pause.

I think so. A little girl's fear vibrated through the words and
infected Greer.

*On my way. Hold tight. Call the police if something changes.
Hurry*

She opened the bathroom door and rushed out. "Emmett!"

The screen door banged shut behind Emmett. He whistled
low. "Unless you're in the mood for a quickie, I'll have to turn
the oven off."

Greer yelped and held an arm over her breasts even though
his eyes and her body were well acquainted. She scampered to
his room and grabbed clothes from her drawer, struggling to get
them on her damp body. She wished she had something more
badass to wear than shorts and a tank top. She needed a leather
jacket and steel-toe boots.

"Ally texted back." She handed over her phone to let him
read while she combed her hair and squeezed out the excess
water. "I've got to go get her."

"*We've* got to go get her."

She looked up from tying her tennis shoes. "You don't even know Ally."

"You care about Ally. I care about you. Ergo, I care about Ally."

She stepped to him, let out a huff, grabbed his shirt, and planted a hard kiss on his lips. "Thank you," she murmured against his mouth.

Emmett turned off the oven while she waited at the door, shifting on her feet. He hesitated before performing an about-face to unlock a drawer in a writing desk tucked into the corner. A matte black gun appeared in his hand before getting tucked into the waistband of his pants.

The situation shaded darker with danger. "Is that really necessary?"

"Cuthburt? Unless it's been cleaned up, then yeah, it is."

They took her car, but Emmett drove. She was too distracted with her worry. She sent Ally texts along the way, updating her with their ETA.

When they were within sight of the tall buildings of downtown, Ally quit replying. Greer sent another text. And another. No response.

"She's not texting me back." Greer tapped her phone on her knee and sat forward. "Can you go faster?"

"I'm not risking getting pulled over considering I have a gun in my pants." He covered her hand jiggling the phone with his. The contact settled her nerves. "Don't worry. We'll find her."

Finally, after what felt like forever but was closer to ten minutes, they turned onto Cuthburt. The streetlights were blinking on in the gloaming, the buildings already throwing portions of the street in deep shadows.

She texted Ally again. *We're here. Where are you?*

Nothing. Greer prayed the lack of response was due to nothing more serious than a dead phone battery.

"Any suggestions on our next move?" she asked.

"Get out and look around?" Emmett pulled onto a side street and parked at the curb, the lack of lighting inviting an enterprising thief to break into her car. Not that there was much to steal.

They walked shoulder to shoulder on the sidewalk, dodging a garbage bag emitting a pungent rotting-meat smell. Trash gathered in corners against stoops as if the street itself had given up. After walking down one side of the street, they crossed to the other to trek back. She tried Ally again, texting and calling, but her voicemail picked up.

"This is crazy. Do we start hollering her name?" She threw her hands up.

"Let's ask first." Emmett nudged his chin toward a rowdy group of men gathered on the stairs leading up to one of the apartment buildings. As they grew closer, the group came into focus as mostly teenagers.

Emmett stepped closer. "Hey, guys."

A lanky, dark-skinned boy who hadn't quite grown into his over-six-foot frame returned Emmett's greeting with a simple raising of his chin. He eyed them both with suspicion.

"You lost, man?" the boy asked in a voice that cracked slightly, putting him even younger than Greer had first thought.

"Not lost but looking for someone."

"You a cop?" The group had quieted and a palpable tension thickened the air.

Greer notched between Emmett and the boys. "Not cops. My friend needs a ride. She told me she was around here but she's not answering her phone. She's about your age, white and kind of Goth-looking. Her name's Ally. Have you seen her?"

The boy in front exchanged a glance with someone behind him. A more mature-looking boy stood at the top of the stoop. "You Greer?"

"Yes. Greer. That's me." She took a step toward him.

"Your girl's in here."

"Thank you," Greer murmured over and over as the boys on the stairs parted to let her and Emmett through.

The single bulb lighting the interior seemed to be on its last watts. The boy led them past the stairs and down the hall to a door at the end. In a low voice, he said, "I was letting them crash until her mom sobered up, but she's pretty messed up."

"Drugs or alcohol?"

The boy only shrugged and toed the door open wider. Greer shuffled over the threshold into a cozy room full of shabby, mismatched furniture. Ally sat on the floor next to where her mom was passed out on the couch.

"Ally," Greer whispered, crouching next to her.

Ally turned, her dark eyeliner and mascara smudged, her eyes huge. Greer hesitated, worried about Ally's prickly, independent nature, but when her chin wobbled, Greer pulled the girl into a tight hug. She was stiff for a few heartbeats until surrendering. Her arms came around Greer and sobs wracked her body.

Greer rocked her back and forth like she would a toddler, shushing her and whispering words of comfort. Emmett came to the arm of the couch and checked Karen's pulse, but when he tried to lift her eyelids, Ally swung away from Greer and swatted his hand away.

"Get away from her." Ally popped up and shoved Emmett,

who stumbled back a few steps before catching his balance. Greer tried to pull her back around, but Ally's focus was on the perceived danger.

"This is Emmett Lawson," Greer said. "I've mentioned him in our sessions, remember? He's my friend and here to help."

"You're not a doctor." Ally narrowed her eyes.

"No, but I went through basic medic training in the army. May I?"

Ally stared at him as if she could ferret out his motivations. Finally, she curled in on herself and in a defeated voice said, "Whatever."

Emmett squatted next to the couch, a little off-balance with his prosthetic leg stretched out to the side.

"What's wrong with your leg?" Ally's voice was flat and distant and strangely conversational.

"Got injured in an ambush. Lost it." He pulled his pants up enough to reveal his prosthetic.

"Sorry about that." After a pause, she said in a quiet voice, "My dad was in the army. He was killed last fall."

"I'm sorry. Too many good men don't come home." Emmett didn't force-feed her pity, only understanding. "What was his name?"

"Javier Martinez."

Emmett froze with his phone halfway out of his pocket. His face had blanched except for two red streaks across his cheeks. He looked like he might throw up.

Greer put her hand on his shoulder and stared up into his eyes. Devastation reflected back. "Everything okay?" she whispered.

He took a deep breath and transferred his attention back

to Karen. She noted his non-answer. Everything was far from okay. With a noticeable tremble, he turned on his flashlight app and shined it into her eyes while lifting her eyelids one by one.

"Ally. What did your mom take?" Emmett wiped his suddenly sweaty face on his shoulder. He was leaning hard into the arm of the couch.

"Sit down, Emmett." Greer pointed to an armchair bearing the permanent impression of its owner. He didn't argue, but took a seat and dropped his head toward his knees.

With worry bearing down on them, Greer snaked an arm around Ally's shoulders. "Any idea what sort of drugs she usually takes?"

Ally stiffened. "She's not a druggie."

"She's a woman who needs help. Let us help her," Greer said.

After a pause, Ally seemed to collapse into herself, her shoulders hunched. "Painkillers. Xanax. Not sure what else."

"Pills, then?"

Ally took a swipe at her running nose like a toddler. "I did something bad."

"What?" Greer asked.

"I took the pills she had stashed and flushed them. I knew she didn't have the money for more. I thought—hoped—things would go back to normal, but it got worse."

"She went into withdrawal." Emmett's statement jolted Greer. It had been more dire than she'd imagined.

"She's been antsy and paranoid, but today was really bad. I skipped school to take care of her. Exams are over anyway. She took off to score what she needed. I tried to stop her." Ally's wobbling chin almost got the best of her, but she took a shuddery breath and continued. "I got Miles to help me find her. He knows where this kind of stuff goes down. We found her wandering around. She was high but able to talk to us and stuff, but then she sort of passed out as soon as we got her in here."

Emmett levered himself up, looking shaky but with more color in his face. "Her breathing and heart rate seem normal, but her eyes are dilated and she's unresponsive. We should call 911."

A tear streaked the black liner under Ally's eye, muting it like a watercolor. "No! She's just passed out. She wouldn't want me to call an ambulance."

Emmett hesitated as if he was preparing to launch an argument. Instead, he said, "Fine. No ambulance, but we're taking her to the hospital."

Without letting Ally mount another protest, Emmett tucked his arms under Karen's neck and knees and cradled her to his chest. He limped to the door. Greer herded Ally after him. The boy from the stoop stood waiting against the far wall, the tip of his cigarette casting a faint glow. He moved forward.

"Thanks, Miles." Ally kept her head down and her shoulders hunched. A note of embarrassment weaved through her fear and worry.

Emmett and Ally shuffled toward the exit. Miles slipped by her to the small apartment, but Greer grabbed his hand before he could disappear. "Thank you for keeping them safe."

"She going to be okay?" he asked low enough for Ally not to hear.

Greer wasn't sure if he was more worried about Ally or her mom. "I hope so. We're going to take her to the hospital."

Miles bit his lip, his gaze skating to the carpet. "Tell Ally I'll see her around. I won't tell or nothing."

The boy knew Ally well enough to know her weakness and her strength was her pride. Greer stopped herself from giving the boy a hug. Barely. She caught up with Emmett and Ally. He took the steps one at a time, his limp more pronounced once he hit the sidewalk and headed to the car.

Once Emmett had Karen loaded into the backseat, he pressed the keys into Greer's hand. The nearest hospital wasn't more than ten minutes away even with the lights to navigate. Once she had pulled out on the main road, she checked on Karen and Ally in the backseat—situation unchanged—then tossed a glance Emmett's way before the light turned green.

"How's your leg?" she asked even though he was rubbing his thigh.

"Hurts."

Ally scooted and poked her head between the two front seats, her elbows resting on top of the seats. "At least you came home. None of this would have happened if Dad hadn't died."

Emmett sank down in the seat, covered his mouth, and shifted toward the window. More than his leg was bothering him, but Greer didn't have the emotional energy to devote to Emmett at the moment. She pulled into the circular drive of the hospital's ER entrance, left the car idling, and ran through the automatic doors to snag the nearest person in scrubs.

"I have a woman who's possibly overdosed out in my car. She's unconscious, but her breathing is normal." Her words stumbled over one another in the rush to get out.

The woman's expression remained impassive, but she directed a young man outside with a gurney. No one was moving as quickly as Greer wanted.

After some tense moments when the doctor questioned Ally and Greer about what Karen might have ingested, Karen was wheeled into a room and Ally and Greer banished while she was evaluated.

Greer walked Ally to a seat. "Can I get you something? A Coke? Coffee?"

Ally sat down, leaned her head back against the wall, and closed her eyes. "No, thanks."

Greer hovered and watched her until it started feeling weird. She turned away and scanned the waiting area. No sign of Emmett. A shot of panic had her run-walking through the automatic doors. Her car was gone. The red and blue from the ER sign cast eerie light around her.

A man approached from the shadowy parking lot, his gait uneven. She let out a breath and met him halfway, walking straight into his chest.

"I thought you'd driven off and left me." When he didn't offer reassurances, she pulled away to take in his grim countenance.

"As a matter of fact, I'm going to head home. No one needs me here."

She thwarted his attempt to shake her off and grabbed hold of the front of his shirt. "I need you here."

The slight hitch to his breathing signaled her words hitting their mark, yet he didn't speak.

"What's wrong? I saw your face back there. You nearly fell apart." This time she let silence apply its unique pressure.

"Her dad was Javier Martinez."

"Yes."

"He was my sergeant."

Her two worlds collided and the aftermath left her reeling. "Ally's dad is the man you tried to save but couldn't?"

His anguish swirled around them like a tornado, affecting her as well. But she knew that if she let him run from this, he would never leave the cabin again. All the growth he'd achieved the last few weeks would be mown down.

"I'm the cause of all of this," he said.

"No."

"Yes. Ally said it herself. If her dad had made it home, none of this would have happened."

"The ambush wasn't your fault. You didn't push drugs into Karen's hands."

He made a scoffing sound and pointed. "That girl is suffering."

"Yes, but not because of you."

"If I'd been faster . . . If I had been paying closer attention to what was going on, I might have been able to warn him. Her dad would be alive. Karen wouldn't be in the hospital. Their family would still be together, and Ally wouldn't be dealing with things no kid should have to deal with."

"You can't rewrite history."

The desolation in his eyes resonated to her like aftershocks. "It should have been me. I had nothing; he had everything."

"That's bullshit and you know it." She shoved his shoulder and life flared on his face for an instant before it was snuffed out. "You want to discuss what ifs? What if I hadn't met you? Where would I be right now?"

"You'd be fine."

"I'd probably have caved and gotten back together with Beau. Or gone out with Ryan. Would you call that better off? I definitely wouldn't be playing music again. I wouldn't have enrolled in school. I wouldn't have a plan for my future. And I wouldn't be desperately in love for the first time in my life with the best man I've ever known."

He took a step back as if she'd punched him in the gut. "No," he whispered.

"Yes." While she wasn't going to deny the truth of her outburst, her timing was spectacularly bad. "You can't turn your back on Ally and Karen."

"I'll only make things worse. Once I tell them who I am, they'll hate me for being alive when Javier is dead."

"Then let them hate you. Maybe that's what they need. Or maybe they need help getting their lives back together. You think you don't deserve to be called a hero because of what happened in Afghanistan, but you have a chance right here, right now to be a real hero, Emmett."

He stared up at the sky and mumbled a string of curses. "You're not being fair."

"None of this was fair. You losing a leg, Ally's dad dying. That doesn't mean we give up."

"But—"

"No more buts. Listen to me: You gave me the courage to get back onstage and face my fears. Once I did, a weight disappeared. I know this is different—harder—but I'll back you up. I promise." When he remained staring sightlessly at the sky, she added, "You can't feel any worse about the situation, can you? Why not try to make it better?"

"Is it even right to lay this on Ally when she has other things to worry about?"

"Ally is stronger and wiser than most people give her credit for. She'll appreciate being treated like she's not a child. More than anything, she wants the truth."

He ran a hand down his face and nodded. "This is my purgatory."

She tutted. "Church of Christ are so *dramatic*."

A spontaneous huff snuck out of him. "How do you manage to make me laugh?"

"A rebellious nature and unchecked sacrilegious tendencies?"

He hauled her closer and kissed her temple. "God, I love you."

She stopped short and looked up at him. "You do?"

"How could I not? I was a goner when you informed me in no uncertain terms that I needed better manners and a bath."

"If only I'd known that's how to attract nice guys, I would have turned to insults years ago." She wanted to keep him diverted, but as soon as they crossed into the artificial lighting of the waiting room, reality darkened the mood.

Would the truth set Emmett and Ally free or would it drive them deeper to ground?

Chapter 20

Every pang and ache in his residual limb on his walk toward Ally felt like part of his penance. The coming storm threatened to consume him. He took the seat next to her, garnering a suspicious, teenager-specific side-eye that already made him feel like she disliked him. Greer sat across from them, her steady gaze giving him a bolster of courage he needed more than ever.

His world had gone topsy-turvy as if God, sensing he had found his footing in Madison, had tugged the rug from under him to keep him off-balance. Greer's defiant declaration of her love had shocked him, yet drawn into sharp focus his own feelings.

After the trauma of losing Javier and his leg, he'd assumed his life would continue in a series of dreary, uninspiring days until he too died. Greer had carved new paths and given him a will to not just live but live well. But his regrets and guilt hadn't vanished, they had just taken up residence in a spare room.

He fought the compulsion to walk out and keep going until

his legs gave out. How was that for heroic? Yet here he sat, his hands clasped between his knees, wondering how to tell the girl at his side he had tried but hadn't been able to save her dad.

"Any word on your mom yet?" Greer asked.

"No." Ally sat back and crossed her arms over her chest.

Emmett couldn't look away from her. Parts of Javier reflected back in the set of her chin (stubborn) and the turn of her mouth (sarcastic). In her, pieces of Javier would live on. It was small comfort, but comfort nonetheless.

"Dude. What are you staring at? It's creepy." She finally met his gaze head-on and defiantly.

"You remind me of your dad," he said softly.

With her gaze glued to him, she asked slowly, "You knew my dad?"

He nodded. "Sergeant Javier Martinez. I was his company commander."

"Why didn't you tell me?" Ally shot an accusing look at Greer.

"Greer didn't know. I didn't either until you told me his name." He cleared his throat. "He was a good man."

"You were friends?"

The chain of command precluded true friendship, but Sergeant Martinez had been an integral part of his company. "His men respected him, and I hope I earned his respect."

Her gaze sharpened. "You were his commander. That means you were in charge?"

"I was in charge."

She glanced toward his leg and pointed. "Did that happen the same time my dad was killed?"

"Yes. He was right in front of me when the explosion went off."

He wasn't sure what he had expected. Tears. Anger. Hysterics of some sort. In a flat, emotionless voice, she asked, "Was he in pain?"

Based on his massive injuries, he must have been in intense pain, but how could he tell her that? Yet, had he really experienced pain? His own injury taught him the debilitating pain came later. In the moment, adrenaline masked all feelings, and mind and body had one purpose: survival.

"I can't say for sure if he was in pain or not, but based on my own injuries, I'd say no."

"Your leg didn't hurt?"

"Not right afterward. Everything goes numb. In fact, I tried to stand back up. Only when my leg wouldn't support me did I realize something was wrong."

"What kind of injuries did my dad have?"

He hadn't expected her to want the gory details. "It's not important. I want you to know—"

"It's important to me. Tell me what happened. *Everything.*"

Her eyes were years—decades—older than her body. Fundamental understanding flowed between them and left them isolated from even Greer, who loved them both.

"It should have been routine patrol. We'd completed dozens without incident. It was hot, but a beautiful day. The sky was blue with a few puffy white clouds. The kind I used to stare up at as a kid and imagine they were animals. I lagged behind your dad. It was when he turned to bust my chops about falling behind that the explosion took us out."

He paused and closed his eyes. "Next thing I know, I'm on my back. My ears are ringing. I can't hear. But I can see the impact of bullets in the dirt around us. I returned fire. After I realized my leg was toast, I crawled to your dad."

"Dad wasn't dead?"

"Not . . . not yet. I grabbed his flak jacket and pulled him with me into a shallow ditch on the side of the road. He . . ." This part was the hardest, and he swallowed down a slug of emotion. "He was staring at me, his hand out."

The dirt under him had turned into bloody mud . . . but some images were only for him to bear.

"My training kicked in. I applied a tourniquet and put pressure on his chest wound, but I could tell his lung was perforated and an artery hit."

"Did he say anything?" Ally asked softly, her hands knitted together and pressed between her knees.

Between the ringing in his ears and the general chaos, he'd never figured out what Javier had been mouthing. Emmett closed his eyes and forced himself back into the moment he'd done his best to bury six feet deep.

He opened his eyes to find himself gazing into a pair of chocolate-brown eyes fringed with the same dark lashes as Javier Martinez.

"*Ally*. He repeated your name until the end."

The impassivity of her expression crumbled beneath an onslaught of grief. He didn't know what to do except take her into his arms and offer comfort. It wasn't enough. It would never be enough.

She didn't shove him away and curse him for his inability to save her dad. Instead, she buried her face in his shirt. He rubbed her back and murmured meaningless apologies. Remembering Greer was bearing witness, he turned his head, fearful of her reaction even though she'd already seen the worst of him.

She brushed tears from her cheeks, her nose red and her eyes puffy, but she nodded and the rightness of his confession settled like the final fistful of dirt in a grave.

When Ally's sobs faded into hiccups, he said, "I wish things had been different."

"Me too." Ally pulled away and took a tissue from a box on a table next to her. "But it's not different. My dad is gone and my mom is messed up. What am I going to do?"

"You mean, what are *we* going to do? The situation may not be different, but some things have changed. You're not alone." Greer squatted on the floor in front of Ally.

A doctor came out and approached them, his movements brisk, bordering on impatient. The three of them stood. "Are you Mrs. Martinez's daughter?" he asked.

Ally nodded. "How is she?"

The doctor glanced at Greer and Emmett. "I'm afraid medical information can only be given to family."

"I'm her aunt and he's her uncle," Greer announced without breaking eye contact with the doctor.

The doctor narrowed his gaze on Emmett, who held his hands up in surrender. "You heard her."

"Physically she'll recover, but her underlying addiction needs to be addressed." He handed over several pamphlets. "I can recommend her for a short-term intensive inpatient treatment which will include therapy. Then it will be up to her to keep outpatient appointments."

"That sounds doable," Ally said.

"Will she be transferred directly from here to treatment?" Greer asked.

"If she agrees."

"What do you mean, agrees? Can't the state force her into treatment?" Emmett asked.

"Unless she's an immediate danger to herself or others, no. Frankly, we see higher rates of relapse from people forced into treatment. It's much more effective when the person chooses a path of sobriety. She has to want to get better."

"You're saying I need to make my mom agree to treatment."

"If you can. When I broached the subject with her, she became agitated. It seems she doesn't want to leave you alone." The doctor gave Greer and Emmett a pointed look. "She made no mention of an aunt or uncle who might be persuaded to look after her minor child."

"Can I see her?" Ally asked.

"Of course. She's awake but still groggy."

Ally took two steps toward the double doors that led to the exam rooms, stopped, and turned around. "Will you guys come with me?" Ally glanced between him and Greer.

Emmett opened and closed his mouth, the ability to speak lost.

"Of course." Greer took his hand, making the decision for him.

A nurse directed them to Karen's room. The thick smell of antiseptic was cut by earthier smells of urine and blood. Even the strict order of the hospital couldn't keep chaos at bay.

Ally knocked softly on the door and let herself inside. Emmett shuffled to the side, staying against the wall and close to escape.

Karen Martinez lay propped on two pillows, her face wan and her lips bloodless. She looked as if she had been sucked dry of life and the will to live. Emmett's knees trembled, and he leaned into the wall, unsteady on his prosthetic.

Ally half sat on the edge of the bed and gave her mom a kiss and loose hug. Greer stopped a few feet behind Ally, the strength she projected to support Ally palpable.

"The doctor said you're going to be fine for now, but you need help," Ally said.

"You'll help me, won't you, Ally?" Karen reached for her daughter's hand. "We'll get through this like we got through your daddy's death. Together."

A tear trickled down Ally's cheek, but she didn't break the intense lock she had on her mom. "You need professional help, Mom. I'm just a kid."

"There are doctors and nurses and therapists trained for this." Greer's voice was husky and gentle.

Karen's huge eyes darted between Ally and Greer. "Who will take care of Ally?"

Emmett's legs carried him forward without conscious thought, drawing everyone's attention. "I will. I'll make sure she's safe."

The color that came to Karen's cheeks only underscored her pastiness, like rouge on a corpse. "And who the hell are you?"

Who was he? The man who'd held her husband as life had leaked from his body into the dust. The man who'd buried himself under suffocating guilt and regrets. The man who needed to atone for the twist of fate that had left him alive while others had died.

"Captain Emmett Lawson, ma'am. I was your husband's company commander. He was a good man. A good soldier." Emmett swallowed and forced the words out for a second time that night. "I was with him when he died."

Karen pressed back into the pillows, closed her eyes, and covered her ears with her hands. "No, no, no," she repeated.

Ally took her mom's wrists and tugged her hands away. "It's okay, Mom. It means Dad wasn't alone. He had a friend with him."

"I'm so sorry, Mrs. Martinez. I should have sought you out as soon as I got home, but now our paths have crossed, I know I'm meant to help you and Ally."

"How can you possibly help?" Karen turned to Ally, her voice childlike and begging. "They want to send me away from you."

"You have to go, Mom." Ally turned to Greer with a beseeching look. It was difficult for Ally to ask for help, and Greer didn't want to let her down.

"School's almost out, isn't it?" Greer asked.

"Three more days, but my exams are done."

Greer moved closer to Ally and touched Karen's knee. "Let Ally come back to Madison with me and hang out. It'll be like summer camp."

Karen didn't answer, but her resolve was cracking.

Emmett stepped in to administer the final blow. "My family owns a horse farm, Mrs. Martinez. If Ally is interested, she can work there, earn some money, and ride whenever she wants."

"I don't know how to ride a horse." Despite her declaration, Ally's eyes sparked with interest.

"I'll teach you. In between mucking out the stables, that is. It's hard work, but you can earn good money. If that's what you want, and it's okay with your mom."

Everyone turned toward Karen. She shrugged and turned away. "Sounds to me like you've already decided so it doesn't matter."

Ally tugged her mom's arm until she garnered her attention again. "It does matter. I want you to be able to concentrate on getting clean so we can be together. Greer and Emmett will take care of me so you can take care of yourself."

"It's been the two of us since your dad died," Karen said.

"But it doesn't have to be just the two of us, does it? We don't have to do it all." Ally sounded like an adult reasoning with her teenager and not the other way around.

Karen pressed into the pillows and tipped her head back, blinking away tears. "Fine. I'll go to rehab while you go to Madison. But what happens when I get out? You're not keeping my daughter." She lifted her head to pin Greer and Emmett with her glimmering eyes.

"Geez. I'm not a dog they're adopting from the pound," Ally said with enough hot teenage angst to fry an egg.

"We're not trying to take Ally away from you. I promise. Emmett and I want to help out until you're back on your feet." Greer was so calm and collected, Emmett could imagine her handling a classroom with ease.

Karen sighed and found a small smile for Ally. "Working with horses and learning to ride sounds fun."

Ally held her mom's hand for a few seconds in silence. "They want to move you straight to the rehab facility."

Karen's face crumpled into sobs, and she pulled Ally close.

Emmett caught Greer's eye and nudged his head toward the hall. They retreated, giving Ally and her mom privacy.

"Offering her a job was sweet." Greer leaned against the wall, shoulder to shoulder with him.

"The least I can do. Where will she stay? I would offer up my cabin, but it's only a one-bedroom. How long does rehab last?"

"Honestly, I don't know. I think my parents would be open to having her stay a few weeks. Then what?"

"What do you mean?"

"Karen gets out with no job waiting, and we send them back to a duplex in a shady part of Nashville? That's putting her on the same spiral to end up right back where they are now."

"What is she qualified to do?"

"Waitressing? Reception? I don't know." She chewed her thumbnail before throwing her hands up. "Who would take a chance on hiring her?"

Emmett hummed. "Wasn't Ryan looking for help at the vet clinic?"

She shifted to face him and took his arm. "You think he would hire her?"

"Maybe if it's framed as a favor to me. Or even better, to you."

"I don't have any pull with him, but you might, seeing as you're both former Madison High jocks."

He gave her a half smile. "I don't know about that. If you agreed to have dinner with him, he'd probably hire Charles Manson."

She gave an embarrassed laugh and tucked her hair behind her ear. "I can't in good conscience have dinner with him because I'm taken."

"Damn right you are." Emmett slipped an arm around her waist and tugged her close, breathing her in.

Guilt still nipped his heels like a starving dog, but he was starting to outrun it. "I thought my life was over when I came home," he whispered.

"I thought my life was over when I came home too," she whispered back.

A laugh snuck out of him. "I guess we had to prove each other wrong, huh?"

"Seems like that's what happens when two hardheaded, stubborn people butt heads. And other stuff." Her laugh was tired but held notes of relief.

Ally slipped into the hall, her eyes red and puffy. "Can you run me by my place so I can pack up some clothes and toiletries for Mom?" The hesitancy in her voice reflected her hatred of being a burden.

"Of course. You can pack your own bag too, because you're coming home with me," Greer said.

"No. Absolutely not. I can stay by myself until school is out. I'm not a toddler."

"If you're finished with exams, then you're finished with school. I'll call them tomorrow morning to let them know the situation. Your summer is starting early." Greer tempered her decree with a smile.

Ally shot a look at Emmett through her lashes. "Were you serious about the job or just blowing smoke for my mom's sake?"

"Totally serious. In fact, you'd better pack clothes you don't mind getting dirty."

Ally's attitude made an appearance, but it held an impish quality. "How much will I make per hour?"

Emmett rubbed his chin. "You can start at eight dollars an hour for a week trial. If everyone is happy—including the owner, my dad—then I'll bump you up to ten. Sound fair?"

"More than fair." Ally stuck out her hand and Emmett took it in a shake.

When she tugged, he held on and murmured, "Your dad would be proud of you, Ally."

A veil of grief came over her face, and for a heartbeat, he regretted his words, but then she said, "I hope so. I think about him every day."

"I do too." While helping Ally and her mom wouldn't bring his sergeant back, helping them would honor his memory.

Greer herded them toward her car and drove to Ally and Karen's duplex apartment. The white noise of a pop song played low on the radio. Greer parked at the curb. As Ally slid out of the backseat, she said, "You guys can wait here. I don't need help."

Emmett could see the indecision threading tension through Greer's body. He put a hand on her leg. "Let her go. She'll be fine."

Greer settled back in the seat and rolled the windows down. The night was warm but not unpleasant. Honking horns and street noise drowned out the subtle sounds of nature.

"Will she be fine?" Although her focus was on the front door of the duplex, Greer's question encompassed more than whether Ally would remember to pack underwear and shampoo.

"We'll make sure if it."

Greer shifted her gaze to him. "How are you holding up?"

"My leg hurts like hell." It wasn't what she was asking and she deserved a real answer. "My heart too, if you want to know the truth. I hope helping Ally and Karen will be the best kind of medicine."

She linked their arms and snuggled into his shoulder. "I hope so too."

A lull settled over the car after they loaded Ally's two duffle bags and the guitar Greer had lent her into the trunk and returned to the hospital to drop one bag off for Karen. With the car eating up the miles to Madison, sniffles came from the backseat. Emmett and Greer exchanged a telling look, but Greer only turned up the radio, giving Ally as much privacy as possible in such a small space.

By the time they reached the turnoff to the cabin, Ally was sprawled on the backseat asleep looking young and blessedly untroubled.

Emmett leaned over the console to kiss Greer, softly and without any intent. "Can you bring her out to the farm tomorrow? I think we should keep her busy."

She glanced in the rearview mirror. "Agreed. We'll be out as soon as she gets up and ready."

"Shoot me a text when you leave the house, and I'll meet you at the barn." He stood at the bottom of the porch stairs as Greer swung her car in a sweeping turn and headed to the road.

A myriad of feelings shot up like new growth in the scorched ground of his psyche. For the first time, the cabin felt less like a refuge and more like solitary confinement. He'd missed having people he could count on, but he'd also missed having people count on him. Now that he'd regained both, he craved more.

Chapter 21

The strum of a guitar woke Greer. The chords were faint with a pause between each one as Ally searched for the proper strings with her fingers. Still, she had climbed the learning curve with impressive speed.

Greer slipped out of bed and crept down the hall to where Ally's door was ajar. The mirror of the dresser reflected Ally sitting on the edge of the queen canopied bed, her full concentration on her chording fingers.

Her voice was soft but had a lovely husky tone that spoke of maturity and a life lived beyond her years. The tone was something innate and treasured, unable to be learned or taught. Greer didn't have it.

Ally got hung up on a key change leading into the bridge and tried out several chords before huffing and setting the guitar aside.

Greer knocked and toed the door open, propping her shoulder

against the jamb. "You might try C to A and take it up a half step. Do you know how to do that?"

Ally narrowed her eyes, but instead of unleashing the storm brewing in her expression, she pulled the guitar back into her lap and strummed. "Like that?"

"Like this." Greer didn't take the guitar but guided Ally's fingers into the correct positions. "Try again."

Ally did and this time, the chords vibrated sweetly. She looked up and smiled a smile of simple joy. How long had it been since Ally hadn't woken to a litany of worries? Any amount of time drowning in anxiety was too long when you were a kid.

"Thanks." Ally stared at the frets of the guitar where her fingers were moving from chord to chord even though she wasn't playing. "For everything."

"I never would have thought we'd end up here based on our first meeting at the foundation." Greer chuckled.

"Me neither. I thought the whole songwriting thing was dumb."

"Me too." Greer sighed and rolled her eyes. "I hate to admit it but my uncle Bill knew what I needed all along."

Ally set the guitar aside and tucked her hands under her legs. "What do we do now?"

"Let's head to the kitchen for some breakfast. Then we'll mosey out to the Lawson place and see what Emmett is up to."

Ally popped up. She wore an old T-shirt, a pair of jeans that had been hacked off above the knee, and combat-style black boots, but her face was fresh and open. Absent was the heavy eye makeup that was part of her usual façade.

In the kitchen, Greer's mama was stirring pancake batter next to the griddle. Fresh blueberries stood at the ready. The smell of bacon hung heavy and made Greer's mouth water.

A wave of appreciation and love flooded Greer. Her parents hadn't understood her desire to become a musician, but they had done their best to support her and hadn't judged her when she'd crawled home.

She came up behind her mama and put her arms around her shoulders, startling her. "Didn't mean to scare you."

Her mama laughed and patted Greer's arms. "Not a better surprise in the world than a hug from you."

She turned and wiped her hands on the hem of her apron, her welcoming vibes worthy of a fifties sitcom matron.

"Morning, Ally. I hope you like pancakes and bacon."

"Thank you for letting me stay here, Mrs. Hadley. I won't be a bother, I promise."

"Please do be a bother. It reminds me of when Greer was a teenager." Her mama picked up a spatula and shook it at Greer like an accusing finger. "On second thought, maybe I don't want another teenager like Greer around."

Ally took a few stuttering steps closer. "Yeah? Did Greer get in trouble?"

"You bet she did. She was a wild one."

Ally shot Greer a puckish half smile.

"Mama! You're going to make me look bad, and I'm supposed to be a role model." Greer snuck a hand out to grab a piece of bacon. Her mama swung the spatula at Greer's bottom and missed. Laughing like an evil mastermind, Greer moved out of swatting distance and took a bite.

Ally wasn't laughing along at their antics but her smile was genuine. She perched on the edge of one of the chairs, not quite comfortable. "What kind of trouble did she get into?"

"She got caught drinking a few times. Smoking. Cutting school. Minor infractions these days, I suppose, but her father and I were . . ." Her mama hummed before saying, "I guess you'd call us straight arrows. It never occurred to us that our child would be so headstrong."

Greer tipped back in the chair and barked a laugh. "I should have tried to be more of a straight arrow. Instead I boomeranged right back where I started."

Her mama raised an eyebrow and pursed her lips. "You just needed to get out and experience life on your terms before you could settle down."

"Is that what I'm doing? Settling down?" Panic went off like an emergency flare, but it faded quickly. Greer wasn't going to listen to the part of her that had set it off.

"What would you call it?" her mama asked.

"Growing up?" For the first time, Greer wasn't focused on herself. She had been selfish in her ambition to make it in Nashville to the detriment of friends and family and boyfriends.

While she wouldn't go so far as to admit she owed an apology to Beau—he was still a lowdown, dirty cheater—the relationship had been doomed from the start. Beau needed a woman who could put all her energy into boosting him. That would never be Greer.

Emmett was as independent and stubborn as she was, yet he needed something from her as well. The difference was she was happy to offer herself to him, freely and without strings. And in return, he offered her something she hadn't known she was missing all these years. Someone who loved her but encouraged her to fly.

Greer steered the conversation into shallower waters while the three of them ate blueberry pancakes and bacon. Bit by bit, Ally relaxed into the chair, her shoulders rounding as she listened to Greer and her mom narrow the list of desserts to contribute to the church bake sale.

Greer's mom stacked their plates. "What are you girls going to get up to today?"

"We're going to clean up the kitchen after that spectacular breakfast so you can sit and read the paper, then head to the Lawsons' farm. Emmett is going to put Ally to work with the horses." Greer swept the plates from in front of her mama and headed to the sink.

"That sounds wonderful."

"Mrs. Hadley. Since I'm going to be earning money, I want to pay you rent or whatever." The soft hesitancy in Ally's voice reminded Greer how young and unsure she really was. The brash bravado Ally wore was a costume that recent events had shredded.

Greer turned to watch the interplay, confident her mama's deft touch with people would leave Ally feeling secure.

"Nonsense. We are pleased as punch to have you staying with us. You save your money for college or to buy yourself something special at the end of the summer." Greer's mama sat back with a little smile. "But if you really want to help, I could use a sous chef in the kitchen. I'm not used to cooking for four."

"You'll have to teach me what to do. Mom and I did mostly takeout or frozen."

"You'll know how to make all the classics by the time I'm done with you." Greer's mama winked. Ally's answering smile held pain and worry but also hope for a better tomorrow.

Greer's mama poured herself another cup of coffee and retreated to the sunroom to work on the crossword. Greer and Ally made quick work of the kitchen and were on their way to the Lawsons' farm thirty minutes later.

"What are Emmett's parents like?"

"His mom is as sweet as can be. I'm sure she's going to want to mother you as much as my mama does. His dad . . ." Greer bit the inside of her lip, searching for a diplomatic answer, and decided to stick with a simple fact that spoke volumes. "His dad is a retired army colonel."

Ally sat up straighter as if the very mention inspired her to watch her p's and q's. Greer was happy to avoid the main house and parked next to the barn. The sight of Emmett emerging in a T-shirt and khakis brought a goofy smile to her face.

Emmett opened Ally's door and gave her a half hug. "Are you ready to meet the horses? We have a new foal that's about the cutest thing ever."

Ally nodded and ran her hands down the front of her ripped, worn jeans shorts. "They won't bite, will they?"

"They might, but it's usually to get your attention, not to eat you." Emmett rumbled a laugh. "Don't worry, we haven't lost anyone yet."

Ally shot a panicked look over her shoulder at Greer but followed Emmett into the barn for a tour. Greer wandered to the paddock fence where a mare snuffled at the ground while her foal cavorted around her with boundless energy. Propping her foot on the lowest rail, she smiled at the foal's antics.

"That colt will likely be worth thousands once it's trained." The familiar clipped voice of Mr. Lawson at her side startled her. He'd come up on her unawares.

She glanced at him from the corner of her eye, but his face was impassive. "Emmett told me he decided to stay."

"I was out of line when I called Amelia. I misjudged you and I'm . . . sorry." Although his economy with words gave the impression of brusqueness, the man would never have apologized if he wasn't sincere. "You've been the best thing to happen to him since he came home."

A slug of emotion threatened to spill over, which would be too embarrassing to contemplate. Mr. Lawson's approval meant more than she expected, considering she'd never had a problem thumbing her nose at authority.

She swallowed several times before she could speak, but even then her voice trembled. "He's the best thing to happen to me too. He's a good man."

"He is. His mother and I couldn't be prouder."

"I hope Mrs. Lawson gets good news this week."

"Thank you, Greer." He stuffed his hands into his pockets and took three steps toward the barn before crisply turning back. "You should come to dinner sometime this week with Emmett."

"Okay. Sure, I'd love to."

Dazed, she watched him disappear as Emmett and Ally made a reappearance. Emmett and his dad paused to talk while Ally joined her. Her cheeks were flushed and the energy thrumming from her matched that of the foal in the paddock.

"That baby horse is adorable. I hope I get to take care of him." Genuine optimism had stripped the angsty tarnish from Ally's voice.

"What do you think so far?"

"I mean, they smell kind of bad and their poops are enormous, but each one seems to have their own personality. I can't wait to learn to ride. Emmett said he'd get me on a horse this afternoon if it doesn't storm."

"That sounds awesome."

Ally smiled and propped herself against a post to watch the mare and colt, her chin resting on her folded hands.

Greer backed away and joined Emmett once his dad had

entered the barn. "She seems excited." She kept her voice low so Ally couldn't hear.

"We'll turn her into a country girl before the summer is out." Emmett looked at Ally with a combination of hope and sadness. "Have you heard from Karen?"

"Not yet. I'm not sure when they were transporting her to the facility. No visitors are allowed for a week. I sure hope this works." Greer had done some reading on addiction and treatment, and the statistics weren't as encouraging as she'd hoped.

"Karen has strong motivation to get better. I believe in her."

Greer rested her head on his shoulder as they watched the mare meander over to Ally, who held out a carrot. "You're not going to believe this, but your dad apologized for calling Amelia and invited me to dinner this week. Can you believe it?"

"Can I believe you won him over with your charm?" He laughed. "Actually, no, I can't. He thinks I chose to stay and work the farm because of you."

Greer shifted to see his face. "You're not staying just for me, are you?"

He tucked a piece of her hair behind her ear and wrapped his hand around her nape. "I'm staying because it's the right thing to do and because it feels good to work hard and give back. Having you near is an unexpected bonus."

She gave him a hug, laying her hand over his heart, the steady rhythm coaxing her own heart into a dance. Their paths had crossed before taking detours through unexpected hardships, but finally they walked side by side toward a future that promised neither happiness nor peace.

But she was no longer fearful. Whatever conflict and heartbreak awaited, they would overcome them together.

Chapter 22

Emmett squeezed the steering wheel and stared at the wooden VFW sign swinging in front of the brick building that used to house the Madison police force. The VFW had taken over when Madison had built a big new police facility on the main highway into town. The eagle crest with VETERANS OF FOREIGN WARS etched around it like a medallion held him hypnotized.

He'd sworn to never set foot in the place, but the last weeks had seen him mature and grow and he liked the man he was becoming. Anyway, the bravery and strength Ally was exhibiting on a daily basis made his fears seem frivolous.

Just that afternoon Greer had taken Ally to visit her mom in rehab. Twelve days in and Karen had medically detoxed and was now getting the counseling and support she'd need once she got out. Emmett needed the support too. Greer had made him realize it was more than okay to lean on someone else. It was healthy and made him stronger, so when someone he loved needed to lean on him, he'd be able to support them back.

His mom's doctor's appointment had been nerve-wracking but ultimately given them good news. A treatable ulcer had been the cause. After cauterization and medication to eliminate the infection, his mom would make a full recovery. The alternative diagnoses still had the power to make Emmett's knees weak.

Even though the doctor and his parents assured him the cause was more complicated than simple stress, Emmett felt the weight of responsibility. He was tired of hurting the people around him.

He pulled his phone out and considered calling Greer for a pep talk, but she and Ally had plans to write songs together that evening and Emmett didn't want to interrupt their flow. The three of them had spent several evenings playing together, but Emmett hadn't played regularly since high school and his skill level had suffered from the long break. Whereas Greer and Ally seemed to talk in a different language when it came to song-writing.

Cradling his guitar and making something beautiful had been a reminder that pain and suffering were only a valley of time and the cycle of life was rarely cruel enough to abandon one there.

He hit a name in his contacts and waited.

"Emmett, my man. What's happening?" Terrance's deep voice vibrated with good humor.

"I'm sitting in my truck in the Madison VFW parking lot working up the courage to go in. Motivate me like our old drill sergeant." Emmett smiled.

"Can't. I'd scorch the ears of the little kids around and prob-ably get a walloping from their mamas." His laugh didn't hold any resentment from their last meeting. "What are you afraid of? It's a bunch of guys just like us."

It was an excellent question. The truth stuttered out. "I don't want to, you know, relive the glory days with them because they weren't glorious."

Terrance heaved a sigh. "Then don't pretend they were. No need to put on airs with those men, Emmett."

Terrance was right, of course. His dad's confession and even the sliver of insight into Mr. Meecham's military history were evidence. "Okay, I'm going in, but I wanted to tell you something first."

"I heard you turned down Colonel Harrison. Almost called to give you hell about it. You have plenty of time to settle down in Madison and take over the farm."

Emmett's experience had given him a new appreciation for time and how quickly the hourglass could run out. Or get smashed altogether. Terrance didn't understand yet, and Emmett hoped he never learned.

"Yeah, well. I'm ready to move on from the military." He paused. "There's a girl."

"Ah, shit. I should've guessed. Pretty?"

"Pretty and funny and doesn't take any shit from me. I want you to meet her before you deploy. Plus . . ." Emmett ran a hand over his jaw. "You need to fill me in on your mom's finances just in case. Can you come to dinner at the cabin next week?"

"Thanks, man." Terrance's voice had lost its teasing edge. "You have no idea what a load off that is."

"I was an asshole for turning you away before, but I'm better now. Trying to be anyway."

He and Terrance firmed up plans for dinner, and with no excuses left to make, Emmett slid out of his truck and made his way to the door. The windows were covered with heavy curtains, and Emmett had the feeling of stepping into a black box when he opened the door.

A dozen or so men turned to eye him as he stepped inside. He recognized several of the older men. Mr. Meecham stood at a short bar and saluted him with a foaming glass of beer. His dad sat at a round table in the back without a drink but talking to two men, one older, one younger even than Emmett.

His dad smiled in welcome but didn't rise. Emmett appreciated his restraint. He had to figure where he fit, if he fit at all, at the VFW. Another man with tats along both arms had his elbows propped on the bar, nursing a beer, and laughing with the man serving the drinks. He looked around the same age as Emmett.

Feeling a little like he was the new kid in school, Emmett approached the bar. "Hey, I'm Emmett Lawson and new to the VFW."

The man swiveled on the stool with a smile. The far side of the man's cheek and jaw was a mass of burn scars, shiny and pink, drawing his mouth into a grimace. But his eyes were untouched and twinkled with an optimism Emmett envied.

"Mason Butterfield. Where'd you serve?"

And with that, Emmett settled next to the man and felt like he'd found a new friend and a place to sit in the lunchroom.

Epilogue

One year later . . .

Greer parked next to Emmett's truck, hauled her backpack out of the passenger seat, and tramped up the steps, her brain mush after taking the last of her spring finals. He'd been at the farm all night with Ally and his dad holding vigil at a foaling, which had suited her fine. She'd studied into the wee hours of the morning and didn't need any distractions of the delightfully physical kind.

Lounging on the couch with an action movie muted on the TV and a beer clamped between his crossed legs, Emmett cradled his guitar and strummed a few chords. Ally was on the edge of the chair, bent over and concentrating on picking a series of notes. She had progressed far beyond Greer's musical abilities over the past year.

Greer dropped her backpack next to the door with a thud, climbed over the couch, and cuddled next to Emmett, feeling as exhausted and wrung out as he looked. But he also looked . . . content.

A far cry from the man who had tried to scare her off with a shotgun. He was different too from the golden boy she'd known and crushed on in high school World History. He was wiser and sometimes sadder, but a week would often pass without a nightmare.

Every day, she blessed her failures because without them, their paths would have never recrossed. Amelia liked to take credit for getting them together, but fate had already been steering them toward each other.

"Did you kill it?" he asked.

"I think so. Grades will be posted by Friday." She took a swig of his beer and handed it back. "What about you? I hope you *didn't* kill anything."

He chuffed a laugh. "Mare and foal are doing well."

"It was the coolest thing ever!" Ally glanced up to deliver her verdict before picking out the notes of the song they'd been working on for the past week. "I think I fixed the bridge. What do you think?"

The combination of her chords and notes were perfect and Greer wondered why they hadn't stumbled upon it earlier. "Yes. Love it."

Greer slipped Emmett's guitar from his lap and joined Ally, the music better than a shot of espresso. Their difference in age meant little when both had undergone trial by fire. They'd written a dozen songs together. Greer performed them during her sets at Becky's, but she'd also sent demos to a contact she'd maintained in Nashville on the off-chance one would get picked up.

When the final chords rang out, Emmett clapped. "That was amazing."

"Maybe this will be the one," Ally said with shining eyes.

"Maybe it will." Greer loved her positivity. The string of rejections they'd received for their songs hadn't dimmed Ally's confidence. Maybe it was because she was still young, but Greer had a feeling Ally's spirit had been tempered into steel.

Ally was thriving in Madison. While she still maintained an edge with her short hair and style, she was softer at her core. Friends seemed easier to come by, although Greer suspected that was due more to Ally's changed circumstances than any significant difference in Madison's teenagers. She worked part-time at the farm and had become an excellent rider.

"Dr. Humphries came by on his way home from work to see how the labor was progressing," Ally said.

Greer raised her eyebrows. "Your mom still enjoying working for Ryan?"

After getting out of rehab, Karen had turned things around. Greer wasn't sure if it was the therapy or if time had simply helped blunt the grief of losing Javier, but Karen was happier and healthier and building a life to be proud of. Emmett and Greer had gently suggested a reluctant Karen settle in Madison, but it was Ally who insisted they stay.

"Dr. Humphries is trying to convince her to get her vet tech degree at the college." Ally continued to strum a meandering melody. While Ryan had been initially resistant to hiring a woman right out of rehab without even a GED, Emmett and Greer had pleaded, and it had ended up working out well for both Ryan and Karen.

"Is she going to do it?" Greer asked, picking up the threads of the new song and joining Ally.

"I don't know. She's not sure she can handle it. Maybe you should give her a call and casually bring up how much you're loving school," Ally said.

Greer stuck out her tongue at Ally. Greer's classes were

challenging and interesting for the most part, but being on campus made her feel like a crone surrounded by fresh-faced, unjaded teenagers.

"'Loving' might be treading too close to a lie. I can't wait to start student teaching, though." Greer still got her biggest thrill working with the veterans at the Music Tree Foundation.

"Mom called and invited us for dinner tonight. You too, Ally. She's trying some new gluten-free casserole." The dread in Emmett's voice made Greer laugh. "Be ready to hit the pizza place afterward."

Ally smirked. "I'll pass. Mom and I are getting Chinese tonight to celebrate the end of finals and the start of summer vacation."

Greer's phone vibrated in her back pocket and she shifted into Emmett to fish it out. She settled into the crook of his arm. "Hello."

"May I speak with Greer Hadley?"

"This is she."

"Hi, Ms. Hadley. My name is Rhonda Wilmore, and I'm with AVX."

"AVX?"

"Yes. I have an artist who heard your demo and is interested in recording it."

"Demo?" Numbness spread from Greer's hand clutching the phone to her lips. She must be experiencing an exhaustion-induced delusion.

"Yes." A hint of confusion crept into the lady's voice. "I am talking with the writer of 'Dark Side of the Mountain,' aren't I?"

Greer met Ally's wide eyes and nodded, realizing after a few beats that the woman on the other end of the phone couldn't see her. "Yes. My partner Ally and I wrote it. Someone actually wants to record it?"

Ally slapped both hands over her mouth and bounced on the chair.

"Indeed. A top-flight artist. I'm not at liberty to mention her name, but let's just say she doesn't like men who cheat."

Carrie Underwood. How could Greer possibly not know the song that had set her life spinning on a different course? "That sounds incredible."

"Wonderful. We would love to meet you and your co-writer face-to-face to talk about licensing."

After setting up a meeting for the following week, Greer hit the *end* button and let out a whoop. "I can't believe it."

Emmett scooped Greer closer. "I'm so proud of you."

Ally stood up and pumped both arms before plopping back down. "Are they actually going to pay us? Did she say who was interested?"

Greer filled Ally and Emmett in on the conversation. "She couldn't say for sure, but I'm about 99.9 percent sure it's Carrie Underwood."

"Are you sure she didn't make a mistake?" Ally asked, her eyes huge. "Maybe they called the wrong people."

"I doubt there's a plethora of songs floating around called 'Dark Side of the Mountain.'" Had the call been a hallucination? She checked her phone's log and there was the number.

"But that was our first song. You sent it in months and months ago," Ally said.

"It's all about timing. Right song and right artist." Reality was taking hold. It was happening. After grinding it out for years in Nashville without even a brush with success, Greer had realized her dream on her own terms. But not without help.

She reached over Emmett and took Ally's hand. "This wouldn't have happened without you."

Ally squeezed her hand. "I couldn't have done it without you either. We make a good team, don't we?"

"We sure do." Greer turned to Emmett and took his face between her hands, pressing a kiss on his lips. "And you."

"What about me? You and Ally wrote the song and deserve the credit." He took her wrist and rubbed his thumb along her pulse point.

The strength of her feelings for this man rampaged through her, too wild to contain. A tear trickled out even though she smiled. "You encouraged me to fly, Emmett. I love you."

"I'm just going to . . . check on Bonnie. Not that anyone will notice," Ally murmured as she sidled to the porch.

"Marry me." Emmett stared into her eyes, the intensity startling.

As if having an out-of-body experience, she traced the path of her life like the old board game. Never would she have guessed the twists and turns that brought her full circle back to Madison, yet somehow being in his arms at this moment felt inevitable.

She was exactly where she wanted to be. Winding her arms around his neck, she touched her lips against his. "I thought you'd never ask."

Acknowledgments

A big thank-you for the team at St. Martin's Press for making books happen! The ability to experience other people's tragedies and triumphs enriches our lives, makes our world bigger, and grows our empathy for others. In my opinion, extensive reading is a fundamental requirement for leadership. From the multiple editors to the cover designers to the sales and marketing departments—it really does take a village. Special shout-out to my editor, Eileen Rothschild, and my agent, Kevan Lyon!

I also want to thank Laura (Merryman) Brown, an old high school buddy, and her husband, who were kind enough to answer questions about making a living songwriting in Nashville. Speaking of songwriting, I learned it is a different skill entirely from writing prose, and I don't have it! I'm even more in awe of the songwriters out there who can create an emotional story in just a few lines. Songs have always been a big inspiration for me in terms of writing books, and even more so now that I can truly appreciate the talent needed to put together the perfect song.

The VFW (Veterans of Foreign Wars) have posts all over the country, including one in my fictional town of Madison, Tennessee. I remember the post in my own Tennessee hometown as being a big gathering spot. As a child it seemed pretty raucous, to be honest. But in addition to the social interaction, VFW posts offer support to returning veterans, including financial and mental-health support, and grassroots advocacy.

Most of us will never experience the tough road military families who have lost a loved one in action must tread. This book is dedicated to the families who rebuild their lives after a tragic loss. I hope I have portrayed the pain and strength with honesty and compassion.